Freddy is a footballer
- England's newest star

He is also
a troublemaker...
an agitator...
a political revolutionary (some would say)

Somewhere down the line
something has to give

Over the Top

Laurie Barth

MINERVA PRESS
MONTREAUX LONDON WASHINGTON

OVER THE TOP

ISBN 1 85863 178 5

First Published 1995 by
MINERVA PRESS
10, Cromwell Place,
London SW7 2NJ.

Printed in Great Britain by
B.W.D. Printers Ltd., Northolt, Middlesex

OVER THE TOP

GEORGE - JOURNALIST

From hacks in macs with bribes on doorsteps to the élite, the literati with their pampered expense accounts and portable fax machines; we all love to spot a star (in embryo). It is a common thread running right through the profession. It can happen any place any time.

Take this little game: a nothing match between Spurs first division wide boys and non-league Eastgate Athletic. Fixed up in haste, to test the injured leg of Peter Stevons, long-time England centre back. No doubt up in the boardroom it had seemed an ideal opportunity to give Stevons a run against grateful, non-threatening opposition. Cigar smoke theory: no one had informed Eastgate of their allotted role. Roared on by their few hundred fans, they ploughed in like peasants dismembering the nobility. Soon Spurs were more intent on protecting priceless limbs than playing football and Willie Warner, the manager, was hopping up and down on the touchline - waving his cigar and cursing. Only Peter Stevons stood firm, a rock among falling pebbles, as Spurs players hit the grass.

Then the magic moment that makes football the game it can be. A long, hopeful punt out of the Eastgate defence, Stevons ready to control the ball as he had been doing for the last twelve years. Suddenly, a small figure pops up from nowhere, takes the ball on his chest. With his back to Stevons he sways left, turns right and shoots. All in one smooth sweet movement. A moment of magic that lingers long after the game had faded.

As the game settled to its script, with Spurs attempting to impose their class and Eastgate their strength, I kept my eye on the little inside forward. Noting his intelligent positioning, his off-the-ball movement and willingness to show himself in all situations. In a way the strength of the Eastgate team worked against him. Time after time he would make runs, only to see the ball hit harmlessly over his head. Nevertheless, he was enjoying himself, snapping at the heels of the England centre back - twisting and turning in the box - looking for that yard of space. He scored as well, a scrappy goal, a melee in the box, but it was the little blonde forward who poked it over the line.

After the match I quite forgot about Peter Stevons and his leg. My mind was full of the fair-haired inside forward, and the way he had, at times, dominated the England centre back. I filed the name Freddy Feather away in my mental index, prepared to trot him out in seasons to come. "Oh yes, first spotted him years ago in a non-league match."

Flick forward through the sports pages a couple of years: somehow, in a search for football's mythical roots, I had become imprisoned in a series of articles covering the lower divisions. A dismal trudge around the Hartlepools, Darlingtons and Rochdales of the football world in search of a purity that never existed. Glanville gets the foreign beat, Macillvanny the glamour, but good old George gets Doncaster vs. Scunthorpe on a cold, stale night in February.

This particular evening, while researching the Doncaster Argus, looking for an angle, an old warhorse ending his days, something, anything. The name Feather, F. plucked a chord. Fairly faint, a high C. I looked closer, Feather F. left back, interesting. There he was, the same compact figure, first seen two years ago; lining up in defence instead of attack. During the game I focused half my attention on the game, half on Freddy. I wasn't disappointed. After tying up the Scunthorpe winger, he began to overlap, laying off quick, incisive passes to his mid-field. The crowd was not in favour, nor was the mid-field. Adroit little passes left them in space that was as unwelcome as it was unexpected. Freddy would deliver the ball and go for the return that never came. He never gave up, never stopped trying to play football. His instant control: the timing of his tackles, the all round thoughtfulness of his play marked him out, for me at least, as the one player of quality in a dismal match.

I have to be careful here, how trustworthy is my own memory? Certainly the views of Manager, Maurice Moore, differed from my own. We might have been watching different matches. He prowled around his office, muttering about 'Work rate, character, doing the business'. When I mentioned Freddy his eyes hardened, his face turned rigid. "On loan from Dockside," he said shortly. "We needed a defender quickly when Don Protheroe did his cartilage." He shrugged. "Feather was all we could get in a hurry, and quite frankly the sooner he's on his bike the better."

"I thought he had quite a good game," I ventured timidly. "After all, the equaliser came from his cross and defensively, he got in some good tackles."

Maurice Moore was not the type of manager who appreciated

contradiction, certainly not by smart London journalists. "Six penny ball player," he snapped. "You heard the crowd, they want to see it in the opposition box and so do I. Anyway the lad's trouble. Lives in a squat with a bunch of Anarchists. The sooner he goes the happier we'll all be, now that's the end of it." He looked at his watch, "We've a job to do here at Doncaster." And he meandered off down the platitudes laid bare by managers of struggling teams everywhere.

I made the long journey back to London somewhat depressed. On the one hand, I had surely seen a player of true quality. On the other he seemed to be going nowhere. Shuttling positions in struggling teams. Eastgate didn't want him - Doncaster couldn't wait to be rid of him. Whatever toehold he had in league football seemed precarious at best. I drove along moralising to myself; if this was the roots of our greatest game then the tree must surely be damaged. Then again Maurice Moore seemed to be hinting at some sort of personality conflict. We all know about the burn outs, the unfulfilled talent, the wasted lives. Maybe Freddy was different. But, always a but, something was impeding his progress. The same something that had so alienated Maurice Moore? Back Freddy went into the index file with a question mark against his name.

The seasons drifted by. My marriage collapsed. I started to drink more than was good for me. Liverpool won the league (again) and an old acquaintance, a friend (I like to think) landed the manager's job at Dockside Town. A struggling third division club caught in the capitol city cross fire between too many clubs and not enough money or support to go round. The most they had ever known was moderate success, back in the 50's. The days of national service, short hair, the maximum wage, the Bushy Babes, Stanley Mathews: another (better?) lifetime.

Ray Hutchinson, Hutch to everyone, was a contemporary of mine. We had entered the football world at the same time but by different routes. He had been a swashbuckling wing half, a fiery figure, who, at his peak, narrowly missed selection for the 1962 World Cup Squad. He played on; slowly sliding down the football snake, until he landed a job as player manager and begun the climb up a new ladder, rung by painful rung. Now he was as clearly over the hill as a manager, as he once had been as a player. To the casual observer, Dockside may have been the tip of the snake's tail but to Hutch it was a foot on the bottom of the ladder.

I was genuinely pleased for him. Six months on the dole must have been hell for a man of Hutch's restless energy. He had been in the game for 30 years. It was his life, as it was mine.

He had arrived quietly (the days of celebration and fanfare a good five years in the past), with four games to go and a minimum of seven points need to stave off the dreaded drop to the fourth division. The crowd was small and cynical. At the first mistake they would turn against their own team with a bitter relish. All they had ever known from The Dockers was struggle (a mirror image of their own lives?). Hutch was cheerful though, the new challenge had restored some of his natural bounce, a new team, a new dream, the possibilities were limitless.

"This team can go places," he assured me. "Look at the history, second division runners up"

"That was 30 years ago," I said repressing a smile.

"But the potential is there," he insisted. "This club has had crowds of 30,000. If the tradition is there, then so is the potential. Anyway it's good to see you, Johnny will be pleased."

Ah, good old Johnny; how could one forget him? As dour as Hutch was perky. For 15 years they had been faithful partners, a relationship closer than most marriages. Whenever, wherever Hutch got a post: from Stockport to Southampton, Hull to Halifax, Barnsley to Benfica, Johnny would go too, stopping just long enough to pack his bags and turn in his U.B.40. Now here they were again, rekindling the flames for yet another cold winter.

For this, their first match, I had the somewhat dubious privilege of sitting on the bench. It promised to be ninety minutes of non-stop blasphemy. Waiting for the teams to emerge, idly leafing through the club programme, (£1 worth of advertisements and out of date pen portraits plus a column from 'That much-travelled manager and well-known football personality.' Hutch himself), my eye was caught by the name of the substitute F. Feather. I looked around. Yes there he was, fair hair poking out of the shelter. Just then a muted roar told me that the teams were coming out. Hutch and Johnny joined me on the bench.

"What do you know about the substitute, the boy Feather?" I asked cautiously.

"Christ George, give us a chance, we've only been here two days, we have to give the first team an opportunity, that's only fair."

"I've seen him," I said "He's useful. What position does he play?"

"Blimey, I dunno, here Johnny. Where does the boy Feather play?"

"Reckons he's a forward," Johnny said tersely. "On the books he's down as a fullback." He returned his gaze to the players, the only people who existed for the next ninety minutes.

The game started and I could feel Hutch and Johnny wilt like daffodils. Dockside were - formless, aimless, lacking in conviction. All self belief beaten out of them by the long season of failure. Leicester City, going for promotion, were quick and eager, they had success to play for Dockside had only avoidance of defeat. With half an hour gone they were already 2 down. The first, a sloppy defensive error, the second an almost inevitable addition to the first.

"Put Feather on, he's useful," I said. Hutch smiled at me knowingly; friendship or not, I was still an outsider.

"What have you got to lose?" I insisted. "Give him a chance, at least see him play." Finally after much nagging and a third Leicester goal, Hutch shrugged his shoulders and sent him on.

The first goal could have been down to luck. A desperate punt out of defence, Leicester caught too far upfield. A run, a shot, no bother. Three-one half an hour left, the Leicester defence more cautious now, still confident, but wary. Ten minutes later, they halted another jinking run on the edge of the box. Slowly Freddy picked himself up, placed the ball, then calmly floated it over the defensive wall into the corner of the net. Leicester put two men on him, pulled everyone back. To no avail. He twisted and turned in their midst causing panic like a bee in a roomful of small children.

The Dockside players drove forward, firing every ball towards their new talisman. Once he took the ball on his thigh, swayed right, shot, only for the ball to bounce back off the post. A minute later, he held the ball on the half way line, chipped it over the advancing offside trap, ran through himself, lobbed the keeper only for another Dockside player to be given offside. When I saw that move, saw the backspin he placed on the ball, I knew this was a player of true quality. There was the thrill of seeing my own judgement confirmed.

The crowd was playing its part after years of sullen silence, they got behind their team. Leicester were falling apart. Once more they hauled him down on the edge of the box. What happened next took place so quickly that I think only Freddy, myself and the referee were aware of the circumstances. From a prone position, he held the ball between his feet, placed it, then, still lying on his back, he flicked the ball sideways. The surprised Dockside player managed to swing in a shot while the Leicester defence were still busy Jerry building their wall. When they realised that a goal had indeed been given, the Leicester team, goalkeeper and all, swarmed around the referee, causing a multitude of yellow a cards to be held aloft. I leaned towards Hutch who was splayed out on his seat like a rag doll. "Told you he was useful," I said smugly.

"What happened, I saw it but I don't believe it!" he muttered blankly. "Tell me we scored, wake me up. No, on second thoughts don't." He stared at the ground shaking his head.

"Three goals in half an hour, that's what happened. You've hit gold my son and don't forget who spotted him first."

The referee blew for time and the Dockers left the field to a standing ovation, sweet music to anyone born outside Leicester. Later, in Hutch's office, still filled with tea chests, we were reliving the match over a whisky or two or three.

"I've asked young Feather to come up, so you'll have a chance to meet your boy wonder," Hutch said, watching me closely. I kept my tone neutral as I replied thoughtfully, "I don't think he's so young, I must have seen him some four or five seasons ago. Maybe he's a late developer. Whatever, he's something special, no?" My journalistic instinct was picking up negative waves.

"Early days yet," said Johnny reluctant as ever to display enthusiasm. "So far we've seen half a match, and just in case anybody forgets, we didn't win." Good old Johnny, give him a diamond and all he would see was coal that refused to burn.

"Johnny, Johnny," I said grandly. "You saw magic out there today, flashes of skill that turned a match."

"Magic is for writers," he jabbed at me. "What about commitment, character. Fancy footwork." He snapped his fingers, dismissing skill and flair.

A few drinks later, Freddy was standing in the doorway. Freshly showered, dressed in a shabby Dockside tracksuit, he seemed stockier, more solid than he had on the pitch. Hutch leapt up and put his arm across Freddy's shoulders. "Brilliant game my son. Where have you been hiding yourself?"

"I've been around," Freddy replied, yielding to Hutch's bear like grip. "I've just taken some time to arrive."

"You're here now son. Stick with your Uncle Hutch and we'll go places. I liked what I saw out there tonight, when your chance came you grabbed it. Listen to me son I've been around. I'm going to build a new team here and I hope you're going to be the centre of it."

Detached, watching Hutch in action I could only shake my head in cynical, silent despair. Hutch built his teams on a fragile base of personal loyalty. Ruthlessly disregarding older, independent players, bringing in younger more malleable ones, firing his teams with a seemingly inexhaustible enthusiasm. Ten years before, at the height of his managerial career, he had taken a young Newcastle team to the brink of a European cup final. But, somewhere behind the Iron Curtain the dream had fallen apart. The team which had worshipped with the innocence of altar boys returned home like whipped dogs.

Years on down the line, it's a new team, a new dream, a gold nugget amongst the stones. I kept a close eye on Dockside as they wriggled their way out of trouble. Freddy scored five more goals, lifted the team and the town. So, when I popped up to Hutch's office I thought I would be seeing a happy man. Not so. "Freddy Feather trouble?" I ventured.

"Who's been talking?" Hutch snapped back.

I had to laugh. "Just the old instinct working," I told him. "What's he been up to?"

You name it and he's pouncing about in the middle of it. He's a fucking little troublemaker." I waited for Hutch to unburden himself. "Just the other day he comes waltzing in, in that way of his and says 'Can we have a rock concert? All profits to go to Famine Relief.' Of course I say no, and he says 'Why not' and I say 'Because the chairman won't sit still for it,' which he won't. Dolton does nothing unless there's something in it for him. And then he says, 'that if money that could have been raised isn't, then those people carry moral responsibility for the lives that could have been saved.' I tell you." He said, "At my time of life I don't need any of that shit." He sat back drained by his near miss with moral responsibilities.

"Seven goals in four games, that's hard to argue with." I said.

He nodded, sighed, sipped at his whisky, did all the things a man does when he's run out of words, and his tether is all used up.

I left Hutch soothing his problems with whisky. Jetted off to Amsterdam for yet another bleak English performance in the European championship.

Each new season brings its own dreams but Dockside, despite the fresh faces brought in by Hutch, started the season in the same dispiriting fashion that the national side had ended it. One had grown used to seeing their name at or near the bottom of whichever league they were in. It took two-third round cup matches against Arsenal to alert the football intelligentsia that life was stirring in run down Dockside. The football world smirked when lowly Dockside travelled to majestic, intimidating Highbury and pulled off a shock draw. The smirks turned to outright laughter when Dockside, on their own territory, took Arsenal to pieces. Freddy scored the winner in the eighty-seventh minute; a free kick floated lazily over Arsenals international defence into the corner of the net.

After the match, Freddy disappeared, leaving Hutch and Johnny to re-emerge into the spotlight like an old music hall act, confounding the crowds, the critics, and maybe even themselves, with the success of their latest comeback. Hutch trotted out the platitudes with all the fervour of a born again Christian.

"We played to our strengths, showed lots of commitment, lots of character." When asked about Freddy he became coyly evasive. "The boy played well, he did his job, but so did the whole team."

Spurred on by a classic cup victory Dockside begin to climb the league table. Driving through the worn out streets on my way to an evening match it seemed like a scene from the 30's, filled with men in cloth caps. It had to be a football match or a hunger march. Dockside were out of the cup, beaten by W.B.A. (a match Freddy missed through injury) but promotion seemed a real possibility. So once again, after a comfortable 4-1 win I expected to see a happy Hutch, once again I was disappointed.

"I hope you never win the cup Hutch," I said only half joking, "You'd kill yourself for sure."

"Hello George." He looked up listlessly.

"Freddy Feather trouble," I smiled. "What is it this time?"

He sighed heavily "What isn't it? You name any sort of trouble and he's there, poncing about in the middle. All sorts I've had, I thought I'd seen it all. But I've never had a Communist, Anarchist, Trotskyist. What other 'ists are there?"

"Ornithologist, philatelist."

"Don't be funny George. Even if I was in the mood, which I'm not, it still wouldn't suit you."

"Sorry Hutch, but don't you think you're taking it all too much to heart. For performances like you're getting you can surely put up with a little politics. So he's left wing, so what? All that means is he's still got his ideals. I wish I still had mine. What happened to all the things you believed in all those years ago?"

Hutch ran a hand through thinning hair. "I don't know George, I'm a football manager, not a bleeding heart social worker."

"Be more specific Hutch," I urged. "Give me an example."

"Example, I'll give you examples, you can have examples till they're coming out of your ears."

"I don't mind that, each to his own. But I do object to pictures of tortured cows appearing on my plate just when I'm about to tuck into a well deserved steak. You know what he did don't you?" A rhetorical question, my cue one of interested silence. "Well we're on the bus going to Stoke or Huddersfield or somewhere equally grim. We've just fitted the bus out with a video and we're all settled in looking forward to a good war movie, a Stallone, and what happens? We switch it on only to find he's substituted something called the Animal Film. Ninety minutes of blood and torture, just the thing to put you in the mood for Huddersfield."

"What did the other players think of it?" I asked, aware of the delicate hierarchy that exists within the confines of any club.

"What did they think! We've now got four bleeding heart vegetarians in the team. All going on about knowing the consequences of your actions, taking down the barriers in your mind, worse than a bunch of ex-smokers. And then there's this benefit thing."

"I remember that was going on at the end of last season."

"Well, it's still going on. Christ I don't know anymore, on one level it sounds kosher. No reason we couldn't hold concerts, providing it's for a good cause. Then just when you're on the point of thinking 'Well okay, perhaps he does have a point,' he'll come out with something like 'The club programme should be made of recycled paper.' Or 'The police should arrest all the racists in the crowd.' Or

'Why doesn't the club operate a crèche to encourage families on match days?' He's doing my head in I know that."

I nodded in sympathy, searched around for something to lighten his mood. "What about his play on the pitch?"

"There's no arguing with it," Hutch said. "The team revolves around him. Christ you've seen him. You've noticed he's been dropping back to mid-field?"

I nodded again.

"I don't mind that, he's too busy a player to be stranded up front. But what I do mind is that he did it on his own authority. Or rather him and his coach decided between them. Ah, didn't know that did you George? You must be slipping. Our Freddy has his own personal coach. An old cripple in an even older overcoat. That's what gets me. Its like we're, me, the whole club, just a stage in some great masterplan." Hutch sat back, his store of indignation temporarily used up. He leaned back in his chair, then leaned forward and poured another whisky. "I don't know, on the one hand there's everything to look forward to. You saw him out there tonight; by his standards that was a quiet game, yet if you know football at all you know he was the most influential player on the pitch. With him we can go up, we can get out of this prison they call the third division. Take him away and we're a struggling third or, God help us, even fourth division team."

"Can you sell him?" said the journalist in me taking over from the fan. He raised his hands. "At this moment in time we'd get nothing. Next season, if his play continues to develop, maybe half a million, or maybe we won't be able to give him away. Even if I could sell him, and believe me it's been discussed, I'm not sure that he'd go. His wife, sorry partner, we've got to say partner these days, anyway she's some sort of bigwig left wing politico, definitely not the sort of woman you want to meet down an alley on a dark night. She'll slice you up and leave you for dead."

"Have you had any direct confrontation yet?" Hutch sat back sipping his whisky retracing unpleasant memories in his head. When he spoke his voice was distant, as if reluctant to disturb painful memories.

"Just one, on the Thursday before the West Brom cup match. I said to him 'Son you go on this demo, you don't play on Saturday.'"

"What demonstration?"

"How the fuck do I know what demo?" Hutch snapped crossly. "A demo for this, a demo against that. Is the sun shining then let's have a demo. I said to him 'Son it's football or politics.' 'I've given my word' he said 'but even if I hadn't I wouldn't buckle down to threats.'" Hutch stopped, sighed, sipped. "Now I've dropped internationals in my time, no problem. I did what any manager would have done. So why," he appealed to me, "Why do I feel bad about it? Well of course we lost," he said answering his own question. "And that brought home just how reliant the team is on him." Stop, sigh, sip. "I don't know, all I do know is he's doing my head in, I know that much."

Somehow, Hutch's tender head survived the tense run in to promotion. The boxed-in little slum area of Dockside held its breath as their team slid up on the rails to clinch the last promotion spot in the very final match of the season. Surely, I thought, as I climbed the stairs to his office, this time it will be the old Hutch, the warhorse restored by the glory of a winning team. Alas the sounds percolating through the corridors were anything but celebratory. A royal row, raised voices, banging on tables, the works, I edged forward.

"On the contrary Hutch." This was Freddy's voice in a tight clipped tone. "I'm perfectly willing to talk to the chairman. I just thought you ought to know the feelings of the players first. You are the manager aren't you, or perhaps I'm mistaken and you're nothing more than the chairman's messenger."

"Don't give me that son," Hutch was struggling for control. "I'm the manager; I manage the team. You're a player; you play for the team. He's the chairman; he owns the fucking team."

"Not good enough Hutch. If the club goes to South Africa and I go along then I become part of a policy that condones Apartheid. If I don't eat South African food then I'm certainly not going to play football in a country that treats the majority of its citizens as second class citizens. I'm not going and that's final."

"Apart from wondering what the fuck you do eat, I don't give a stuffed duck's fart if you go or not. But you've conned the rest of the players into taking your side."

"I really resent that Hutch. You're saying footballers are too stupid to make up their own minds, or change their minds once the issues have been presented. I haven't conned anyone but I've told them where I stand and I've said that on this issue there is no neutrality. If the club goes to South Africa then everyone associated with the club is legitimising a corrupt, racist regime. You can threaten the players all you want, but even if they change their minds I won't."

I could imagine the two of them eyeball to eyeball over the desk, Hutch's whisky bottle acting as referee. There was a silence.

"I'll make you Captain if you come." I cringed with embarrassment to hear an old, respected friend stoop to such clumsy wheedling. Freddy's laughter was, in its way, more cutting than anger.

"My price is just a little higher than that Hutch. One other thing, on this issue I don't keep my peace, not like the West Brom match. If I'm transfer listed, everyone will know why."

"I see," said Hutch. "Now you think you're bigger than the whole club."

"No, but nor do I think that the club is bigger than the suffering of a whole population. The Dockers jaunting off to South Africa is not only immoral on its own but it's an insult to the people of this area and to the black people who work in this club. You've got the players' statement, you want me to deliver it?"

"Leave it with me, I'll think about it. Now get out."

"Hutch is that the way to talk to your star mid-field performer? I do hope that this little difference won't come between us."

"Get out!"

I admired the man's control as he struggled to maintain his voice.

"One last thing Hutch. Don't think on it too long - don't do anything cute, like booking the tickets and thinking we'll go along because we won't."

"Piss off."

I dodged behind a corner as the passageway echoed to the sound of a door being slammed. Re-emerging into the gloomy passage I greeted Freddy as if he was the last person I expected to see. He smiled in return, "Hello George, if you've come to see Hutch, tread carefully he seems a little on edge today."

"I'll take it easy," I said, foolishly pleased that he remembered my name.

"Actually," he continued, "I would like to thank you for the good things you've written about me, it's much appreciated."

"That's how I've seen it," I said. "You won't know this, but I first saw you at Eastgate at least six years ago, and then at Doncaster."

His whole face lit up as he laughed. "Oh don't remind me, I've done my best to forget Doncaster. Every time I go back it's like something out of a horror movie."

"Freddy," I said, "I don't wish to seem pushy but Hutch has told me something of your political views. If you want to go public or even need a sympathetic ear, give me a ring. Here's my card."

He studied it for a moment then put it in the pocket of his shabby Dockside tracksuit. "Very nice George, your own card." Then he sauntered off down the corridor, not a care in the world. They had all landed on Hutch's, increasingly bowed shoulders.

"So tell me George, what should I do?" he said, his fingers wrapped tightly around his third division Manager of the season bottle of whisky. His hands shook as he poured us each a quintuple. I raised my eyebrows in surprise.

"First of all I think you're undoubtedly drinking too much. Secondly," I raised my hands, "he's right. South Africa is an appalling decision. Apart from anything else you'll be crucified for it. Think of it, demonstrations, petitions, boycotts all aimed at you. Because Sam Dolton won't be there when trouble lands. At best you'll be tied to him, alienated from the community. Your decision Hutch, good luck with it."

I wouldn't be a Manager. I might swap my life for one game in the fourth division, but a Manager: Never.

FREDDY

"Feather, Boss wants to see you now." The ill-disguised pleasure in Johnny's tone told me that trouble was waiting up the stairs.

"Can I shower first?"

"Now means now, not tomorrow, perhaps I wasn't making myself clear." The other players watched, stifling smiles, as I trooped off the pitch and followed Johnny like a naughty schoolboy up to the Headmaster's office. I knocked and went in. Hutch sat at his desk pretending to immerse himself in paperwork. Johnny stood guarding the door. I waited while they went through their little ritual. Finally he looked up: surprise. He sighed deeply, shook his head from side to side, looked me up and down.

"We don't ask for much out of life son. A winning team and we've got that, touch wood. Promotion would be nice; who knows, if everything goes smoothly we might even get that. Look, you see that?" He pointed to a giant bottle of whisky standing in the corner. "You know what that is?"

"Your weekly drinks ration."

"Christ, you're a lippy little sod. It's a little bonus from Bells, Manager of the Month. You'd think wouldn't you, that with all these good things coming our way we'd be happy men? But we're not, are we Johnny?"

"Definitely not Hutch, definitely not happy."

"And do you know why we're not happy?" Hutch said. "Well I'll tell you." Somehow I thought he might.

"Do you know how many clubs we've managed? Tell him Johnny."

"At least nine, ten if you count two spells at Leyton Orient."

"You hear that, ten clubs, and everyone with their own pet problem. I've had womanisers, drunks, gamblers, poufters..."

"I don't think you should refer to people in those terms," I said. "The correct term is gay. And if there's a problem, perhaps it's yours."

Hutch sucked in a deep breath making a whistling noise through clenched teeth, a sure sign of his agitation. "So here we have the nub of the whole problem. You're a troublemaker son. A nice lad in many ways," he added reassuringly. "But you've got a big mouth and it's always on the move. Well, now it's stretched itself once too often and in the wrong place."

"Oh Hutch, do get on with it," I said wearily. "I haven't got all day, I've children to collect from school."

"I fought for you son."

"What, in the war?" I said disbelievingly.

"Up in the chairman's office."

"What's the chairman got to do with any of this?" I felt a tightness across my stomach, chairmen are to be avoided at all costs. "Besides being a corrupt, foul-mouthed, capitalist swine."

"Ah, you have met then." He said with a rare trace of humour. He took out two pieces of paper. "I've got some good news and some bad news, which do you want first?"

I thought for a moment. "Is the good news better than the bad news is bad?"

Hutch balanced the two pieces of paper.

"It's pretty close. But all things considered the good is only good; while the bad is fucking horrible."

"Alright tell me, I can't decide, just say your piece."

He settled his bum on the seat, leaned back comfortingly. "I wonder, have you ever met the chairman's wife? A charming woman? No, never been invited over for sherry? I have, just the once mind. A lovely place, a mansion out Middlesex way." He leaned forward. "Between these four walls you might be right about the chairman. He's a hard son of a bitch, but her Ladyship, now there's a woman with class. A magistrate, you know."

"I didn't."

"Oh yes. Now there is nothing her ladyship likes better than to go out riding on a Sunday morning, with her lovely teenage daughter."

"The plot thickens," I said, just to get a word in.

"Anyway," Hutch went on, ignoring me, "there's her ladyship and her lovely teenage daughter galloping across the Middlesex Moors on a sunny Sunday afternoon. Any bells starting to ring yet son? They ought, because it seems that your particular path and the path of her ladyship were doomed to cross."

He looked at me, shook his head, had another sip of whisky. "As I say, there's her ladyship engaged in her favourite pursuit when, stack me, what d'you think happens next?"

"Get to the point Hutch," I said, although I knew better than most how the story turned out.

"Hutch? Hutch? My friends call me Hutch. Johnny calls me Hutch, but when I think of Johnny I don't get a headache. YOU call me 'Boss'." He leaned forward drummed his fingers on the desk, "Just tell me in your own words what happened next. You know just so I'm clear in my own mind. You never know, what with her ladyship being a magistrate and all she may have missed out on a few details. Take your time, no hurry."

"They're hunters Hutch, just about the scum of the earth." 'Calm down Freddy,' I told myself.

"Surely not lost for words?" Hutch said in tones of mock surprise.

"An historic moment. Johnny, remember this day."

"Etched on my mind Hutch."

"Very droll," I said. "You want to know what happened or not?"

"I know what happened. The chairman has told me in the most graphic detail. Her Ladyship and her friends and her lovely teenage daughter were set upon by a gang of punks, yobbos, and one professional footballer, who launched themselves out of a nearby wood: blowing trumpets, waving banners, and proceeded to attack the riders. When the police arrived, there was chaos, bodies on the ground, but no yobbos."

"Sabs is the word, short for hunt saboteurs. Sabs, get it right."

"I do apologise. Although the sabs had vanished into the mist, luckily or unluckily, depending on your point of view, her ladyship and her daughter both recognised one of their attackers. Apparently the very lovely daughter has, or had, a poster on her bedroom wall. I believe Mummy has torn it down now."

"Mummy didn't mention the fact that they tried to ride us down, or that they used their whips. I suppose it must have slipped her mind. So what happens now?"

"Let me see." He leaned back on his chair, sucked in all the available oxygen, placed his fingertips together in a reflective pose. "As I see it, there are two alternatives: you can of course apologise - crawl in the chairman's office on bended knees and grovel for forgiveness. Repent your ways and promise that nothing like it will ever, ever happen again."

"Or."

"Or, you can pick up your cards on the way out. Sacked, I believe is the phrase."

"He can't do that," I said. But even as the words formed I

recognised their hollow emptiness. Hutch hammered home the point.

"He's the chairman son, he can do anything he wants. While we work here he owns us. We're well paid for the privilege, but he has the power of instant dismissal. Who should know that better than me? You tell him Johnny."

"Six sackings, two resignations, two mutual consents," said Johnny up to date with all the latest historical news.

"Think about it son," said Hutch. "Oh, before you go, I almost forgot, don't you want to hear the good news?"

"Surprise me!"

"You've been called up to the England squad. You report to Joe Doughty at the Hendon training centre at," looked at his watch, "three hours from now. Just enough time to pick the kids up from school. Now piss off!"

Johnny politely held the door open for me. As I passed through our eyes locked for a moment. If I was hoping for sympathy I was sadly mistaken.

"Go on son, piss off!"

* * * * *

I am not by nature an introspective person. From an early age I knew how to keep my deepest feelings hidden even from myself.

This emotional immaturity, had been covered, up to now, by physical activity. Movement over thought, a restless energy that rushes ahead of the most careful planning.

Standing under the shower, looking out over the deserted changing room, it seemed as if this delicate balancing act had just caved in on itself. Picked for England. The very words made my head spin with a wild elation: justification for a life plan in its fourteenth year. This surge of triumph was quickly displaced by a despair that seemed to leave me helpless and unable to move.

I was being dragged between the conflicting emotions. I think I must have suffered a mini breakdown. My mind opened up like pages from a photo album; each picture capturing a moment in time, releasing its memories from the coffin of the past.

Eleven years old, overweight and lonely, frightened to go home to an already half-pissed Father. My place of safety, an old, deserted garage behind Loveridge Road where I could kick a ball in and out of the rubbish; where I could drop into fantasy and be anyone I chose. Even at eleven I had a clear idea of my position in life, somewhere near the bottom of the pile.

This particular day, the ball ran free to the single foot of a man wearing a dark overcoat; heavy for a warm spring day. He stopped the ball, then leaning into his crutches, he swung his one leg in a surprisingly graceful movement. I don't know why I wasn't more frightened of this strange looking man. In his huge coat and tatty cloth cap pulled low over his face, he must have seemed the perfect child molester, scouring stray plots of land for victims.

Somehow the act of kicking a ball brought us together.

Loneliness recognising its reflected self. This chance meeting swiftly became a ritual. The two of us meeting after school, losing ourselves until the sun went down.

He even came to see me make my debut as goalkeeper for the school team, standing silently on the touchline away from the other parents. It was a day when the forces of life conspired to pour humiliation on one of its lowlier subjects. We lost 11-0. A goal for every year of my life. Ian Hamilton scored 9. Two direct from in-swinging corners that floated over my flailing arms. He dribbled through our whole team and pushed the ball through my legs. He did as he wished and with every goal I grew smaller and he larger until he filled my whole vision.

After the match we walked home in silence. The end of fantasy; life was too grim, too real. Finally he broke the silence that had lasted the length of several streets.

"It's time to take a hard look at yourself Freddy." The very last thing I wanted to do. Mirrors revealed that I had the breasts of a developing girl, thighs pale and flabby, a little winkle hidden away within the folds of flesh.

"It's almost the end of the season now," he was saying. "That leaves six weeks of cricket and six weeks summer holiday. If you trust me and if you're willing to work, in those twelve weeks we can make you into an athlete." I looked up at his unshaven face. I would have trusted anyone who showed an interest in me.

It worked just as Alf said. Every day after school I would rush to the garage, and for three hours, I ran wearing heavy boots. I skipped, lifted rocks, sprinted, ran some more. Sometimes I went down on my knees and was physically sick while Alf stood by, silently waiting for me to recover, then went right on calling out his instructions, stopwatch in hand. This was our secret, the rest of the world never stopped to notice. Wearing the same outsize clothes I was still called 'fatso, barrel, tubs', but inside the fat uniform, a new thin me was pushing through.

The pictures flick through the years. I am fifteen proud in my new kit, lining up alongside Ian Hamilton for East London schoolboys against the South, the first step on the representational ladder. Training has never stopped. During the summer months Alf and I would catch a bus to the marshes where the local teams were in pre-season training, running off the inactivity and the alcohol.

"Can I have a game, mister?"

"Oright son. Where d'you play?"

"Up front."

At first the men treated me lightly, but I was small and tricky, a rabbit dodging in and out of elephant's legs. It wasn't long before I became a legitimate target for crude, clumping tackles, a compliment in itself.

For this match I felt fit and fast, but it was all lost alongside the genius of Hamilton. We were moths to his flame. He towered over us all. Already a schoolboy legend, signed to Chelsea, his future assured.

After the match, elated by victory, it took some time to realise that Alf's silence had an edge to it. I jabbered on, seeing only the well-timed tackles, the perceptive passes. Finally, on the bus home, I caught his mood! As we sat together yet miles apart, I felt angry, betrayed.

"What's wrong Alf? Okay I didn't play that well but we won didn't we?" He said nothing, his eyes turned away staring out of the window. I could hear the sound of his breathing.

"Come on Alf," I pleaded. "Tell me what's up." He kept his head turned, refusing to look at me.

"It's nothing to do with you Freddy," he said finally. "I'm genuinely pleased for you and I don't want to spoil your day."

"So tell me, maybe I can help."

For the first time he turned towards me and I could see a sadness in his eyes. "It is to do with you Freddy, in a way. I was watching you out there and I realised that there is nothing more I can do for you. You remember what we said when we started out? 'A nippy little inside forward.' Well that's what you are, we've achieved everything we set out to do."

"I thought we were friends Alf? You're my best friend." I was practically begging the man.

"Look at me son, I'm a cripple. I shouldn't be your best friend. You've become dependent on me. Maybe I've encouraged it, without meaning to. Now it's time to stop. I haven't anything more to give you. It's time for you to live your life and me mine."

I stared up at him, hearing the words but unable to take them in. Perhaps he was joking, but Alf rarely joked and one look at his grim profile was enough to tell me he hadn't changed his ways.

"I thought this match was just a beginning. What about all the plans we made? Look how far we've come, and it's all down to you Alf." I could feel the tears stinging the back of my eyes as I searched around for something, anything, to make him change his mind. "Alf, I'll do any thing you want."

"There's only one thing I want and no one can give me that. I want my leg back. Can you do that for me Freddy?"

We got off the bus without speaking, my mind racing with desperate half thoughts. Finally I asked, "Alf, am I good enough to be a pro?"

He rubbed his nose with his hand, a sign that he was thinking.

"No."

"Will I ever be?"

"It's possible."

"Why can't we come to some sort of deal then? A business deal. You continue to coach me and I'll pay you a percentage of my future wages. We can draw up a contract."

He didn't reply but he did continue to rub his nose. Nor did he speak until we reached his house. Then he said, "Come inside, I've got something to show you."

I put the kettle on, trying to act normally, as if nothing had changed, waiting for him to make the next move.

"Go to the cupboard under the stairs, bring me what's inside."

I dug around in the dark, cobwebby, cupboard until I felt a large box. I dragged it out and carried it to Alf. He held the box in his arms, cradling it almost. Without looking at me he unpacked the box. "Know what this is?" He asked.

"It's a false leg." Placing the box on the table, he unfurled his empty trouser leg, rolled it up until his stump was revealed. It poked up in the air like the end of a sausage.

Still without speaking, he fitted his stump into the leg then rolled his trousers down. He slotted the end of the leg into a shoe, stood up and walked around the small kitchen.

"You're not the only one who's been practising," he said.

"It's fantastic Alf!" Suddenly I began to cry. The tears simply streamed down my face.

"How long have you had it?" I managed to say at last.

"It's lain in the cupboard for ten years. I used to take it out and look at it, but then about six months ago I put it on, just like that."

"Does it hurt?"

"The only thing that hurt more was when they cut it off. It hurts but it's worth it."

"And does this mean you'll go on coaching me?"

He gave one of his rare laughs and somehow I knew it would be alright.

"How did you lose your leg?"

It all came out. Ten miners trapped by the collapse of a main shaft. The knockings from above which caused another collapse and the cutting off of the air supply. The long, slow, painful death. One by one, until only one miner remained alive. Hauled into the glare of the television cameras, the unctuous words of the waiting politicians, the tears of the waiting relatives. Alf's voice was expressionless, he might have been describing a shopping trip to Sainsbury's.

"I was ready for death - calm, accepting - better me than those men with families. When they dug us out after three or four days, I didn't want to live. All I could see then and for years after was the dead faces that stared through the gloom of our coffin. All I could hear was the crash of voices telling me how lucky I was to be alive, even when they were cutting my leg off. Then they offered me money, 'Three days in a living tomb: one man's incredible story.'"

Guilt at living had driven Alf away from his home to the crowded anonymity of Dockside - a half life, a living death.

"Meeting you brought me back Freddy." He laughed softly to himself.

"Tell me."

"Your youth was some of it, but more your sense of helplessness, like a little lost puppy. Before I knew it I had a reason to get up in the mornings."

The realisation that someone actually cared for me, little fat Freddy brought more tears to my eyes. Ten year later, the tears still fall, mingling with the water from the tepid shower.

Somehow, without any memory of how, I was on my pushbike, cycling to Alf's house. Over the inevitable mug of tea I unburdened myself. Expecting anger, at Dolton, at myself, at everybody, Alf's calm acceptance caught me by surprise.

"How can you just sit there?" I said. "We've got to do something."

"Any suggestions?" he replied with just a touch of malice. "No, well it's a good thing that one of us thinks with more than his mouth."

"Don't go mysterious on me Alf. I couldn't cope with it. I need someone to tell me what to do."

"One thing we want from you, just one, think you can manage it?"

"Not until you tell me what's going on in your devious little mind."

"Alright." He stopped for a dramatic pause. "We're going to take Dolton on. Hear me out, because I've been working on this for some time." He poured more tea, took a sip. "Dolton is a cheap little crook. Propped up by family money he sees himself as a working class boy made good. In a way this is true, he's kept all the faults of the working class, the ignorance, the prejudice, the narrow mindedness, the refusal to accept change, and dropped all the virtues. Make no mistake, he's a nasty piece of work, and in his own sphere he wields a certain amount of power. But he may have overreached himself."

"How? How has he overreached himself?"

"Two ways," he said, emphasising the point by holding up two fingers. "Firstly, he's been greedy. His butcher shops, his travel agencies, the scrap yard, make more money than any one person could reasonably want. God knows how, but he's even managed to marry money. All this isn't enough for our Sam, he's got cash flow problems so he's been sticking his fingers into the club's money. Don't worry about any of this Freddy, we'll go into the details later."

"Wait, wait, wait, what's the second thing? Tell me I've got to know."

"Our second weapon is you Freddy. Dolton has no real conception of the depth of local feeling. He thinks he's popular. Even more, he takes credit for the success of the team. He wines and dines on it. He eats only the best, mixes with the mighty; but everyone in Dockside knows him as a cheap little crook, like his Father and his Father's Father. With a lot of preparation and a little bit of luck, his small town dynasty might prove rotten enough to cave in completely. He won't go quietly mind, he'll scream and at the last, he'll squeal for mercy.

"That's when we stick the boot in," I said.

"So what's my role in all of this?" Impressed by Alf's analysis, I was eager to throw myself into the fray. He sat back caressing his mug of tea.

"From you," he said slowly, "all we want is a hat trick on Wednesday night. Think you can manage it?"

"Right. One other thing, so small it's hardly worth mentioning, but what if, hypothetically speaking, I don't get a game? I could easily spend the whole match on the subs bench, then it's thank you and on your bike!"

"You'll play Freddy, I can feel it in my leg." He smiled that rare sunshine smile. "Now go and get ready."

Which book to take? There is that Biography of Marx that I've been meaning to read for weeks, his bearded face stared up from the bookshelf. Maybe a thriller for easy reading, or even a Phillip Dick before he went off his trolley. Oh look, there's a book on bridge technique. Somehow nothing seemed satisfactory, perhaps there's time for a quick trip to the library.

"Wha'cha doing, babe?" Elane's voice made me jump.

"Nothing."

"I can see that," she said. "The point is, what should you be doing? Are you packed?" I nodded. "Have you been to the toilet? Cleaned your teeth?" She looked at me carefully, shaking her head. I sat hunched in the passenger seat of Alf's Robin Reliant. Elane and Alf talked across me as if I were some kind of idiot child.

"I've made a map," Elane said to Alf, handing him a square of paper, "that even Freddy should be able to understand. The journey should take two hours, any longer and you're in trouble." Alf nodded silently,*p his knuckles showing white on the tiny steering wheel, then we roared off at ten miles an hour to do battle with the London traffic.

Three and a half hours later we pulled up outside this huge

complex. Alf and I shook hands solemnly, aware that for the first time I would be without his guidance. A realisation that filled neither of us with confidence. The door to Alf's Robin wouldn't open so I squeezed out of the window, landing in a heap on the floor. As I rose, brushing my knees, a massive security guard stood over me.

"Who're you sunshine?"

"Freddy Feather, footballer."

"Never 'eard of you, go on, on your bike!"

"No, really I am, honest."

"Got a Pass?"

"A pass absolutely, got it here somewhere." He hovered, a cynical expression on his face as I went through all my pockets, twice. "Must have left it in the car," I said attempting a winning smile.

He smiled back. "No pass, no entrance."

"I take your point," I said. "You can't have any old riff raff walking up here, but perhaps we could compromise."

"Okay."

"Phone the office. There must be somebody expecting me. After all you don't want to be known as the man who cost England the World Cup."

He considered this. "What did you say your name was?"

"Feather, Freddy Feather. You'll be hearing it a lot." Such bravado, I surprised myself.

We waited, not talking, waiting for something to happen.

Long minutes passed in silence until a tracksuited figure, whom I recognised as Vic Smith, England's coach for the last hundred years, emerged from the hotel and military-marched up to us.

"You Feather?" he said in an unfriendly tone of voice. "You're late, two hours and forty-one minutes late."

"I'm sorry, but my father is ill and I had to see him at the hospital before I left."

Vic Smith looked down at me. "I haven't heard about any illness."

"That doesn't mean he isn't ill," I replied before I could stop myself. Vic Smith didn't pursue the matter. He gave me another of his disapproving stares. "Inside." He jerked a thumb. "I'll see you later."

Framed photographs of past England teams stared mockingly from the walls of the highly polished lobby. Clutching my shabby holdall I had no idea of what to do or where to go. If no one sees you, perhaps you aren't there at all. Stupid thoughts: think of Elane and the girls, think of Alf and our dreams. 'Think of the sack,' muttered a little voice. 'Think of how small and frail you are. They are going to find you out you know, expose you for the pretender you really are. Did you really think you'd get away with it? You're not good enough, never have been, never will be.'

'We'll see.' Oh God, I'm talking to myself.

To still the nagging little voice I pushed at a door marked 'Private'. There before me, in all their glory, sat the England football team; faces only seen from the television. I coughed, not a single head turned. Just as I suspected, invisible.

At the nearest table three players, Andy Shatlock, Norville Reid and Pete Martin, were picking up freshly dealt brag hands. Pete Martin, football's current 'jack the lad' won the hand and swiftly dealt another. This time Big Norve kept his hand over the cards, going 10p blind, forcing the other two to throw 20p into the kitty. Andy Shatlock stacked his hand but Pete Martin went with it until the table was crowded with small pieces of rolling silver. Norve picked up his hand and threw 50p into the kitty. Pete Martin raised the stakes again and Big Norve threw his cards in. He was bluffing Norve, you should have gone on and nailed the bastard. As the England captain gathered the cards to deal another hand I coughed. An apologetic, excuse-me-but-here-I-am sort of a cough. Interrupted, Andy Shatlock turned his head.

"Didn't you see the sign? You a journalist?" he added in a hostile tone. Looking back at three blank faces, a vague feeling of anger started to rise.

"Actually, I'm from the Ministry of Defence and I'm afraid I've got some rather bad news. There has been a nuclear pile-up just half-a-mile from here. The whole area is under quarantine until everybody has undergone rigorous testing. All this is very hush hush and is being handled at the very highest levels. The P.M. has already been on the phone to the German Chancellor and I'm afraid the match has inevitably been cancelled. Still, the way you lot have been playing lately that's probably good news." I smiled at three blank faces who, finally, were giving me their full attention. If they didn't fully believe, there was enough doubt on their faces to tempt me on.

"The important thing is not to panic. With any luck the security forces will be out of here in two or three days and we can all go home. On the other hand..." But there was no chance for the other hand to be opened, at that moment I felt a weight on my shoulder bony fingers digging into flesh.

"Lads, this is Freddy Feather, he'll be with us until after the match." Well thank you, that makes my position clear. "Here's a tracksuit, be out on the pitch in five minutes." We all watched as Vic marched away then Pete Martin turned to me. "Freddy Feather who d'you play for then?"

"Dockside."

"Oh yeah, third division ain't they?"

"Second, we were promoted last year. You guys winding me up or what?" Big Norve, six foot two of bone and muscle, gave a deep laugh, then he held out his hand. "That's the way it is round here man, bodies come and go."

"Welcome to the execution," added Pete Martin.

Vic caught hold of me as I stood on the touchline. "Listen son," he said into my ear, those bony fingers digging once more into my arm. "I want you to mark Colin Westley, give him a dose of what the Germans will be dealing out tomorrow. Don't do anything flash and you'll have done a good job for England." He smacked me hard on the bum. "Go to it son."

Playing Colin Westley must have come hard to Joe and Vic. He was, after all, an artist, a free flowing player, an exquisite passer of the ball, a dainty, delicate player with none of the attributes so beloved by coaches; running power, tackling, marking. In a way, Westley represented a bowing to public pressure. All of these thoughts flashed through my mind as I took up my position alongside him, cast in the role of the destroyer, the mid-field hatchet man. As we played, Vic's bellow kept us company. "Mark! tackle! cover! Run! Stick with him!" Then it happened - a fifty-fifty ball. Westley's foot came down a fraction late, and I felt the judder run up my leg. For a moment Westley stood, then he slowly toppled like a tree.

Trainers rushed on from all directions. I watched as they carried him off. The only person to speak was Vic. "Well over the top son." Hands on hips he stared down at me. "I said mark him, not cripple him. Who sent you here? Hitler?"

"Don't be so bloody stupid!" I shouted back. "I went for the ball fair and square, carrying out your instructions. His face reddened. He was standing so close that I could see the veins in his forehead throb. He stood for a moment - then made a lunge for me. Fortunately, Andy Shatlock and Norville Reid got hold of him, but we stood, faces no more than a foot apart, I could feel his hot breath. We might have remained locked in this pose more or less forever, but Joe Doughty came up.

"Take a rest Vic," he said in his quiet way. Shooting me a last, venomous glance, Vic went off. Joe Doughty turned to me, "You'd better take Colin's place in the centre of mid-field." He smiled a sad little smile. "You're just about the last mid-fielder in the country still on his feet. Get out there now and play your normal game."

Freed from Vic's presence I ran with the feeling that if this was my last time in the England set up, then I might as well enjoy it. When the session was over, Joe came up and put his arm round my shoulders.

"I know you've had some trouble son, but I want you to put all that from your mind. Tomorrow you'll be playing for England." He gave me another of his sad smiles and strolled off.

Steve Simpson, the Leicester City winger was my roommate. As we were the only second division players in the squad, somebody thought that we would have a lot in common.

"You've done alright ain'cha?" were his first words. "Crock the star and walk into his place, alright for some."

"You'll get your turn," I said.

"Nah, the only way I'll get on is if we're two down with 20 minutes to go. Then it's fling on a winger. Sick of it all really. I wish they'd just leave me at home. He put some earphones on, "I'm going to crash for an hour, wake us up at 8 will you?"

"What happens then?"

He smiled across at me. "The night before the big match meal. In your best suit, and don't be late."

An hour to kill. I rummaged in my holdall for a book. *Intercourse* by Andrea Dworkin, a chilling analysis of the patriarchal society. *Sexual politics* by Kate Millett.

And of course, Karl Marx, due back to the library three weeks ago and still unopened. The bearded face stared up at me, disapproving and accusing. Three of the most uninviting books in the world. Elane's little joke.

At eight o'clock sharp, we were all gathered together like overgrown schoolboys in the dining room. Everything arranged, all personal decisions, such as where to sit and what to eat, already made.

I stared at the menu: prawns, steak, gammon, veal, liver: you name it and it recently died. Somebody resembling authority, black jacket, white shirt, black tie, lurked in the background. Walking over I said quite pleasantly. "Excuse me, but I'm vegetarian and I wonder if you might have something more suitable in your kitchen." He looked at me blankly. Flicking through his mental index, coming up with a blank where my face should be - the question lingered behind his glasses. Suddenly Vic was there, as if he had somehow teleported across the room.

"What's the problem?" he said shortly.

The manager looked across at me, indecision skimming once more across his eyes. Shuffle the blame, share the blame, shift the blame to whom? To me.

Above all, don't upset Vic; football managers come and go, but Vic goes on forever, imposing his granite rule on team after team after losing team. Hotel managers disappear overnight if Vic so much as casts a flicker of disapproval their way. The night before a match. 'The Match,' everything must run smoothly, not a hitch. Vic hates hitches.

"I was just telling this, er, gentleman here," the manager said hedging his bets, "that there is nothing on the menu for vegetarians."

"You a vegetarian then?" Vic leaned forward hands on hips.

"Yes and I'm quite capable of organising my own meals thank you."

"So what can you rustle up then?" His attention switched back to the manager who, fortunately for him, had managed to string a few thoughts together.

"Macaroni cheese, an omelette, some fish pie left over from lunch."

"I don't eat eggs or fish and I loathe macaroni cheese. Talk to me I'm here." Now Vic turned the full weight of his gaze my way.

"So what exactly do you eat?"

"Well, actually Vic, I've a very varied diet. There's only one rule, that nothing on my plate has been slaughtered or experimented on."

We stared at each other, one of those timeless moments that s-t-r-e-t-c-h. Who did he remind me of? Not his looks as much as his manner - the rigidity that ran up his spine straight to his mind. Talking football, Alf and I would often speak of Vic and the chill influence he and his kind have spread across British football. In the midst of soccer misbehaviour, Vic could be heard calling for the reintroduction of corporal punishment, of National Service, a return to the days of old fashioned discipline, of turn up trousers. A face floated up from the past: Sandy Henderson, an old charge nurse of mine. Vic's twin in all but appearance. Sandy too needed just one glimpse to hate me on sight - almost on principle.

"I've heard stories about you," Vic muttered through tight lips. "You've got yourself a bit of a reputation haven't you?" The words hissed across the room.

"I don't know. Have I?" Thirty odd pair of eyes stared, as once more we stood in direct confrontation.

"I'm sure chef can find something suitable in the kitchen. Why don't we just go and look." The manager gave a ghastly smile. "It's just that we weren't informed you see," he added, dragging his excuses onto the stage for future reference. Vic stared at us surprised at this new alliance, then satisfied that he and he alone had solved the problem, he nodded once and strode off.

As I sat down at last with an ideologically sound avocado salad and pot of tea all to myself, Big Norve turned to me and said, "I don't think Vic likes you man."

"I wouldn't say that. Don't you think the situation was handled with poise and dignity?"

Andy Shatlock turned from the other side and said, "What you got to ask yourself Freddy is, are you alright in the head?"

The night before the match was not a restful one. Morning came at last, the sun poking into corners, exposing those things best left hidden. I was lying on the floor doing some early morning stretching exercises.

"What the fuck you doin'?" Steve Simpson said sleepily. "Jesus how can I have a wank with you poncing about on the floor?"

"No wonder you never make the team, all your energy's up here. There's a great career smeared all over the sheets."

"Bollocks."

Faint at first, then growing stronger as the day slowly, slowly unwound - something intangible in the air. Tension? Only to be expected. England's most important match since the last most important match.

Beneath the strain, behind the over-jolly camaraderie, weaving in and out of the air, never staying still long enough to be identified, was something more than the expected pressure. It was there during the training session, still hovering as we gathered in the recreation room for the final team talk.

Vic was there of course, looking down on us, clipboard at the ready. Joe Doughty, "Uncle Joe," stood by a blackboard, his back to us. He turned, his sad eyes reaching out. Now I understood the prevailing mood of vague depression. Not defeat. No manager or player could allow that thought to slip into the daylight. As he faced us, his hunched body seemed to say it all. His tracksuit hung across his tubby frame, the worry lines etched into his face were visible across the room. A man preparing himself for the worst, hoping for the best but not really believing. Too many matches, too nice a man for the killer job in football. The Michael Foot of British football, a worthy man in the wrong job at the wrong time.

Vic looked okay, straight and firm, no sagging flesh on his body. But, come the final whistle, Vic was the enforcer. The mood comes from the manager, and Joe Doughty looked like Binky the Clown at one children's party too many. Perhaps the whole scene was purely imagination, but seeing him in person was poignant, almost moving, crucially different from the fumbling figure of fun seen so often, mumbling through yet another England defeat. Stand up Uncle Joe, a man who has used up his store of joy. You wanted to beat the Germans if only to bring a smile, however fleeting, to his face.

"Okay, lads, this is it, the big one. Win it and we're on our way. The W.C. trail - something to tell your children and grandchildren."

The Match (The Commentator in his box)

Brian: Good evening viewers. It's a warm autumn night and 80,000 people are packed into Wembley stadium in the hope that England can put past performances behind her. Find some form for a match that we must win. Alongside me I have Ronny Buckman, former England captain, who will be giving us the expert view.

Ron: owing to injuries, this is a reshaped England team, how do you think we'll cope with the experienced and very skilful German team?

Ron: Can we do worse, Brian? It seems that we're going through one of those times when England are losing at everything against everyone. The Australians have just slaughtered us at cricket, the All Blacks at Rugby. One does feel that if we put out a tiddlywinks team against The Baffin Islands, we would be beaten there as well.

Brian: It does sometimes seem that when a side is doing badly, as we are, that the little bits of luck that all teams need just aren't there. In this match for example we have lost Colin Westley, probably our one player with pretensions to world class. We've been forced to bring in inexperienced replacements. Perhaps if we run through the England eleven you can give us your expert analysis of each player in turn. In goal we have Pete Renvoize.

Ron: We've always had a tradition of good goalkeepers; Renvoize is a solid rather than inspired keeper, he dominates his box. If he has a weakness, it's in one against one situations.

Brian: We've got a traditional flat back four of Bobby Faulkner, Trevor Garner, Jim Craig, and the captain Andy Shatlock.

Ron: It most be said that the central defence has been vulnerable ever since the glory days of Bobby Moore. Here we are playing Big Trevor Garner; what is this, his sixth cap? And he has never seemed safe, good in the air but lacking that little bit of pace against top class international teams. Alongside, Jim Craig has been looking a little jaded lately. Perhaps he hasn't fully recovered from the pounding he took in the European championships. The right back, Bobby Faulkner, is thirty-three now and there must be question marks against him, especially when faced with a winger of Hottges's pace. Captain Andy Shatlock played alongside me in my last match for England. He has been a good servant to his country and his club across the years.

Brian: A mid-field three of Norville Reid, Larry Hamilton and the one real surprise of the team; Freddy Feather of Dockside Town.

Ron: Yes, you're right Brian, all the players are familiar; they may not be your personal choice but at least we know them. Except for the boy Feather. Alright I grant that he is a late replacement for Colin Westley, and injuries have ruled out Neil Clarke and Gerry Chapman, but it does seem to be a selection that smacks of desperation.

Brian: I must confess that I haven't actually seen him play, but he has scored 12 goals so far this season for Dockside.

Ron: And I must confess that I haven't seen him either, but there is a difference between calling a young player up to the squad for experience, and actually pitching in a player who has never even played in the first division. In fact this is his first season on the second division.

Brian: In fact he's not so young. It says here that he is 26, which in football terms is relatively old to be making your international debut. The story is that he was called up for the under 21s and the selectors were just as surprised as us when they found out his true age. Still here he is and we all wish him the best of luck. Now the front three of Les Godfrey, Ray Archer and Pete Martin.

Ron: Godfrey and Archer are both fast, direct players who thrive on good service from mid-field. We don't have Westley to provide that and, to me, it looks as if the balance of the side is wrong. Pete Martin we all know; if anyone is going to unlock the German defence it will be Martin.

Brian, Finally Ron, how big a match is this for England and for Joe Talsin?

Ron: I would say that this is a very important match indeed: lose this one and we are as good as out of the World Cup. It's possibly the last chance for Joe. But I tell you that I wouldn't do his job, not for anything.

Brian: Finally Ron, who have we to watch out for in the German team?

Ron: All of them Brian, but perhaps especially the mid-fielder Steiner, the winger Hottges, and coming from deep, the sweeper Horst.

Brian: Thanks Ron; now the teams are lining up for the kick off; the referee, a Frenchman, Monsieur Depaulle, blows his whistle and we're off! It's Archer to Martin back to Feather for his first touch in international football, he gives it to Craig, who puts a long ball deep in the German half.

I finish tying my laces, then pick up the shirt, letting it run through my fingers. Vic Smith comes over for a final word. "Okay son, you know what we've been working on, you stick close to Steiner. Do the same job on him as you did to Westley and we'll be well chuffed." I stand up and he smacks me on the backside. The clatter of studs on the dressing room floor like tiny hooves. The long walk up the corridor, and the roar as we emerge into the floodlights. Kicking a ball, right foot left foot against Pete Renvoize. My first glimpse of Steiner as we change ends, a hunched over figure wearing long baggy shorts; his trademark. The strolling assassin. Alf has warned me about him.

We kick off and the game falls into an early pattern, the Germans conceding the mid-field as they retreat to the edge of their box. For ten minutes or so we apply pressure without any real chances. Slowly the Germans start to come forward. Horst the sweeper carrying the ball out of defence - Steiner lays off quick short passes. It takes all my concentration to keep him in range. He tempts me into the tackle, showing me the ball. I refuse to be drawn. I stay close cutting down his angles, allowing him possession whilst restricting his space. Limiting my ambitions to stifle his.

Brian: Twenty minutes gone Ron, your impressions?

Ron: Much as I predicted Brian. We are battering away at the Germans defence, lots of effort, but not one real chance at goal. Reid is making runs; Hamilton is making runs but going nowhere. Godfrey can't get to the byline, and all the while The Germans are growing stronger and stronger. The young boy Hottges is giving Bobby Faulkner lots of trouble.

Brian: Just a moment Ron, it's Germany on the attack, Hottges has gone past Faulkner, he cuts it back to Steiner. Oh he's gone past Garner who sold himself. He chips it over Craig and its Muller who heads it in at the far post.

Ron: Lovely bit of play by the boy Steiner, one wonders where his marker was.

Brian: He's back there on the ground Ron, I didn't see anything, I wonder if he's hurt.

Ron: He will be when Vic Smith gets hold of him.

Pain, nothing but pain all up my leg. I was tracking Steiner when this hulking brute comes from nowhere and deadlegs me with his knee into my thigh. I go down like a tree, can only watch from the grass as Steiner drifts past Garner and makes a goal.

The Germans run past my body, joy on their faces. My team-mates approach more slowly, heads bowed, eyes not meeting mine. As the feeling returns to my leg, I can feel my anger grow. In the end the goal is down to me. The next time I get the ball instead of pushing it short to Larry or Norve I carry it myself. The effect is immediate; Norve and Larry run off dragging defenders and creating space. I swing a curling ball to Pete Martin who takes it on the turn and shoots.

I know, I know, I have to mark Steiner but I can do this and more. Steiner has the ball and I can see Hottges shaping for another run. I slide Steiner, wedging my body between him and the ball, I drag it back and regain my feet in one movement. The minder comes in wildly but I slip him and move into their half. Swinging left I clip a reverse pass to Les Godfrey haring down the right. He gathers the ball at full pace heading for the dead ball line as the defence makes frantic efforts to get back into position. Now it's all slow motion.

I see the sweeper move across as Les prepares to swing in a cross. The retreating defence is caught off guard as the ball comes hard across them. Eyes on the ball I leap tensing my neck muscles, catching the ball just right.

A goal! A goal all the way.

Brian: It's a goal...! No, I think the keeper may just have got his fingers to it. It's come back off the crossbar, a clearance sends it into England's half, and it's Steiner on the ball. He's round Garner who once again has sold himself. It's a one two with Hottges. Oh, the England defence is all over the place as Steiner calmly goes round Renvoize and puts it into the net. Ten seconds ago we were all almost cheering an England goal now it's 2-0 to Germany and the World Cup is looking like a distant dream. Ron, what do you make of that?

Ron: It's a tough old game, Brian. I tell you what, I wouldn't like to be in the boy Feather's shoes. Steiner may have had a quiet match but twice he's got away and bang, bang it's two nothing, and as you say, the World Cup slipping away.

Brian: Ten minutes left to half time, can England come back?

Ron: That's asking a lot at this level. It could have been 1-1 instead its 2-0. That's football.

Am I doomed to lie here on the grass watching Germany score? At the end of the day that goal is down to me as well. Don't believe me, ask Vic. Les and Pete pick me up and ruffle my hair.

"Hard luck, nice try," says Pete.

"Yeah, just keep pushing those passes through. Christ that's the first decent pass I've had all season."

"What about Steiner?" I reply.

"Fuck Steiner. Let's go out and win this fucking match."

The moments are ticking away as I feed Andy Shatlock on the overlap. He cuts inside and is chopped on the edge of the box. Without Westley, we've done nothing from dead ball situations. Norve and Larry dither as the defensive wall lines up. Fuck it, I run between them and curl the ball over the wall into the top corner of the net. Oh yes! There is a silence then the England team jump all over me and I can hear the crowd going wild as I raise my fist into the air.

Brian: Out of nowhere England are right back into this match. What a goal! Oh the crowd's going mad! Out of nowhere England have scored. Ron?

Ron: Well Brian that's football for you. What have we had? A dozen free kicks and nothing. I tell you that ball must have swerved at least five or six yards. If I'm right that is the first free kick the lad has taken all night and what a time to do it.

Brian: Indeed, because there goes the half time whistle.

In the dressing room Vic seemed numbed by the news of our goal. Having left the bench a few minutes early to sharpen his tongue for a right lashing, he was suddenly faced by eleven jubilant players and a beaming Joe Doughty. When he learned that it was indeed I, who had scored from a free kick I had no business to be taking, his face turned a deep shade of red.

"Your Father's not in hospital at all. You don't even have a father."

"I couldn't help it," I laughed right in his face. "You're right Vic, but who cares, we scored we can win."

"We'll play the way we trained otherwise I'll have you off so quick your head'll spin.

"Come on Vic," Pete Martin said. "He's giving us the best service we've had."

"That's right," added Les Godfrey, "that ball to me was inch perfect."

Vic stared from one face to another; then he swung round and with an open palm smacked me across the face, sending me sprawling onto the floor. I lay there looking up at bare legs and Vic looming over me. Behind him I could see the startled faces of the other players. "Referee! book that man," I said and the tension fell away.

"Jesus I'm sorry," said Vic wiping blood off my face with his sleeves.

"Jesus may forgive you," I said. "But I want a sponge first."

"Time lads," called a voice from outside. As I went past Vic into the tunnel, I leaned over and whispered, "Smack me on the bum one more time and I'll fucking lay you out."

Brian: Ron a quick word before the second half.

Ron: Well Brian, we've got to attack. You can bet your life that the Germans will be packing their defence and...

Brian: I'm sorry to interrupt you there Ron, but it seems as if England have made a substitution at half time. Ross Stapleton has come on and I'm just looking to see who has gone off. It's not Andy Shatlock which means that England will be playing with two left backs. It looks like mid-fielder Larry Hamilton. What do you make of that Ron?

Ron: Most peculiar, I'll tell you something else that's odd. Look at the boy Feather. There's blood all over his shirt. Something interesting has been going on in the England dressing room.

We tore into the German defence. Andy Shatlock had taken over Steiner and was feeding me with simple short passes. Big Norve was making powerful surging runs deep into the German defence, whilst up front Pete Martin and Ray Archer were moving across the box dragging defenders with them. But the Germans didn't cave in, or alter their style. They continued to play their way out of defence with neat little passes, keeping possession, slowly regaining composure.

Brian: Renvoize rolls it out to Faulkner who turns it inside to Shatlock, a short one to Feather who takes it on over the half way line, lays a pass through the defence to Martin. Martin holds -lays it back to Reid, inside to Feather who chips it first time over the German defence. And it's Archer sliding in at the far post for the equaliser. Ron, what a beautiful goal. From one end of the pitch to the other without a single German player touching the ball.

Ron: Well Brian, the boy Feather is everywhere: attacking, defending, laying out passes, this has become a performance of passion and power. England are playing like they believe they can win and it's been a long time since we've been able to say that. That was a classic goal, the ball moving from one end to the other without, as you say, a single German player touching the ball.

Brian: How do you see things going now? Bearing in mind that before the match started the whole country would have settled happily for a draw.

Ron: Well Brian, I've said it before, football's a funny old game. Half an hour ago, we were two nothing down and the game as good as over. Now it's a hell of a match. Twenty-five minutes to go and I almost believe we can win it.

Now the Germans are really pushing forward. The sweeper brings the ball out of defence. Steiner moves further forward. Down our right Bobby Faulkner is being given a torrid time by the pacy German winger, whilst Ross Stapleton is also suffering against the more measured approach of the German mid-field. I would have liked to have swapped them over. Steiner is everywhere, pushing and probing, drawing Trevor Garner into no-man's land. When the ball goes dead I trot over.

"Trev, you know you've been firing in these long balls?"

"Yeah, that's what I've been told to do."

"I appreciate that, but how about varying it a bit? You're an intelligent player you can do it. Just push a few short, see how it goes." He looked down at me. "Who to?"

"To me, Trev, to me. You get the ball, you give it to me." As the game settles into its pattern of attack and counter attack, it seems as if it is Me vs. Steiner. The other players respond to our promptings. Not that it is easy, this is above anything I have ever played in. The gaps close so quickly they are gone before they have opened. I can feel the minutes ticking away. Once more I swing left and lay a reverse pass out to Les Godfrey, shuttling down the right. He takes it at full speed, goes past his full back and is chopped by the sweeper on the edge of the box, about six yards in from the touchline. We line the ball up and see what is on. Garner is at the near post for the flick on, Craig is hovering near the edge of the box waiting to use his power. Fifteen or sixteen bodies all jostling in the box. Norve turns to me, "What now, oh great white chief?"

"Okay, Norve, you run across the box, take out the man on the wall, swing in to the penalty spot. I'll run over the ball to the goal line, you push it to me Andy, and I'll get it across to Norve who is just arriving at the penalty spot. Okay, let's synchronise watches. Go Norve."

I run over the ball, make for the touchline, hoping to get a yard. As Andy pushes the ball through, I can see the defender shaping to block my cross. Maybe we'd get a corner. I drag the ball back with my right foot, switch to my left as the defender slithers past. The intention is still to find Norve on the penalty spot. As I prepare to cross I sense the keeper move out to cover it. I dig my foot under the ball, half floating it, half chipping it, falling over as I watch it drift over the groping keeper into the far corner of the net. There is a silence, just for a moment, as the defence look round for someone to blame. Then the England players leap at me and I can hear the crowd going mad.

Brian: My word Ron, that was a magnificent goal! The angle must have been very tight indeed

Ron: Well Brian, what can you say? What a performance! It makes you proud to be English. On this performance who is to say that we can't win the World Cup.

Now the Germans are dishing out the heavy stuff. Steiner's minder clogs me and gets a booking. I can almost anticipate the pain there will be tomorrow. Big Trev pushes me a short pass. I lay it to Norve - take the return to Martin and back again and I curl one from twenty-five yards. Muller tips it round the post. Then the Germans are free down the left. The winger goes past Bobby Faulkner, cuts it back to Steiner and I just get a foot in to block the shot. Then all too soon it is over. I shake the referee's hand, swap shirts with Steiner. We salute the crowd and walk down the tunnel; the cheers echoing behind us. The best match I have ever played in, the best football I have ever played.

The dressing room is spilling over with jubilant bodies. People are laughing and singing. Men clutching cameras and microphones are trying to squeeze in through the doorway. Uncle Joe walks round embracing players. When he comes to me there are tears in his eyes. "Well played son, well played. The T.V. people want to speak to you, how do you feel about it?"

"I don't know Boss, I've never been asked before." From the corner of my eye I can see Vic staring at me.

"You played like a true international son, now go out and behave like one." Uncle Joe gives me one of his sad smiles.

So I had a shower and went out to face the cameras and the man with the microphone.

They pulled me and turned me and finally thrust a microphone at me.

"Freddy your first international for England, two goals; how does it feel!"

"I don't know, has it really happened? I remember walking down the tunnel and my thoughts must have been the same as everyone else's. 'Who's Freddy Feather? What's he doing in the team? Surely some mistake.'"

"What about the first goal, can you remember that?"

"Yes. This was something worked out before hand by The Boss and Vic. The fact was that I represented an unknown quantity to the Germans, but the surprise would only work once. Up to that point I hadn't taken a free kick in the match, so it seemed the perfect moment."

"And your second goal, another free kick, but a very different type of goal."

"Slightly different, no surprise factor. I remember it was out wide on the edge of the box and my first intention was a chip to the near post, but as I ran in, I saw the defence shift slightly. It was one of those moments where the body takes over from the mind, acts almost of its own accord. I hit it across them as they moved forward, and there you go."

"What about the change in tactics at half time. It seemed you had a much freer role."

"Again that's down to The Boss and Vic Smith. They realised that the match could be won." Racking up the brownie points.

"Finally Freddy, what about all the blood on your shirt?"

Indeed, what about it. "I'm just accident prone always have been," I said. "Coming out for the second half I walked into the door." Now Vic Smith owes me one. "Before we go, can I just say hello to my family and to all the people of Dockside, who are probably sitting in the same state of disbelief as myself."

ELANE

Diary - Sept. 24th Tuesday.

Rachel eight weeks old. First day back at the Unit. Went okay. I think.

Inadequate words: even with a little hindsight and the best of intentions, these words are just a screen behind which all sorts of activities seethe and flourish. Drag the curtains back just a little and out they pop one by one.

First up is guilt: misshapen, destructive, weakening the structure like dry rot. The guilt that comes with the act of deserting one's baby, however valid the reason. I defy all but the most entrenched feminist, the type of sister who makes Andrea Dworkin seem almost cuddly, to leave their baby in the arms of a disapproving Mother, without a twinge of well-deserved guilt.

What is it about West Indian. Mothers that makes them so expert in the dredging up and passing across of silent disapproval? It could of course be the legacy of suffering, the ten hours a day planting cotton, the miles walked from the river, water splashing over from the five gallon oil drum strapped to her back. Perhaps, and this is a truly terrible thought, it comes automatically with Motherhood.

Whatever the historical circumstance, my Mother lived her role to the full. Standing in the doorway, Rachel in her arms, her gaze, heavy with reproach, followed me down the street. Once round a corner I felt free, my step lightened, just the guilt to contend with.

I am sure that I seemed calm, professional, almost brisk. I know what people say.

'You have a problem, go see Elane. Good old Elane always there with the right advice. Her own life may be a bit dodgy, but for you my friend she'll know exactly the right thing to do.' Internally, nerves jangled with every step that took me further from the suffocating safety of the family home.

Dockside Psychiatric Unit, where I work for half the week, is an overpoweringly unimpressive. structure, jutting out from the crumbling masonry of the huge General Hospital like a tacked on afterthought. The G.H. may be falling apart but it does possess a certain Victorian grandeur. It has a history, it has healed and killed generation upon generation. The Unit, whilst it may actually be made of bricks and mortar, gives the impression of corrugated iron, chipboard, black plastic sheeting, of cheapness. Inside, nothing seems changed, my absence has altered nothing.

The night nurses, propped up by endless cups of coffee and the occasional cat nap, are nearing the end of their twelve hour shift. Their descent into sleep is crossed by the not yet fully functioning day staff, who squint through the haze of their first cigarette. The thin walls echo to the sound of early morning smoker's cough.

This first hour is probably the worst - certainly the most depressing. The patients/inmates/residents/clients - labels shift with each social clime - step into the day with varying degrees of reluctance. No one is here because they have succeeded in life. The air is thick and drowsy.

Walking through the passageway, searching for familiar faces, I glanced in at the window of one recreation room. Expecting to see twenty or so early morning insomniacs, I was taken aback by the sight of patients stretched out on the floor. A mass drug overdose was the first thought, but a closer look revealed a simple exercise session. Through the sound-proofed windows the scene resembled a silent pantomime. People stretched and twisted their limbs, mouths moved in silent moans. There were even the one or two faces I recognised: Mrs. Schlitzkrull, gentle, smiling grandmother of three - spare time kleptomaniac - struggled on the floor with the best of them. Danny Collier was in the front row, sweat trailing shiny tracks down his face. I knew Danny, born into casual violence, using up his chances with the abandonment of an alley cat.

I walked on to the office, where Fraser Clarke the Charge Nurse looked up and smiled. "Elane, wonderful to see you." He came over and hugged me, a simple gesture, but one which moved me deeply. No matter that I earned respect from colleagues, it is always warming to be welcomed as a person.

"Nice to be back, Fraser." We exchanged small talk for a bit. "Yes Rachel is doing fine, Mother's doing her bit. No Rod and I aren't together." I was ready to rear up at any imagined criticism, but there was only concern in Fraser' voiced.

"The exercise regime is new," I said. He raised his eyebrows in a familiar gesture. "That's down to Freddy. You'll meet him later, everybody meets Freddy sooner or later. Talking of which, you'll be coming to the team meeting."

Ah, the famous team meetings. Seated in the cramped office, surrounded by nurses, therapists, social workers, all of us members of Dr. Lepoise's team. I was reminded once again how, even though theory and practice may miss their connection, the system does chug forward, and once in motion, its own bureaucratic momentum keeps the whole show rolling, slowly, down the tracks.

It felt strange to be waiting once more for Dr. Lepoise to make his entrance. Strange because it all seemed so familiar. So much had happened, yet here I was, quite as if nothing had changed: a baby from nowhere.

Dr. Lepoise our resident psychiatrist and team leader finally strode through the door. His lateness a reminder that his time was, in some subtle way, more valuable than ours.

Seated in his prestigious swivelling chair Dr. Lepoise looked every inch the compassionate leader of our caring team. Maybe the image was the man, but our clashes had been too real and too deep for any respect. His very posture reminded me how much I disliked the man with his trendily cut, just too long hair, his sharp-as-a-razor suits. His arm round the shoulder, fingers straying to the breast. My thoughts drifted, snapping back at the mention of one of my clients.

"So we come to Danny Collier," Dr. Lepoise was saying, drumming his fingers on the desk. "I understand Danny is playing for the hospital in a cup football match. Apart from the ethics of a patient acting as a representative of the hospital, I feel that Danny is an unstable, possibly psychopathic young man. He picked up Danny's thick file. "There's nothing here to indicate that Danny is emotionally mature enough to accept even limited responsibility."

Fraser wriggled on his wooden chair. No Charge Nurse likes to go up against his boss. "Danny has been behaving well lately. His drugs are down. And really I felt that this was a ward level decisions."

"I don't think that 'psychopathic' is a fair label to put on Danny," I said. Heads swivelled my way. "His background is such that casual violence is almost a way of life. It's his struggle against peer pressure that has caused instability. If Danny has become involved in team events here in hospital, then that is surely a positive sign."

Dr. Lepoise swung round ponderously, like a bull elephant facing down the latest upstart in his herd. He stared at me over half-rimmed glasses, "Ah, Ms. Serle." He dragged the sound out, making an insult of it. "How nice to see you back. Someone taking care of the baby I trust?"

"No, it's parked outside next to your Mercedes," I snapped back before I could stop myself.

"I understand," he said dismissing me. "That one of our nurses is playing in this football match."

"Nurse Feather," Fraser replied. "And I'll be on the touchline just in case."

"Ah yes, Assistant Nurse Feather. He of the early morning exercise programme. And what does Assistant Nurse Feather have to say?" I turned and briefly caught the eye of a fair-haired boy whom I recognised from the exercise sessions, had mistaken for one of the patients.

"I think Danny has made progress," he said in growly, cockney tones. "Maybe this game will give him the feeling that the entire white establishment isn't against him. We all agree that Danny has a hair-trigger temper which he's trying to control. To be fair he has worked hard. He isn't the sullen individual he was when he first came in. I don't know, it may not work, but if we withdraw our promises whenever he reaches out a hand then don't we justify his belief that it's all sham? That all we, the establishment, are doing is going through the motions."

Faced with this solid front Dr. Lepoise gracefully withdrew. There were no illusions as to where he would be when trouble came; working on the pages of his latest, learned paper, introducing a group of impressionable students to one of the few inner city Psychiatric units in the country.

After that little hiatus, business proceeded fairly smoothly, until the very end. Dr. Lepoise gathered up the files, joggled them into symmetry.

"Any other little surprises I should know about before we call it a day?" he said with the merest hint of sarcasm.

"Just one small thing," Fraser said in his quiet way. "We've organised a... ah... bridge club. When I say we, I mean Nurse Feather, under my supervision of course."

Dr. Lepoise stood with his arms halfway through the sleeve of his leather coat.

"Well," Fraser continued rather nervously. "We... em... er

invited a team from the local Bridge club in for an evening, and now we've been invited back for a return fixture."

Dr. Lepoise slowly wound his scarf round his neck. "I'm rather keen on bridge myself. Bit of a player actually. Tell me who's in this team. I take it you are nurse Feather. You appear to be involved in everything that moves within these walls."

"I'm playing and Mrs Schlitzkrull. She learned to play in a concentration camp."

Did she? I've been her social worker for two years and I didn't know that.

"And there's Billy," the young nurse was saying. "We've rigged up a special board for him so he can operate the cards, and John Woodcock, the guy who shot his leg off in Northern Ireland. And young Shona is down as first reserve. The club have said they will pre-deal the cards, so it'll be an evening of contract bridge."

Dr. Lepoise looked thoughtful. "That's most enterprising. I don't suppose there's a spot for me in your little team?"

There was a silence. "That sounds reasonable," replied the fair-haired nurse slowly. "But who would we leave out? In all fairness I don't think any of the patients deserve to be disappointed, which I suppose leaves only me. Whilst I appreciate this might be a brilliant career move, I simply can't bring myself to make the gesture. I've worked hard setting this up; I believe in its therapeutic value. What can I say Doc? Maybe next time."

They stared at each other across a hostile silence. Then Dr. Lepoise straightened his coat collar, gave a final tug to his scarf and left the room.

As other staff members drifted away, I lingered, hoping for another word with Fraser.

"Sometimes I think you inhabit a different world to the rest of us," he was saying angrily. "A comfortable velvet world where you can gad about blithely humiliating your Boss, and nobody takes offence." He stopped for breath--a mistake.

"Why should I let him waltz into the bridge team? Next thing the local press'll be down here. Jolly little photographs. 'Look what we're doing for the local loonies.'

"Shut up Freddy, for once in your life just button it." Fraser sighed deeply. "These are compromises you make, it's called survival. You're not stupid Freddy, and you care about the job and the people here; yet all this, your livelihood, is put at threat because of a stupid bridge game. You don't compete with Dr. Lepoise. As far as you're concerned he's God. You don't notice he's there until you cross him, then it's too late, your life has just caved in. Boils, the plague, the sack. I need a cup of tea."

There was a moment of mutual embarrassment as they turned towards the door and saw me, but Fraser in his more normal manner smoothed the moment over.

"Ah Elane, this is Assistant Nurse Feather. Freddy meet Ms. Serle, our social worker with special responsibilities for psychiatric patients."

"That's a mouthful, does your job have a title?" Freddy said to me.

"Not really, it's the job that no one else wants."

Fraser laughed. "Well I want you two to work together. Freddy can keep you up to date on the current status of your clients and you can order him around. One strong lad, willing but not too bright."

So the curtains have parted a little. A new player has entered the stage. Pressing against my common sense, demanding entrance into my life, unasked for and definitely unwanted.

Having passed through that bleakest of times, a love affair turned bad, there was no space in my life for a man. Forced to concede that my judgement was suspect to say the least; I no longer believed in love or relationships. Even worse was the realisation that I conformed to a growing pattern, that of outwardly strong, capable, professional women who, time after time, make disastrous decisions in their personal lives. I needed no man in my life, certainly not a white boy, both younger and shorter than myself.

With the armour of these decisions to protect me, Freddy and I established a fairly successful professional relationship. Not entirely so, partly because working within mental illness involves scaling mountains of prejudice and administrative obstruction; where initiative survives by stealth. And partly because the air between us would sometimes crackle with unspoken thoughts.

Returning to the unit for my half week, I would eagerly await the next Freddy story. They came in a steady flow. One time he took several elderly patients blackberry picking. Mrs Schlitzkrull told me how they took over the kitchens to make fifty pounds of blackberry jam. Of course they burnt the jam, completely ruining a set of saucepans - the smell lingered for days. Most of these episodes were fairly comic in themselves, but sometimes Freddy's wild energy threatened to lash out of control.

I came in one day to find Fraser pacing the floor, the weight of the National Health Service on his shoulders.

"You know what he's done now?" was his greeting. I smiled preparing myself for the latest. "You know how the Industrial Therapy Unit works? Firms send in all the rubbish jobs. Bottle tops, the stuff that no one else will touch. Patients sit there for six hours and that's called therapy and the firm picks up an award for civic responsibility. We all live with this. It's a fact of life. But not Freddy. He marches straight in, calls the whole thing a disgrace and says he can get better jobs. You know where this leaves me?"

"On the fence."

He gave me a sharp look. "In the middle is more accurate. Would that I could sit on the fence, there are worse places to be." He stopped, shook his head. "I've got Sandy Henderson of I.T. doing a Scottish war dance on the carpet and what can I say? I know how he feels. How would you feel if some upstart, only been in the job five minutes, strolls in and said your whole area of responsibility was a sham?" He leaned back breathing deeply. "You know," he sighed, remembering yet another story. "We sent all the students and auxiliaries to see a film on depression. At the end when they asked for questions and comments, you know who gets up and says he thought he was going to see an educational film, not an hour long advert for the latest wonder drug, bought and paid for by the drug companies."

"So why do you put up with it?" I asked, although I more or less knew the answer.

"Because he's the best young nurse I have ever worked with. There is a natural empathy there and not just with his own age group; elderly patients love him. It gives me no pleasure to pay this Elane, but when he comes in, burning with new ideas, he shows that the job can be done better, even within the system. His very presence, always busy, always smiling, tells us that we've all become lax. And not surprisingly people feel threatened. Sandy Henderson may be justifiably angry but he knows that bottle tops isn't therapy. But then we're in the job twenty years; Freddy will be lucky to make twenty months."

"That close is it?"

"You don't go about offending people with such gay abandon and expect them to forgive you. He's only lasted this long because I'm around to cover his tracks."

"So where's wonder boy now?"

"Out coaching the hospital football team for tonight's match. With an ex-patient, an old codger called Alf. You ever meet him?" I shook my head.

"No I thought not." Fraser looked thoughtful. "Pity because there's something going on between Freddy and this old guy. I don't know why I keep calling him that, he's really not that old, fifty or so, but he seems old if you know what I mean. Anyway, there's definitely some sort of a relationship between them.

"What, you mean they're gay?"

He laughed. "The first thing that came to my mind. But no, something else. Take the way the two of them have taken over the hospital team. Are you interested in football at all?"

"Afraid not."

"It doesn't matter, the point is they have taken hold of a moribund thing and breathed life into it. We could very well win the inter-hospital cup. Nothing very grand I know, but within its limitations, it's really quite exciting; the whole hospital is bubbling. Freddy has even arranged to have a live commentary piped over the hospital radio. The interesting point is watching Freddy and Alf interact. They have a relationship, not father son, certainly not lovers. Teacher pupil perhaps. Freddy actually listens to Alf."

"All very mysterious," I said. "Have you asked them?"

Fraser sighed, "I don't really want to know. Come to the match tonight. You'll see something of what I mean. They have signals between them. It's almost as if Freddy on the pitch is a living extension of Alf on the touchline."

"I was thinking of coming anyway. Danny Collier is playing isn't he? What are you smiling at?"

"Me? Nothing," Fraser said innocently. "Come along, you'll be surprised."

By 7.30 the crowds had gathered round the sloping hospital pitch.

Fraser was right, it seemed as if the whole hospital population had turned out. Youngsters with limbs in plaster, geriatrics in wheelchairs, I half expected to see bodies on trolleys trailing drips.

To be fair, my attitude was one of benign cynicism. There is limited pleasure in watching the male sex at play. Rod was a footballer, and snooker and darts, anything to be out of the house away from me. As I look back on our relationship I see how I denied him his little pleasures, resented his absences, displayed no interest in his small triumphs; generally played my full part in the destruction of whatever we may have had. Maybe motherhood has mellowed me after all.

Fraser popped up at my side, rubbing his hinds together. "Glad you could make it."

"Tell me Fraser, what is it about football that turns grown men into little boys?"

"If you're going to talk like that then I'm going to stand elsewhere." He said. "Just watch the game, get an insight into the male psyche. Look, there's Alf over there. He pointed to a gaunt figure who, in an old overcoat and cloth cap, almost blended into the gathering gloom. A shabby man I thought, an image that has remained through the years.

The match itself lingers as a blur. Twenty males chasing a ball with the vigour of puppies pursuing a bitch in heat. No wonder most men are so useless around the house, all that energy wasted. The peculiar, faintly pornographic group cuddle after every goal. Yet and yet, reluctantly, the excitement somehow seeped through my clothes, until I too, much to Fraser's amusement, was straining forward, eager for a hospital victory.

Various emergencies and accumulated days off kept me away from the unit for two weeks. I returned feeling guilty at having missed the increasingly strenuous exercise sessions. But the dayroom was quiet. The air still and heavy. Making for the office I found Fraser leaning over his paperwork, cigarette in one hand, cup of tea growing cold on the table.

"What's happened to the exercise sessions then?" I asked.

Fraser turned his head slowly. "You've not heard then?"

"Heard what?"

"Freddy's gone."

"Gone? Gone where?" As I said these words I realised for the first time how much I had come to care.

"Gone, as in no longer here; absent, given his cards, on his bike, unable to grace us with his presence, the sack. Gone," he finished sadly.

"Why?"

"How many reasons do you need?"

"Fraser, just tell me what happened and when."

He swivelled in his chair, took a drag on his cigarette, took a sip of his cold tea. "I wasn't there you understand, the first I knew was the summons to Dr. Lepoise's for a right going over. It seems, and this is the official version mind you, that Freddy ran amok in the local Conservative club, threatening G.B.H. to some very prominent people."

"The local conservative club." I could only echo Fraser's words. "What on earth was Freddy doing there?"

"Bridge."

"Ah," enlightenment, "he made a scene at the local conservative club whilst playing bridge with with..."

"Going well so far." Fraser said "Finish it off, throw in the very worst, add to it and you've probably captured the scene." He sat back, placed his fingers together in imitation of Dr. Lepoise. "At a conservative estimate, no pun intended, the regrettable behaviour of Assistant Nurse Feather has not only dragged the reputation of Dockside Psychiatric Unit into the mud, but has probably cost the hospital at least fifty thousand pounds in outside sponsorship. Precious hope now for the new minibus, and I fear that the library will remain but a far off dream." Fraser unlocked himself from Dr. Lepoise. Took another swig of his tea.

"If you really want to know what happened, ask Mrs. Schlitzkrull, she was there."

"Oh yes, dear. I was there," Mrs. Schlitzkrull said calmly, her long fingers playing with the crochet on her lap. She seemed in the stable midpoint of her manic depressive cycle. As calm and rational and pleasant a middle-age lady as one could wish to meet. But, oh, the chaos she trailed when her gears started upward. Propelling her into a wild activity that maybe made sense to her, but left everyone else drained and empty. The dark sister to this frenzy lay in waiting, ready with its embrace whenever she stepped over the edge.

Backwards and forwards, up and down, year after year. And yet no trace of this struggle in the serene lady, who sat before me, daintily drinking tea. At times like this Mrs. Schlitzkrull seemed one of the wisest people I have ever known.

"It all started so well," she said shaking her head. "We had tea and little cakes. Freddy and I were playing against a husband and wife team. I never think that couples play well together. Do you play m'dear?"

"I'm afraid not."

"A shame, such a restful game."

"It sounds it."

"I love to play," she said. "So soothing. Freddy and I were going to enter some tournaments together. Anyway as I was saying, we dealt the cards and Freddy and I started to win. Not by much. We would make our contracts and they would just miss theirs, and the better we played, the more abusive the man, Harry I think his name was, became to his wife; blaming her for their failures. The poor woman, I don't know how she put up with it. This must have gone on for about two hours. The man Harry was drinking and slowly getting worse. Then suddenly, I don't quite know how, the conversation was onto politics and South Africa. Well I don't know much about apartheid my dear, but I lived through Nazi Austria and the concept of racial superiority is one I know well. His wife tried to pacify him, but by then things had gone too far. People were on their feet, waving their arms about."

"So what did Freddy say? He didn't hit anyone did he?"

"No, no, no. But who can remember all the words spoken in anger. In the end of course, we had to leave. Freddy was very upset, practically in tears. Thought he'd let us down you see." Mrs Schlitzkrull looked up, her clear blue eyes meeting mine. "What will happen to him my dear? Such a nice young man. Always so cheerful."

As I walked around the wards, there was a little battle going on inside my head. The voice of reason kept saying 'Let it go, get on with your own life. God knows you've enough to cope with. Babies, nappies, sleepless nights.' But behind this common sense something deeper was stirring, like a sea creature waking in its ocean bed. By mid-afternoon the restlessness had grown, the need to get out of this airless, colourless building.

According to the phone book, the only Feather lived on the other side of the Docks. A half-hour walk took me through the market to a messy sprawl of streets. As I looked around to ask someone, I saw him up a ladder, leaning over, the very sight brought a smile to my face. I watched from the gate as he cleaned and polished the windows. He climbed down, knocked at the door, no answer. He pushed a card through the door, turned and saw me.

"I think you missed a bit up there," I said. Freddy said nothing. "I thought I'd see how you were getting on." No reply. "So how are you getting on?"

"Okay thanks."

"I heard about you getting fired. I'm sorry."

"Yeah well, these things happen."

"You want to talk about it?"

"Nothing to say really."

By this time my patience, never my strongest suit, was running out. "So you're doing alright then?" I offered.

"I guess."

"I'll see you around then." I was halfway down the street when I felt a hand on my shoulders.

"Look, I'm sorry, it's just that seeing you there, so unexpected, made me shiver all over. I mean I wanted to say something devastatingly witty, but nothing came. I've got to keep talking now, otherwise I'll shut down again." He wittered on at me while I looked him over. He hadn't shaved, or combed his hair by the look of him. But it didn't matter; I was so pleased to see him.

"So you'll come then?" he was saying.

"I suppose so. Come where?"

"To the football match of course."

"What? You mean I've traipsed halfway across the most crime-infested area of London to watch a football match with you?"

"Almost," he replied with a smile. "Actually you'll be watching, I'll be playing.

"It gets more romantic by the minute. Go on, dazzle me some more."

"Please," he said, "I do appreciate you coming here. It feels as it my life has taken a definite upward turn. But this match means a lot to me, and if you were there it would make it even more special."

To punish him, I introduced him to Mother. Whilst Dad studied the racing results from his paper. Roseanne fussed about Freddy, disguising her interrogation behind a never ending flow of tea and home-made cake. This harmonious racial interaction was shattered by the arrival of my two younger brothers.

'Da Brudders' burst into the room in a cloud of smoke, the smell of grass smothering the final traces of Roseanne's cooking. Freddy's eyes widened in horror at the size of the enormous spliff waved before him as Da Brudders circled, sniffed and investigated.

"Hey, man, I seen you, " said brother number one.

Freddy nodded. "Down the gym."

"That's right, you shift some weight man."

As the room filled with smoke, Freddy and Da Brudders discussed such things as muscle tone and weight to body ratios, until Dad surprised us all by laying his paper aside and actually speaking.

"I know you," he said in his quiet voice. "You're Freddy Feather, you used to be a footballer.

"Still am hopefully," Freddy replied "I'm playing tonight for Eastgate. First match for eighteen months."

Da Brudders became even more excited. "You a footballer? Hey, we come and cheer you on. Hey Bro, get on the phone. Tell all the brothers, we're going to a football match. Cheer on Elane's new boyfriend."

By the time we boarded the bus to Eastgate, we were accompanied by twenty or so very stoned dreadlocks. The blasters went on and the spliffs came out. When the conductor fought his way upstairs, the bus was vibrating and visibility shortening by the minute.

"Hey man, we're all guests of an international superstar, you should be honoured to have us on your Bus."

"Is that right?" The conductor, a gap-toothed, wiry little man, seemed unimpressed.

"Yeah man, up front, that's the dude. We're his fan club."

The conductor loomed up out of the smoke like a survivor from the field of battle. "Freddy!" his face lit up in a gap-toothed smile. "When did you become an international superstar?"

"Give it time Jacko, a bit of time."

"So it's true you're playing tonight then. How's the leg?"

Freddy stretched his leg, patted it, "We'll see tonight. You be there?"

"Some of us got to work. Keep the country running. I'll catch the second half."

The music throbbed, as the bus crept on through the city streets. We sat in silence, thighs touching. Then turned and spoke together. "You first," he said smiling.

"Look, I realise this is a big night for you, and that you've been through a bad time lately, but I still get the feeling that something is bothering you. Am I wrong?"

Freddy looked at me. "You're right as always, there is something I haven't told you and I don't know why." He stopped.

"I know you're not married and I don't think you're gay, so what is it?"

He laughed. "I don't know how to say it. I don't know what's wrong with me. My mouth's all dry, and the music is going round and round my head. I've got all the thoughts but they don't appear as words when I want them to."

It was my turn to laugh. "Freddy, I think you're a little stoned." His eyes widened.

"You think so, actually I feel quite magical, except for this raging thirst."

"I've got just the cure for that." I leaned over and kissed him in a not quite sisterly manner, moistening the inside of his mouth with my tongue, running my fingers up and down his thigh. "You need a shave," I whispered.

"Window cleaner stubble, very fashionable."

Eastgate is a tucked away little pocket of Dockside, a mixture of rising prices and falling buildings, a colony of middle-aged in hippie dress. Organic health shops, neighbourhood watch, left wing book shops. The down and outs still live on the streets but in a better class of alleyway. I shouldn't mock, it's where I would live if I could afford it. We got off the bus and joined the thin dribble of people who looked as if they had somewhere to go. Freddy seemed to grow more nervous with every step. The boy had things on his mind. Finally he turned and said, "I'm going to introduce you to someone. It isn't that I should have told you about him, more that I should have told him about you. It isn't like I've kept you a secret or anything, but there was a moment this afternoon when I could have said that I was bringing someone to the match, and I didn't. I could've said that and with each step I wish I had."

Too late now we were approaching a ramshackle old stadium. I wouldn't have believed anything could be so old and still be standing. Waiting for Freddy, as my subconscious told me he would be, was the shabby man. Freddy went up to him. "Alf this is Elane. Elane, Alf." Then he disappeared through a door leaving Alf and me staring at each other.

"Freddy has mentioned you from work, I didn't know you were interested in football."

"I'm here aren't I?" Already there seemed to be an atmosphere of hostility between us.

"Well whatever, would you like to come with me and see the match?" We trudged up concrete steps that smelled of stale underwear, emerged into a gloomy light. We sat for a moment in silence then the players came out of a tunnel to a half-hearted cheer from the spectators. You could hardly call it a crowd. I leaned forward.

"You know I was a patient in the hospital," he said softly.

"Is that where you met?" I asked. He laughed quietly as if to himself.

"You know I've feared this day knowing it must come, now it's here, it's almost a relief."

The conversation seemed to be moving into areas I had no wish to probe. More to change the subject than anything I said, "Tell me about the football Alf, show me what's going on down there."

"This match is to put us back where we were eighteen months ago."

Had I been abducted, forced to watch the match at gun point, the conclusions would have been the same. Freddy was quite simply the outstanding player on the pitch. He moved with a grace that was beyond the other performers. The significance of this, if any, was unclear as most of the players seemed to be sliding down the far side of their prime, but within its own context it was impressive, rather like trotting off to the local theatre and seeing someone of real talent take command of the stage.

After the game, Alf and I waited for Freddy in a mutual, preoccupied silence, standing there like rivals. The arrival of Freddy dispelled all that. He came out from the same chipped and peeling wooden door bubbling over with excitement. Alf's dourness and my own bad temper melted beneath his enthusiasm.

"What about that goal then? The way I cut in from the touchline and hit it twenty-five yards at least, and then the free kick curling and dipping. It felt so good." Alf leaned forward and ruffled his hair.

"You played well son, go out and celebrate. I'll see you in the morning, and we'll go over the things you didn't do so well." Then he turned and walked away, hunched figure fading into the city night.

"Anywhere special you want to go?" Freddy said brightly.

"I'm bloody freezing. What I really want is a cup of tea and to soak my feet in a basin of hot water." We had started to walk down the almost deserted street, stopping when we came to a street corner cafe.

"Tell me this young Feather," I said when we were seated. "If I hadn't come looking for you, would you ever have searched me out?" He looked thoughtful.

"I don't know. You're a truly formidable woman. I don't think I could ever have allowed myself to think that someone like you would be interested in me."

"Why not?"

"You're so... so..."

"Black?"

"No."

"Butch?"

"No."

"Old?"

"No." He looked down into the cup of tea that had finally arrived. "So astonishingly beautiful; so in control, so bad-tempered. Sometimes it seems like you're in a perpetual state of crossness at me."

"Am I Freddy?" I leaned over and touched his hand. "I think that's because I don't want to admit, even to myself, quite how much I care." I looked around the café; dirty walls, steamed up tea urn, stale cakes under a plastic tray. There were two other couples there, huddled intensely round their table, and the inevitable loner, the one with nowhere to go. This time I didn't see the sadness, somehow this dingy little cafe seemed desperately romantic.

"So tell me Freddy, in all the months we worked together, you never mentioned how much football meant to you." He sat there drinking tea from his chipped mug, his face open and vulnerable.

"It was a dream," he said softly. "A private dream, a faraway dream."

"And now?"

"I don't know, I truly don't. I'm playing again, and that's good, but something about working in the Unit has taken away the single-minded drive that anyone needs to succeed. Working with you has shown me that there's more to life than football. There is too much pain floating about in the world for me to hide within my own private dream. I miss it, not the pain, but the feeling at the end of the day. That possibly, just possibly, I might have done something useful with my time."

I smiled, partly at his passion and naïveté, but also because there was something stirring in the back of my mind.

"I think young Freddy, I might have just the thing for you."

"Yeah?"

"And something for me as well," I admitted. "I'm involved with the local community centre. Ever go there?"

"You jest, I've passed it, but you don't go in wearing white skin."

I nodded in reluctant agreement. "You're right, but it's my dream to change that. As far away from me as playing for England is for you, distant but not impossible."

"So what do you want from me?" he said warily.

"Freddy, so young to be so cynical." Inside my mind I was thinking, 'I want everything from you Freddy boy, body, soul and body again.' "We've got a nice layout at the centre, pitches with flood lights, but it's a mess. What we need desperately is for someone to come down there and take charge. I think you're just the person."

"Alright, when?" Such touching faith.

"How about tomorrow?"

Freddy walked me home and the big night out ended with a chaste kiss on the doorstep. I felt his body trembling against mine. Lying in bed, going over the evening the way one does, I realised Freddy was right. It would be hard for a white boy to come into that closed community.

Dockside is a modern day ghetto, not a bad one as ghettos go. All the usual signs: dirt and dogshit, and broken glass that seems to grow through the pavements. Prostitutes on every corner, the high speed flow of traffic that turns crossing the road into an art form. Of course the poverty, the grinding hardship that makes getting out of the trap almost impossible. But above all the throwing together of eight or nine different communities. The racial lines that criss cross through the area, marking territory. Black pubs and white pubs, the prostitutes are white, their pimps black. Woe betide the white dealer who steps onto black turf. The white police, thought of as the enemy. Councillors are white, authority is white. Yet, unlike other ghetto areas, there is a degree of racial harmony. People may not mix, but at the very least, they do live together, mingling in the shops, and the markets. Probably the only place that people really mix without any thought of colour is in the infant schools, but even there one can see the innocence melt away like snow on the city streets as the kids make their way through the system, learning how to hate. With these thoughts spinning round my head I finally fell into a sleep.

When Freddy was introduced to the fifteen or so black teenagers who made up the usual crowd at the centre, the feeling of resentment was quite plain. As the evening wore on, my looks out of the window became less anxious. Word scurried about the town, more and more teenage kids began to show up. Even 'Da Brudders' appeared in their silky tracksuits and Reebok trainers (where do they get the money?).

The days speeded up, as they do when one has a sense of purpose. The centre creaked with the strain of so much activity. The local teams entered some tournaments, and Freddy brought Alf down to help with the coaching. In their turn the kids became Eastgate, or rather Freddy supporters. I have it on good authority that when the crowds first showed up, the staff were down on their hands and knees counting and recounting the money. Unable to account for the extra few hundred quid that swelled the takings.

The centre must have acquired a reputation, because the police paid us a visit. They poked about, sniffing the air, demanding to see "The man in charge". They left to cheers and jeers, but the episode decided me that the time had come to place the whole operation on a more professional footing. That evening I called a meeting. Myself, Denice, Cathy, Leroy, Alf, Freddy and a friend of Freddy's, an overweight Anarchist called Animal Jim.

"I've called this meeting," I opened hesitantly, "because I think we've reached a crisis point. We can be a force for good or, as I see it, we can be overwhelmed and eventually closed down."

"Just because we've been gone over by the law," said the always aggressive Leroy. "So what? What can they do?"

"They can close us down that's what," I snapped back. "We're not here to make ourselves into martyrs, but to give the kids somewhere to go." I softened my tone. "We've got an opportunity here to create something worthwhile. I must confess I don't exactly know quite what because I've never been involved in something that has so much potential for good or bad." As I looked around at the faces, I realised once again that in the journey from thought to speech, a vital ingredient had been mislaid.

Surprisingly, Alf was the first to reply. "I think you're right, lass."

'Blimey,' I thought. Alf thinks I'm right, there must be a catch.

"But there are two, no three points I want to make." He went on "Firstly, we've got over a hundred kids out there, and we simply can't accommodate them all. We need more space. Secondly, there's drugs on the premises. You may well sneer lad," he said savagely to Leroy, "we've seen you smoking drugs."

"Listen man," Leroy said with that irritating sneer he had perfected. "You ban the weed and you lose the kids, simple as that." He leaned forward, poked a finger at Alf. "What I can do is make sure that no hard drugs come inside, no crack or smack. But the weed. The weed is the weed is the weed."

"Leroy is right, Alf." I said as gently as possible. "The kids here both white and black have all been smoking for years, we have to accept it." There was a silence until Denice suddenly said, "I'm thinking of standing for council. If we mobilise, get elected. then maybe we can reach an understanding with the police, also we'll be in a much stronger position when it comes to getting funds." Ambitious woman Denice.

"Good idea," said Alf, "Let's get hold of the levers of power."

"You stand as a Marxist," Denice replied. "I'm standing as a green, inner city governmentalist."

Alf smiled, a rare enough sight in itself. "I'm an old Labour man myself, but if we hit them with an unexpected coalition then all the better!" All seemed to be going so well, too well.

"There is one thing I'd like to bring up," said Freddy. "Well not me but Jim here. Go on Jim speak your piece."

"I've sat here listening to a whole load of fine words, but it's all crap."

"That's the way Jim," muttered Freddy. "Butter them up first." So we sat and listened to Animal Jim damn our ideals to hell. According to Jim: to be a Socialist, you must be vegetarian, not necessarily the other way round, all sorts can be vegetarian: Hitler was vegetarian. But respect for all living things is integral to Socialism.

If I really searched I could dig out flaws in this argument, but in the meantime I was only too pleased to hand over the community food franchise to his raggle taggle animal rights organisation.

Over the years I must have attended hundreds, it feels like thousands, of meetings. A meeting to form a committee, a meeting to decide when to hold the meeting to form the committee. People can't make it to the meeting, better have a meeting to decide what to do about the meeting.

Denice, is a meeting junkie. She feeds from the strength of like-minded people, feels the need to take charge.

Personally I am more insecure. When it's time to put the chairs away my feeling is usually one of dissatisfaction. Surely something more could have been achieved. This particular meeting lingers in my mind. Decisions were made. Standing for council, becoming a meat free zone, rare enough in itself. But there was something more; a feeling of possibility, maybe we had the weapons to wrest control from the worn out power base that made decisions over the local community.

As these meetings settled into a routine, so vague tensions began to solidify. Leroy and Alf were separated by age, culture, colour, even dress sense. Denice also disliked Alf, by proxy, her real feelings reserved for Freddy. Denice has been a good friend across the years, but she plays on and strains that friendship almost wilfully at times.

"I think we have become over dependent on Freddy. We're saying to the kids let's demonstrate against bombs, apartheid, high rents whatever, because Freddy is going to be there. And Freddy is a fantastic footballer so Freddy must be right." A valid criticism in its rather petty way. Even Denice was surprised when Alf supported her. As gaunt as ever, his shadow fell across these gatherings like the spectre of Death to come, there to make sure that frivolity, compromise, human weakness were kept well away from the agenda. A party man toes the party line, but when that party has betrayed you, betrayed itself, then the line becomes tighter, more inflexible, the words summoned from a distant past when there were no shades of grey.

"You're right lass, any movement that cannot survive on its own merits deserves to fail. You have to make use of the weapons you have... But be prepared." Elliptical words from a man without guile.

I once asked him, "Where does Marx stand on nursery facilities for working mothers?" He didn't answer, treated me to one of his vanishing smiles. Two weeks later, out of nowhere, he said, "Marx would be in favour of anything that freed people from state controlled drudgery." End of conversation.

At the end of this particular evening I said to Freddy, "What was all that about; 'Be prepared.' What does Alf know that I don't?"

"I've had a few offers," he replied looking at his shoes, at the ground, anywhere but at me.

"What does that mean, offers? Who's offering what to whom for what?"

"It means," he said slowly, "that someone is willing to give me the chance to play football at a higher level."

"Where is this higher level?"

"Glasgow."

"Oh, you going to take it?"

"I don't know."

"And when were you going to tell me?" I said trying unsuccessfully to keep the edge from my tones.

"I don't think I was going to tell you. What I've been struggling with is not using it as a threat."

"You've lost me," I said. "What threat?"

"It may have escaped your notice, but I am in a state of considerable personal turmoil. I feel that I'm not important to you as a person. I've become a tool. These offers I've had aren't an opportunity for advancement, although they are. I see them as an escape from feelings I can no longer handle." His voice had fallen to a mumble. "I want to be more than a weapon in your struggle for change. I believe in that fight, I want to be a part of it. But..."

"But..."

"I love you Elane; at least I think I do. I know that I respect you, and I like being with you, you're warm and funny. But..."

"But..."

"When I'm lying in my bed, and I think about you, I don't see you as a politician, or a crusader, although you are both of those things. I see you coming to me taking your clothes off. I'm sorry I realise that diminishes your role, but I simply can't help it, these are my night-time feelings."

"You're sexually frustrated," I said. "You think its about time I came across?"

"Whatever, I would hopefully have phrased it more gracefully, but I guess you're right. Is it painful being so right all of the time? If you must know there are two other reasons just as valid as my sexual feelings. I really don't think I can leave Alf. If he came with me, it would alter our relationship. Plus I really don't want to go. I like it here. It's my home. I'm involved in something worth being involved with?

Afterwards, you know, afterwards. I turned to Freddy and said, "How come if you're so good that people come all the way from Glasgow. Then how come the local team doesn't want to know?" I heard him sigh into the darkness.

"Dockside is a fucked-up little club, the personal play thing of Fingers Dolton. Name ring a bell? Dockside is the natural step up, but it has to be soon, or do I settle for what I've got?"

"So how good are you Freddy?"

"I don't know. In my fantasies I can do it all. In reality there simply hasn't been the chance to test myself." I couldn't see his face but the uncertainty in his voice was clear enough. "Glasgow Rangers don't want to know about me. If I don't come up to scratch, it's on your bike, back to the non-league, a failure. The thing is I'm happy playing for Eastgate, but inside it's like a fire burning, and I don't like it. I would far rather be happy than driven. I like it even less that it seems to be either/or. Glasgow and loneliness, Eastgate and mediocrity. Listen, all I'm doing is rolling the possibilities round, the truth is I can't leave Alf and I won't leave you. Christ, it's taken me twenty-one years to lose my virginity."

"Was it as good as your dreams?"

"In my dreams I never wore a condom, somehow the question never came up."

"Ah, but this is reality Freddy."

He laughed. "Never got stoned either. That's a definite plus, I think." Then more seriously, "Never thought it could be so good. Since you asked me I have to ask you the same. How was it for you?"

"You're young Freddy, lots to learn."

"Oh?"

"Come here boy and I'll teach you all the things that Mama likes."

A golden time, a time when all things seemed possible. Maybe we couldn't change the world but, sure as hell, we could have an effect on our own locality. Alf, Leroy, Denice, even Animal Jim were manipulated onto the local council. Working together they began the take-over of key committees; Housing, Planning, Roads.

Local elections proved that we had the machinery to get people to the polls. The kids told their parents, who came to the centre to see what all the fuss was about, some got involved; all were grateful to know where their kids were at night.

To cap it all, Dockside signed Freddy up. In a way they had little choice. 'Who is this Freddy Feather? Why are the crowds chanting his name?' They came round to Freddy's house while I was there with Rachel. Two jowly white guys in their fifties. I saw the look that passed between.

'Who's this woman? Who's kid is this?' Freddy and I listened to their spiel, selling Dockside like a second hand car. Their hopes and plans. The big break, LEAGUE FOOTBALL. 'Stick with us kid, we can go to the top, listen to us, learn from us, sign this.' Then they brought out a dog-eared contract, passport to glory.

Three months later, they were gone, replaced by a younger version. New jowly faces, new plans that did not include Freddy. He told me about it, the call to the office, maybe even a first team place? "Sorry Kid, afraid not. We're going to put you on long term loan to Doncaster."

"I don't wanna go to Doncaster," fighting back the tears.

"Read the small print kid, you go where we say."

"Then I quit."

"Walk out this office kid and I'll make it my personal business to see that you never play for anyone again, ever."

"Why won't you give me a chance?"

"You've got a big mouth kid. We've been here two weeks, and all we heard is your mouth. I'll be honest with you, you're giving me a headache, you got the sort of voice that could derail a train. Listen, it won't be so bad, the manager there is an old mate of mine, Maurice

Moore, he's been in the market for a full back."

"I haven't played fullback for over a year."

"Don't tell Maurice."

"You're a right pair ain'cha?"

"That's right kid. Now go clear your locker. Hang on I almost forgot, here's your train ticket, Doncaster one way."

Six months of holding on, holding out. Freddy living in a squat somewhere in Doncaster, one ghetto to another. Our movement, our precious, fragile movement sliding downhill and all we could do was try to slow the descent.

Freddy's absence affected us all in different ways. Enthusiasm for football fell away as Dockside returned to its usual slump. Leroy and Animal Jim drifted back into their own things; Leroy into Legal Aid work and Jim into his Animal Rights movement. I hardly saw Alf. He retreated into the gloom, curtains closed, door locked, emerging only to continue his work with Eastgate. Only Denice seemed inspired, filled with a manic energy and wild improbable plans: inner city farms, carnivals, de-selecting the local M.P. I stayed low, hibernating the winter away, taking care of essentials. Surviving the winter waiting for the sun to come through. Roseanne was not pleased.

"Hey girl, when you going to get off your ass? You wait around for your man and you be waiting forever."

"I'm not waiting for any man."

She gave one of her wicked cackles." Sure you are girl, you pining like a lovesick child."

"Go away Mother."

"You been playing hard to get girl, like you so precious or something." She gave her head an expressive shake. "Always been a difficult child."

"Thank you, Mother."

"That's alright child, that's what mothers are for."

Freddy came home one weekend and never went back. True to their word the management turned him into a non-person. There was nothing we could do except wait for the court case to roll round and watch as Dockside slid nearer to the fourth division.

Early in April, Fingers Dolton, going for the Guinness book of Records, sacked his management team and installed a fresh set of jowls. Freddy was recalled to the club, and the merry-go-round started up again. Faster and faster, clinging tight as the world became a blur. Faster and faster until realisation dawned. Leap off into the unknown, or stay trapped, inside the whirling, turning, spinning; rolling existence that threatened to wipe away my identity.

ALF

In that one moment, when that goal went in, we were united, joined in common emotion. Elane threw her arms around me, old enmities forgotten, at least for the moment. Despite the celebrations, the hugs, the excitement, something in me remained withdrawn, a small voice whispering, 'How can we use this? Where does this fit in?'

I know what they say about me. 'Grizzled old ideologue, a cold man, fighting past battles.'

"Marxism has moved on Alf," they tell me. "This is the 90's." It may be they are right, that I lack the warmth of personality to cross the barriers that lie between us. Age and faith and, let's be honest, colour.

The past is filled with hope betrayed, lessons not learned. The history of the left is one of struggle, of failure. There's an old joke: Man goes into the library says 'Where's the section on Revolutionary Socialism?' The librarian says 'Just around the corner where it always is.' Not very funny, I agree, but in this particular struggle - at this moment in our history - we have the opportunity to seize control over our lives, to turn that corner. If we are united, if we can only learn from our past.

"What you really mean Alf is, ask no questions while you shuffle us around like pawns in your own private game." Leroy's tone is aggressive, as always, and I don't have the words to sway him.

"It's true," I said, "that we have the ammunition to damage Dolton. Thanks to Leroy, we have detailed evidence of crooked accountancy, falsified expense accounts including, may I say, a mistress, if that's not too old fashioned a term, and most damaging, club contracts given to dummy corporations owned by Dolton himself. The decision we have to make is what to do with the information we possess."

Denice interrupted me. "What decision, there is no decision. The guy is a crook, we send him to jail. You don't make deals with the enemy." Denice's anger is her fuel, now it is directed at me. Memories of harsh words spoken across the council table. "The problem is you." Pointing the finger. "Keeping information back, doling it out in dribs and drabs."

"Everything I know is here. All I'm saying is we must have an awareness of the consequences of our actions. If we reveal our information and Dolton is displaced then the club will be taken over by asset strippers, and the major asset is Freddy. If we reveal and Dolton manages to buy his way out of trouble, then Freddy still goes. Is that what we want?"

For me this was a long speech, but I had more to say yet. "Last week, yesterday even, I would have agreed with you but today, the balance of power has shifted. We have seen one of our own score two goals for his country. It's my belief that using this in conjunction with the information already in our possession, we can force Dolton to change his position. Let him keep his status, it means nothing."

These are bright people here: social workers, lawyers. Why can they not see? How many defeats must we suffer? Why this need for confrontation? Can they not see that without planning and tactics and preparation, we will be crushed like the Levellers, swept aside like The Chartists, forgotten like the nine dead miners of Abertarey.

"It seems to me that all you're saying is 'The man stays in charge.' Nothing really changes, the time is never quite right. I want to hear what Freddy has to say. I'm not saying I don't trust you just that you keep too much inside." Leroy's words hit their target. I have ambitions and dreams, I see a place for myself. None of this will I reveal, these are private thoughts.

"Freddy will be phoning soon," Elane said quietly. "Why don't we hold our decision till then." I looked around, this was a young peoples' room, if I left there would be a lightening of spirit.

Back at home, I put on the video of the match, stopping, rewinding, wishing I had been there. Time fell away. The doorbell dragged me from my dreams. It was Leroy. He stood there a smile on his face.

"Freddy phoned, he said you have his support and total trust, he said to go ahead with whatever you have in mind." Leroy looked hard at me. "I just want to say, count me in." He held out his hand.

The next evening was the specially convened shareholders' meeting. I stood in the empty rooms, waiting for people to arrive. Looking up at the podium; my mind went back twenty-five, twenty-six, twenty-seven years. Another hall, crowded with angry miners and their families, fists raised. Through the crowds came the men from London, men in smart suits, men who had never worked down a mine. They got up on their podium, wasted little time on promises, got right down to threats. Gave us a stark example of where the power lay. We lost that battle. In truth, we never had a chance. They owned our homes, our shops, they owned our lives. I swore then that if the chance ever came again I would be better prepared, with weapons of my own.

Well the time has come. The issues are not so pure, but it helps to see the whole as class conflict in miniature. Dolton is capitalism: small town, seedy, corrupt local capitalism. His empire propped up by paper deals, money moving faster than the tax man can follow. Basically, Samuel Dolton is a stupid man, he cannot see how fragile his empire has become. He will not see the tide until the waves are over his head.

The room is filling. Old friends greet each other, smelling something in the air. Now Dolton comes, with his cronies. He walks arrogantly through the crowds, shaking hands and back-slapping. Behind him, head bowed slightly, walks Hutchinson. He stares round the room like a hunted animal. Then Freddy comes in, and the room explodes with noise, cheering, stamping. A warning to Dolton that all is not well in his world.

Twenty-seven years ago, in many ways it seems like yesterday, the bitter trail of broken promises led to surrender and in turn, to death. The faces blend as those far off days return.

Tim Kirkwood, chairman of the supporters association, gets up to speak. He has little knowledge of the issues behind the issues. He introduces the faces, realises he has nothing more to say, sits again. Then Dolton rises; he is confident. In his time he has seen off pickets and rivals and unionisers. He is a man who makes his own reality. He truly believes that the men and women in this room hold him in respect, even love him. He sees himself as a benefactor.

"I don't need to introduce myself. I know you and you know me. My family and I have looked after this club for thirty-five years." Who could disagree; thirty-five years in which the fall of the club has been mirrored by the decline of Dockside itself. Thirty-five years of short sighted failure, and the man could actually boast about it.

"We are naturally pleased when a player has success. But when that player returns and the only thanks for the opportunity he has been given is to march into the manager's office and demand more money, then it is time to say that no individual is bigger than the club."

I looked at Hutch; would he support his master if the price was right, say one percent of any transfer fee? One percent of a half million is five thousand; men have sold their souls for less. Dolton placed an arm round Hutch's shoulders.

"This club is firmly on the road to success. We have a good team and good management. As Chief Executive I cannot allow the greed of one player, however good that player may be, to disrupt the smooth running of the club." He sat down confident in his self image, perhaps he even believed it.

Freddy stood up, the weapon we never had all those years ago - one of the weapons. If deals were to be made, they would be bargained out behind the scenes.

"There's no point denying that Mr. Dolton and I are suffering from a severe clash of personalities." Start off slowly, proffer the olive branch. "However, it must be said that signals seem to have become crossed. I haven't asked for more money. My contract is for £15,000 a year. Mr. Dolton's contract pays him £30,000 as chief executive of the club, plus an unlimited expense account." Careful Freddy, just a hint of the stick. "Whatever our differences we agree on one principle. The club is bigger than any individual. We should be able to put aside our differences and work together for the good of Dockside."

Dolton had stopped listening. He leaned forward studying the big brown envelope that had appeared on his table. He opened it, took out his reading glasses. Watching closely, I saw the look of shock that passed across his face. This was a crucial moment. If he had the intelligence to understand the threat, he would survive. If he tried to bluster on then we would bring him down, send him to jail, make the best of the consequences. Dolton exchanged hurried words with his companion, their eyes flicked out across the room, fell on me, moved on. They huddled together, then suddenly got up, pushed their way through the crowds and left.

"What now?" Denice demanded. The meeting had come to an end. Dolton had gone and people milled about dissatisfied and angry. "At ten o'clock we phone him, present him with our demands," I answered. I thought I would be nervous, where did this feeling of exhilaration, almost joy come from?

"I don't understand this need for secrecy," she said. "Why don't we tell him who we are and what we want?"

"Let him wonder," I answered gently. "Let it prey on his mind. 'Who are these people? What do they want? How come they know so much?' So far Freddy is unconnected to all of this, that's a weapon to keep in reserve."

"What if he doesn't answer?" Denice was persistent, one of her weapons.

"He will," I said quietly.

"But what if he doesn't?"

"Time is knocking on Alf," Leroy said. "Where we going to make this phone call from?"

"My house."

"What if he traces the call?"

I hadn't thought of that, the modern world catching me out. A loose thread that could unravel and come right back to me. Too late to worry now. "My house," I said firmly.

Three of us, myself, Freddy and Leroy sat in my kitchen, waiting as the minutes ticked slowly away. Thankfully, Elane had persuaded Denice that there were other important things to be done. She left muttering things about blackmail being better left to the boys, heavy irony in her tone. There was respect for her. During the bad times, when Freddy had been sent on loan to Doncaster, spirits were low. She had worked hard, making sure that the foundations, so swiftly laid, were strong enough to survive.

"I got to admit I'm a bit nervous," Leroy said. "My Mum would have a fit if she knew what I was doing. 'My son the lawyer' sounds better than 'My son the jailbird'. You're quiet Freddy."

"I wanted to take Dolton apart up there.""

"I know," I said. "But this way is better." Ten o'clock - time to make a telephone call. The phone was snatched up on first ring, "Yes."

"Samuel Dolton?"

"I represent Samuel Dolton. You are the people responsible for the file containing certain allegations against my client?"

"Samuel Dolton is responsible for the contents of the file."

"Yes well, you say you have more?"

"We have enough hard information to send your client away, to ruin him in this town, to drive him out of football."

"When can we meet to discuss the situation?"

"There will be no meeting, no discussion. We will present you with a list of demands which you can obey or not." Silence at the other end of the phone, background whispers then the voice again, "The evidence of any theoretical wrong doing will be returned to my client."

"All this information will be in the files." I put down the phone, turned to Leroy. "Time to deliver."

"Man, you're cool about all of this. I mean I've got to admit to the odd flutter or two, but you it's like you're born to it."

"I'm nervous son."

"I'll take your word for it," he said putting on his jacket.

Freddy and I were alone, not a situation that occurred too often these days. I understand. He has a family now, responsibilities, but it is hard nonetheless. There are things I want of Freddy but I do not know how to put my wishes into words.

"You video the game?" he said. I nodded. "Let's go see it then. I'm sure you've got a whole list of things I did wrong.

"Some," I said.

The video room is my sanctuary. A concession to the technological world. In here I can find peace. The years fall away as we watch the football. There is a mutual recognition that after thirteen years we have finally achieved something. If it all ended tomorrow, we would still have achieved something, together, that no one could ever take away.

Hours later, when Freddy had returned to his family, I still sat before my video, running the match again and again, searching for something, proof of my own existence perhaps. I do not like these thoughts. I know the pattern. They lead to introspection, twisting and turning down the alleyways of memory, taking me back, always, to the despair that has ruled so much of my life.

Without me, without my assistance, my guidance, there would be no Freddy Feather, international footballer. This I can say without arrogance, in the knowledge that without Freddy I would be dead, or worse. Locked inside hospital walls, victim of an overpowering, all embracing depression.

When I was down, trapped in what I think of as 'The Pit.' When all the drugs and the electric shook treatments could no longer shift my mood. When I had reconciled myself to the dark, had achieved a quiet contentment inside my dark cell. When all I wished was to be left alone, in peace; I woke one day to the sound of a voice. Not wanting to hear, I closed my senses, but the voice grew from a whisper to a demand.

Irritated at this intrusion into my world I turned, and through the darkness saw a tiny point of light. I turned away, angry at this violation of my solitude, but the voice refused to let me go, forcing me to turn once again towards the light. Peering up through the long, dark tunnel, I saw a hand reaching down for me, and the voice was saying, "Take hold, I'll pull you up." I resisted with all of my strength, but the voice was too strong, too selfish, would not leave me in peace. Finally, reluctantly, more to shut the voice up than anything else, I took hold of the reaching hand and allowed myself to be hauled up into the cold, harsh light of the world.

Looking back through the years, it is possible to see those times when events took over from life. Those terrible days in the tunnel where I could only watch as comrades passed away, were killed, murdered by capitalist greed. A terrible death, so slow, so filled with pain, that the desire for life was replaced by a longing for death. As each hour went by, so the life force faded, then drifted away, leaving behind the shell. For years the only emotion that remained was guilt at being alive, and below that a desire for revenge.

I numbed myself to all feeling: the loss of a leg, a permanent reminder that I lived while comrades died, that somehow life was a betrayal. I existed in this fashion for fifteen years until a small boy sneaked through my defences, taught me how to share, became my reason for living.

Now... now I have ambitions, and a newly discovered ruthlessness, powerful enough to turn these dreams into reality. So when I say that without me Freddy Feather international footballer would not exist, this is no more than a statement of fact. This person, this creation, before me on the screen, is living proof that dreams, hidden away in the recesses of one's mind can overcome reality.

Four years ago, this very week, Freddy broke his leg. A nothing match. The London Cup. Eastgate vs. Chelsea Reserves. A day out for us, a chance to take on the big boys. They had Ian Hamilton in their team. A lad so filled with natural talent, that it seemed nothing could stop his progress.

In the first half they were all over us. Our enthusiasm and endeavour no match for the pure skill of Hamilton. At half time I put

Freddy onto him. "Mark him out of this game." As the flow of the game started to shift, I knew that Freddy had the ability and intelligence to make it to the very top.

Then a tackle, Freddy first to the ball, Hamilton coming in late, over the top, cold blooded, deliberate, a tackle designed to maim. I was on the field before the referee even noticed. As they stretchered Freddy away, our eyes locked and in a voice filled with pain he said,

"Why did he do that?" All I could reply was, "Because you're better than him." Ungrammatical but true.

This incident laid waste to any so called normality. Those barriers, so carefully constructed, were swept away as the depression crept over my body, through my mind, almost welcome for its familiarity. I turned myself over to the mind men, submitting to electric shock treatment, gobbling down pills as a normal person takes aspirin.

The calendar said three months had passed before I regained control. Winter had turned to summer. My front door key was rusty, and the smell, like a dream returned to haunt me. Flesh turning rotten like a slab of meat in the gutter. Freddy sprawled on my settee, leg in plaster, brandy bottles lay lopsided on the floor.

He almost lost his leg, irony there somewhere. The poison feeding on neglect.

More time in hospital followed by the slow build up to full strength, never knowing if things would ever be quite the same.

It took its toll, this rebirth of feeling. Seeing another person's pain, saying the right words, silencing the doubts. It brought on another breakdown, another visit to the land of shadow. This time Freddy searched me out, hounded and bullied me back into the world.

Leroy implies that I have somehow planned all this. The club taken over as a result of a carefully constructed, deep laid conspiracy. We started to investigate the finances almost two years ago. Freddy had been loaned out to Doncaster and, once again, control was slipping away. Almost immediately Leroy and his team of lawyers and accountants began to unravel all sorts of irregularities, until the whole club was revealed as no more than a money-making machine, churning out deals in all directions, all for the benefit of one man and his dog.

I didn't plan it, there was no blueprint. But Leroy is right in that I planned for it. Gathering weapons for a day that may never come.

What now, as I sit here in my room, projecting my thoughts forward? I want to be a part of Dockside, maybe the reserves, or the youth team, a chance for me, for Alf Evans, before Freddy slips away completely.

A successful club can lift a town. This is historical fact. For too many years Dockside, the town, has been a victim. The money men move in with their plans for redevelopment. New houses, new factories. On paper it all looks wonderful, a new start. In practice, some people make a lot of money, and the new houses and jobs somehow fail to materialise. An old, old story, familiar as capitalism itself. No more; even as I sit here in my sanctuary, peering through the possibilities, I know that the next few months will be crucial.

Samuel Dolton must be crushed beyond thoughts of revenge, yet he must still have something more to lose. In this particular case, his freedom and reputation. Yet our people; the Leroys, Elanes, even maybe especially, Denice, must keep their innocence, their belief. I have tried to protect them, as a result I have become a keeper of secrets, a blackmailer, a manipulator. The moral high ground is far behind me; now I move in the mud, threatening people over the telephone, enjoying it.

VIC

If Vic had his way, if he was The Boss, then Feather would not have made the England Team. Simple as that. A squad member - maybe - on the bench, possibly. But the fulcrum, the hub, the centre of the team. No way. never. Football at this level requires commitment, guts, an inner discipline. Vic said as much to Joe, "He'll let us down. When it really matters, when we need him, he won't be there."

Joe returned his gaze. "There's a personality clash here, Vic," he said gently. "I'd hate it if team spirit were disrupted because of it."

Was there the mildest hint of threat behind these words? Was Joe really saying, 'Don't back me into a corner over this. My dream is stronger than yours. Joe had changed, no doubt about it. Take this Bridge game for example. Whoever heard of a manager partnering a player across the card table. It offended Vic's sense of rightness, was bad for team spirit.

"Another thing," he said to Joe. "What about these tracksuits then. I know he's lifting them. They haven't gone walkies by themselves."

Once again Joe gave him the sad stare. "Vic, if we make it to Brazil then I'll buy him a warehouse, out of my own pocket."

"That's not the point Joe." Vic was really pissed off by this not so petty thievery. His sense of rightness assailed him from yet another direction. "We're talking discipline here. Are they all going to go around lifting whatever they fancy? He can't be allowed to get away it."

"Alright Vic," Joe said in tired tones. "I'll have a word."

But Vic knew he wouldn't.

As England moved with increasing speed down their World Cup trail, as the 'Get Togethers' became more frequent, so Vic's dislike grew. There wasn't any one thing he could focus on, come to grips with, rather it was everything. His just-crawled-in-from-a-Salvation-Army-jumble-sale appearance. That ever present smirk, he'd knocked it off once, could do it again no problem. That voice, braying on about this that and too much of the other; scraping away at his nerve ends like the grizzling of a small child. Most of all, Vic despised the way Feather set himself up as somehow better than his fellow professionals, better than the game.

Vic was a good family man, proud parent to three married children, indulgent grandfather. He believed in home, family gatherings, Sunday dinners. Sometimes, catching a glimpse of Joe's loneliness, he felt pity stir. He had somewhere to go, away from the pressure, away from football.

Vic had this ritual. He could date it back twenty-two years to the very day. He'd just been sacked, for the first but not the last time. He'd even had to give up the club car and catch the bus home. People had looked at him, they'd known. He reached home, all his emotions boiling and bubbling, building up into something explosive.

When he went into the living room, all those years ago, Mary, his wife, was sitting listening to the radio. Mentally drained, he sank onto the sofa and let the soft voices float over him. It was The Archers and gradually he hooked into the story. Joe Grundy was still a young man. Walter Gabriel and Mrs. Perkins and Dan Archer still alive. When The Archers finished, he tried to talk, but Mary shushed him and for the first time in his life he found himself listening to Woman's Hour.

First item up was a piece about middle-aged redundancy. The voices seemed to speak right to him, clarifying his own feelings. Yes, that's how he felt, like someone had taken a hammer to his self esteem. And frightened, he could admit it, fear of the dole. And angry, oh yes anger at the ignorant know nothings! But there was also comfort in knowing that he wasn't alone. More highly qualified, more desperate people than he were biting the dust. Since that day this had been his and Mary's shared secret. Other couples had their place or maybe a piece of music. He and Mary had The Archers and Woman's Hour. Whenever football allowed, Vic would make tea and sink into his spot on the settee. It was a meeting place for the marriage.

This particular day, the day when Vic's anger moved over the line into obsession, he had made the tea like always, caught up with the escapades of Shula, Nelson and Lucy, a trial to her father that young lady. He let his mind drift as Woman's Hour came on - the programme had got a little radical for his personal taste - when his attention was jerked back to the radio.

"Our special guest today is Freddy Feather, best known as an international footballer, or perhaps as a left wing activist. Welcome to Woman's Hour, Freddy."

Vic could hardly trust his ears. He looked round to see who was playing this sick joke. No joke, Jenny Murrey's comfortable voice droned soothingly on.

"Freddy, most people know about your skills on the football field, and most football fans are aware of your political views. But there was a moment last season, just after your arrest, when you transcended sport and politics and somehow you touched a common chord. I'm referring to the moment when you spoke directly to your children via the television cameras. How did this come about?"

Vic sat as if superglued to his spot. He wanted to get up but couldn't move.

"This wasn't anything rehearsed." Oh, that voice. "But it had filtered through to the jail that the gutter press had invaded my home. They were doing the usual things, sticking their microphones through the letter box, asking my kids how they felt now their Daddy had been arrested. My kids were terrified, as was my mother. So when the opportunity arose, without thinking I told them to clean their teeth because that's what I do. I'm a fanatic for teeth."

"Is this the one you're always on about?" asked Vic's wife. He nodded, unable to find words. He felt betrayed, let down by an old and trusted friend.

"At this time your partner was working in Zimbabwe, and you were, to all intents and purposes a single parent. How did you cope with this role?" Partner! What's all this partner business? Vic thought. Other men have wives, Freddy has a partner.

Still the words poured out, in his living room, invading his life.

"I had it a lot easier than most, lots of help, lots of support. One of the major problems was prising the kids away from their Grandmothers, saying to them, 'Hey I can do it. I may only be a man but I can do the job. I don't want to build up this single parent business. As Elane made perfectly clear when she returned, if I'd been a woman, no one would have batted an eyelid."

My God, Vic thought, when will somebody see through all this crap? Not today, obviously. Jenny Murrey was already into her next question.

"Were the children affected by their mother leaving?"

"They took it with remarkable maturity, much better than I did. The youngest, Abigail, was two at the time, battling against potty training. She'd wee on the floor then look you right in the eye as if to say 'What you gonna do about it then Fat Boy?' From the day Elane left she never weed on the floor again. Don't ask me what goes through their minds."

Still Vic could only sit, his head moving back and forth like a nodding dog.

"Your sense of family is obviously very strong. Is this because your own life as a child was so unsettled? I know your father left home ten years ago."

"I'm only surprised that the tabloids haven't dug him up yet. 'Freddy Feather's Father found sleeping in gutter.'"

"You sound bitter. Are there no good memories of childhood?"

"My dad was a drinker. A big, angry presence in the house. I used to come home from school praying 'Please God, don't let him be in.'"

"Is this the beginning of a pattern? Like fat children turn to comedy to ward off the ridicule, so you turned to football?"

"Yes, a lot of truth in that. From my earliest memory, it was me and my football against the world. If home had been a happier place, more of a shelter, I wouldn't have been driven to the streets. My obsession with football would probably never have developed."

"What about girls. When did they enter the picture?"

There was the sound of Feather laughing, a sound Vic knew only too well... never expected to hear it in his own living room.

"I was an underdeveloped child. When my mates were going out with girls, I was still kicking my football. The neighbours used to say 'Oh, he'll shoot up' but it never happened. I stayed locked in a fantasy world where everything that might happen, happened to Freddy Feather, a creation of Freddy Feather. Reality was hazy, the dream was real. I didn't emerge from this state until I met Elane. Is that clear at all?"

Not to Vic, all he could hear was the sound of Freddy's voice filling his head. What if he turned on the car radio in the morning and heard that voice baring its soul from under the dashboard?

"We've spoken briefly about your partner. She is a prominent community worker, she's also Black. I just wonder if this has caused any problems for you?"

"No."

"You won't elaborate on that?"

"No he bloody won't," Vic said loudly. With a huge effort of will he heaved myself from the settee and turned the radio off. Silence, blessed peace at the flick of a switch, comforting and warm in its nothingness.

"I was listening to that," Mary said in a cross sort of way. "I don't know what you've been making such a fuss about. I think he's sweet."

Vic looked at her and thought 'Thirty years of marriage, how little you can know a person.' He knew one thing for sure. Never, never would he listen to Woman's Hour again. Not if they tied him down with chains. A few months later, when they shifted the programme, Vic felt no sympathy. Serve them right if it had been cancelled altogether.

Vic could acknowledge his feelings; but Feather still wouldn't be in his team. On football terms: none of this sweeper nonsense. Not that Vic had anything against the system as such, as he'd said to Joe, he had nothing against continental food either but, 'Give me fish and chips over frog's legs any day.' Vic knew Joe's problem. Joe had been a ball playing defender, he saw Feather as some sort of spiritual heir, fulfilling his own dreams.

Take this Moscow episode. The whole squad gathered in this crummy hotel, miles from anywhere, snow falling outside. A key time in any visiting team's itinerary. Food, facilities, entertainment, everything has to be right. Vic had always found that a bit of the old 'siege mentality' helped 'Us against Them.' A quick in and out job. It was the same in the old days, motor up to London thinking 'We'll show these big city bastards.'

Vic was counting heads when he saw Freddy edging to the door. "Hey you," he called, "where d'you think you're sloping off to?"

He turned, "You speaking to me? I thought the Chinese had invaded." There were a few sniggers from behind.

"Get yourself back in here," Vic said in a low, dangerous tone. "This is rest and recreation, nobody leaves without permission."

He looked at Vic insolently. "Please Sir, I've got permission from the Headmaster. I promise to be back by tea time." Of course, by this time, everybody was looking, footballers love confrontation. Everyone except Joe, who still had his head buried in *The Daily Mirror* crossword he'd been working on since Gatwick.

"Joe," Vic called. "Feather here says he's got your permission to go gallivanting all across Moscow."

Joe dragged his eyes up, looked at Vic over his spectacles. "Oh, ah... yes... Goodness is that the time? Did I not mention it Vic? Must have slipped my mind. Young Feather here asked me weeks ago, then we had this letter from the Moscow Academy. It seemed ah... good politics to accept. Building bridges and all that."

'We're here to win football matches,' Vic felt like saying. 'If we want to build bridges then we'd have brought shovels and hard hats.' But that sort of thing is best kept away from the players. "Anyone else got any visits lined up?" He turned to the giggling players. "Lenin's tomb, a quick trip to The Bolshoi? No? Then up to your rooms." There was a chorus of groans.

"Practice at 5.30 sharp. Be there. And you," Vic turned back to the door, but Freddy was gone.

If fate had thrown out those cards just a little differently, then Vic would have been The Boss, and Feather would never have existed.

FREDDY'S DIARY

I fear that I have no inner self. There, my first ever entry in a diary. The first attempt to peer beneath the surface gloss to see what, if anything, lies beneath. Already these few words seem pretentious. I can see the problem. Does one write as well as one can, searching for vivid images, subtle metaphors, deep meanings? Or does one attempt to catch the flow of feeling as it pours out faster than the hand can write?

First things first. What has driven me to the pen? A form of confessional which, to say the least, has always seemed self indulgent. Elane confides in her diary to an almost obsessional degree. For half-an-hour every night she would retreat to her inner sanctum leaving me to wash up, and put the kids to bed.

It is Elane's departure (as good a word as any) that has provoked this feeling of crisis, of malfunction. On the surface I am coping quite well thank you, flourishing some might say. But inside, the realisation of her absence has shattered something vital, leaving an imbalance. With a sad little wave and a 'Goodbye lads, I can't cope anymore.' A part of me has withdrawn from the whole. To cover the gap, the hard, cocky, ruthless side has grown. Oh how he has grown, like a rogue child released from captivity, or the Arsenal back four from their cage. He has grown so big, so fast, there is no room left.

So clear is this effect, that I have taken to calling myself Freddy 1, and Freddy 2. F1 and F2 for short. These words are a desperate attempt to resurrect F1, to push him back into the power balance.

I understand why Elane left: no one should turn down a year in Africa. I can even understand it from a socialist, feminist perspective. She has been smothered by the explosion of my fame. All the phone calls are mine, she has become Freddy's woman, lost the battle to be a woman in her own right. If our relationship is to be saved then she has done the right thing. None of this was clear as I sailed on, the model 'New Man' changing nappies with the best of them. F2 has always been there. His is the voice that mutters, 'Is it my fault if I can't give birth or breast feed?'

"Everything you give is handed down from above," she said, during one of 'those' talks. 'Everything I take is seized from below.' If these are her feelings, how can I say different? It isn't that I resent her going, although there are times in the night, when real bitterness bubbles up. But I miss her, I miss her laughter. God help me, I even miss her temper - no one ever called Elane placid or easy going. I miss her friendship, her advice, and yes of course I miss her body, that smooth skin. Oh, just everything.

Back to the breakdown (I see F1 has been quite cunning, or fortunate. It's night, F2 is sleeping, lightly, slightly disturbed, he senses threat, but it's okay, Fl is used to skulking.

A dose of manic depression almost fits the bill. A memory. Do I leave stray memories in? Fuck it, it's my diary. Mary Carthy, six, seven years ago. Mary was manic depressive, almost classical textbook. Catch her in the middle and she would be the sweetest middle-aged lady you could ever wish to meet. Then the move upwards, changing gear into hyper activity, then downwards, stopping briefly at normality, into depression. Then slowly, painfully, upwards again, every step an effort, dragging heavy legs through normality and up again into unmanageable mania.

So not manic depression: I don't move up and down the scales of human emotion as Mary did. Nor is it a Captain Kirk division of the personality into good and evil. Nor is it a hearing of voices, although there are voices, but they are mine, engaged in their own struggle.

It took me by surprise, things seemed to drift away. Duties, life around the children, were done. Everything else, everybody else became vague, shadowy, not quite real. Compassion fatigue on the doorstep. Tiredness, lethargy, a retreat into a hermit like existence, (hermitry?). All fairly consistent symptoms of a common or garden depression. Then something else, not me, seemed to take hold of my body, dragging it up, out of tiredness, into relentless new activity. I can look in the mirror and Freddy 2 stares back. It's me yet it isn't. My eyes aren't quite so cynical, my smile not so polished. This is a hard man, too young to be so old.

Of course, F1 asked for it. F2 could never have moved in, had not F1 shrivelled away from the world. Shrivelling being the right word as F1 had taken to wanking off at least three times a day. If events had not been taken out of hand, it's possible he could have wanked himself to death. Lots of sound, psychological reasons for this: feelings of rejection; a desire to punish Elane, 'See, look what you've reduced me to.' Even a common sense removal of sexual tension, lessening the likelihood of falling into temptation: whatever, the result was to leave F1 walking round like a human zombie, drained of energy, deprived of fluid, bursting into spots. Fertile territory for a predator as skilled as F2.

Yet he is successful, let F1 be the first to acknowledge the sheer weight of his triumphs. Within the game, the professional world in which he moves, he is openly recognised as operating at the highest level, a figure on the international stage. He's good and he knows it. But F1 knows that the sheer joy of playing has lessened. It's all business now, elbows in the ribs, knee in the thigh, another three points, hauling an inadequate team towards promotion. Last season, the referees association presented me with a fair play award, a little silver whistle. Alas no more silver whistles for Freddy Feather.

He has used his status, his smile, and his artificial charm to carve out a national position, a posture, international footballer/left wing dissident. And he loves it. At public meetings he is assured and witty. Sometimes, because of who he is, even inspiring. Famine relief, anti apartheid, animal rights, gay rights, squatters rights, everybody's rights. He has his own local radio programme. Poor F1 can only hang on for dear life as this juggernaut of human energy rolls on.

His own head a jumbled mess, F1 watches from inside. He feels envy; yes F1 is jealous. How clear the world is to F2. No compromise, no shades of grey. Why is it all so much fun for F2? Life isn't this easy. Gratitude; F1 can sink into the comforting clutch of self pity as F2 takes up the slack, embracing all the 'right' causes, carving out a public following. Taking part in 'The Struggle.'

And fear, real fear that he will be lost forever, as his voice grows smaller and fainter.

Second Night

It's easy to see how one slips into this diary writing. It is the ultimate 'Me' book. Since starting this, I've been obsessed with memories that I thought had been successfully cut away, snip, snip, like a placenta, never to be seen again. But that isn't how it is. Memories, the past, stay with you, dragging behind like unwanted luggage.

Onward, backward, into memory, into me. After the broken leg, after weeks in hospital they finally sent me home, leg plastered up from ankle to groin. Home, a prison: chief jailer, my Father. Dad. No! I never called him Dad... he was never a father. He was a huge, hulking, gone to seed, ten pints a night, roll home, where's my supper, stick it in, pass out, sort of a drunk. I hated him, without really knowing it, without knowing anything else. If, today, I saw him in the gutter, begging for pennies, I'd spit on him. Now, with the wisdom that comes too late, I see how I was a threat to him. Back then, as a kid of eighteen, with it all before me, I couldn't understand his frustrations. All I knew was a mixture of fear and loathing. 'Everyone quiet, your dad is home.' How many times had I heard that sentence down the years?

Months went by in a living limbo. Casual, suppressed violence, a similar situation being lived in at least a dozen houses down our street, nothing uncommon, almost a cliché.

So this night, my father comes in and starts acting out his role. Most times I can slip off before he's really noticed me, like tiptoeing round a vicious dog. Maybe it was a full moon or something, possibly an early guest appearance from F2. There was some sort of argy bargy in the kitchen. From the stairs, looking through the banister rail, I saw my mother fall to the ground. Nothing that hadn't been seen and lived with for years. This time - and I can see it so clearly, once removed, like a film - I hobble over to Mum, help her up, turn to my Father and say, "God, you are a fucking animal." There is a silence. Mum clings to my arm. Then he turns my way, a little smile on his face.

"Oh you're here, thought you'd moved in with your cripple up the road." He moves in closer, towering over me with his bulk. Jabbing a finger in my chest, forcing me back into the kitchen, working himself up. "Mr. High and Mighty, with your football, not so high now, eh? Not so fucking mighty." All the time poking me with his finger. Awkward with my leg, I stumble back, reach behind for balance, hand clutches onto the kitchen knife. Still he comes on.

"So, what you going to do now you haven't got your precious football eh?" I see my mother cling to his arm, she says something I don't hear. Probably 'Leave the boy alone.' Something like that. He shakes her off, I bring out the knife and he laughs, lifts his hand. I slash round arm, the tip of the knife slices through his belly. Then we stop, frozen, assessing the situation, knowing that things will never be the same again. There is a thin red line across my father's belly. For a long moment it seems to hold, then red leaks, seeps, floods from his stomach. He clutches at it, trying to pour it back. Blood dribbles through his fingers, splashing onto Mother's working class, spotless, linoleum floor.

My Father, I can't think of another word for him, clutched at his skin, trying to hold it together. Our eyes locked and all sorts of dramatic thoughts passed between us. I remember him turning, leaving. Then there was just Mum and me, and the blood trickling across the not so spotless floor.

Mum and I had a serious talk, long overdue, past its sell-by date. She was surprisingly firm. Easy to say it was the stubbornness of the weak, but my mother isn't weak, a victim perhaps, but she held her family together. Probably not worth the effort, but she did what she understood as her duty. She raised her children, she endured. Mother decided it was best that I leave. Her choices had been made many years before.

"Come with me," I begged. "Christ, he's been ruining your life for over twenty years. Take your chance while it's here." She just gave me one of her looks.

I piled some things into a bag and hobbled off to Alf's place. No one there, so I broke a window round the back. Climbed in, found a sleeping bag, threw it on the floor and collapsed. At different times I must have gone out, to cash the Giro, buy food, but there is no memory. Nothing, until one day, the sound of a key in the door. Alf returning from God knows where.

I think that little episode qualifies as a breakdown. Different circumstances, but the similarities are there: withdrawal, an inability to make decisions. Then there was Alf and good old Mum to be determined for me. Now there is F2.

Third Night

A good evening for F2, two goals in a win against Norwich. His 'Fuck it, life goes on' philosophy seems to be a real winner.

And doesn't he love it. Everybody's little darling, mixing it up with left wing comedians and rock stars. At the centre of events, a maker, a doer, a star. But it isn't me. It isn't the 'me' I wish to be. Everybody forgives his excesses. Nobody sees him truly. F2 is an opportunist, determined to prolong his moment. I don't like him. I don't like the person I am turning into.

Where is he come bedtime, when the elders gather round, to drink my tea and tell me what I'm doing wrong?

"You should'a been firmer boy," Roseanne says. "That Elane, she never been happy, even as a baby. She need a firm hand that girl." Her own children, Elane included, have brought little but sorrow. Still, she's not the sort of woman to let that interfere with the giving of free, unwanted advice. Then there is mother, who seems to have developed maternal urges from nowhere.

"Oh let them stay up a bit longer, it's still early."

"It's an hour past their bedtime," F1 says weakly.

"I'll tell them a story," says Alf, the third in this 'Trinity of wisdom'.

"Now, which story do you want to hear?" The girls run by me, poking little pink tongues out in triumph.

"Tell us the one about how you lost your leg."

"Freddy boy, did you say you'd put the kettle on?" says Roseanne.

Oh yes, Freddy put the kettle on, we'll all have tea. How many times has F1 sloped off leaving them to it. Returning hours later to find them still gossiping in his kitchen.

Where F2 really excels, is inside the Peter Pan world of football. That all male, foul-mouthed, disgustingly crude, extremely cruel world of overgrown, overpaid, over-idolised adolescents.

All workplaces have their own quality. The general mood of hospital life is one of small mindedness, the nurturing of petty offences. Which is sad, when one considers the value of the work, maybe it's the bad pay, the conditions, the claustrophobia? Whatever, hospitals are petty places to work. Wherever you go, of course, there is always someone on your back, and footballers are, without any doubt, the cruellest gathering of individuals outside the Inquisition. It's all push, prod and probe for that weak point.

Dig it out, expose it for all to see. Worried about the size of your dick, (not you Norville, you ain't called Big Norve for nothing) don't let on man, don't let on. Nobody messes with F2, his retaliation comes in hard and fast, over the top and early.

It is F2 who deals with the Vic Smiths of this world. All football management deals in a 'Good cop-bad cop' scenario. Usually it's the coach who plays bad cop. Occasionally it's reversed, sometimes they're both bad cops.

Vic Smith is the hardest cop in town, not above cracking heads, or planting evidence. He hates me and F1 is genuinely frightened. To F2, he is a joke, a clock to be wound up until a spring goes.

This is the world of F2, newcomer though he is. His territory has been staked out. He's one of the lads.

Fourth Night

F1 here, still trying to get a grip on things. Just this afternoon I thought I had a real insight.

The realisation that my life divides into three sections Home/Public/Football: with a different personality for each. F1 is allowed supremacy in the home. He is a houseperson, he deals with the kids, meals, etc. F2 is boss on the field and in public. As I sit writing this, it obviously isn't profound at all. Everybody splits their life into sections. Work/play/sleep. On the dole my day shifted into two. Twelve hours up, twelve hours in bed, an eminently reasonable arrangement. I could let this shift system roll on because it's working. It needs an F2 to deal with the gutter press. It is going to need F2, maybe even an F3, to confront Hutch in the battle that is surely coming.

F2 is a man of frightening ambition, and tunnel vision. I don't like him. Normally I could go to Alf for advice, but it seems that Alf and F2 get on swimmingly, their vision peers down the same tunnel. F1 has little faith in Alf's rigid dogma. The people aren't going to rise up against the capitalist monster. F1 lends his name to causes because he believes in them, he dabbles in politics because he believes you must line up on one side or the other. F2 never does anything without thinking 'What's in this for me,' and Alf, he's thinking, 'How can this aid the revolution.' I even believe that F2 is using Alf. If it came to the crunch, I believe F2 would ditch Alf.

In my growing years, I learnt from Alf a socialist view of history. I remember when the first doubts crept in. It was in the hospital where, ironically, Alf had led me. I did a lot of reading. R.D. Laing's 'The Divided Self' and 'Sanity, Madness and the Family.' Simplified down, this view of madness as extreme sanity, the only sane reaction to life in an insane world, was a persuasive philosophy, until I came to work on the wards. Then all I saw were damaged people who wished only to rejoin life on the outside. I maintained respect for old R.D. but the vital faith had vanished. So it was with Alf. I can work for change, but I don't think I can beat my head any longer against Alf's revolutionary wall.

F2 rarely stops to thinks. He acts, relying on personal charisma to leap across the flaws in his argument.

"One person's wealth is many people's poverty," he says dogmatically. Ye'es, but F1 knows this wealthy couple, who are so right wing that, to them, The Guardian is the blueprint for the next Communist revolution. In some ways they are the other side of Alf's rigid socialism. The extreme right and the dogmatic left. Probably the only two groups left who believe in revolution at all. This couple set up an Aid agency that has raised over a million pounds for refugee camps in Tigray and Eritrea and other places where more 'respectable' agencies do not tread.

"Alleviating their own guilt," says F2.

"Easy to say," F1 replies. "Without their hard work, people would have died. Without them, medicines would not have got through."

"Every penny raised by charity is another load lifted from Government. All it does is bolster the system that caused the starvation in the first place."

This argument horrifies F1. "Is this what we've come to? A gigantic game of bluff with people's lives as the stake?"

At least this shows F1 beginning to fight his corner. He is emerging, and not before time.

Q.: What is the difference between a reason and an excuse?

A.: Not very much.

GEORGE

We all seek the exclusive, the scoop, the big one. It's scoring the winning goal at Wembley. To sit on a story is journalistic sin number one. Missing the metaphorical penalty in the last minute. I have the story. The others have bits of pieces. They listen in the sidelines, sniff around the rumours, but cannot put the pieces together.

"Come on George," they plead, plying me with drinks like shabby Casanovas. "Spit it out man, you're down there on the touchline, what the fuck is going on?" I smiled, drank my whisky before they could snatch it away. Another round, and it's the old arm around the shoulder, whisky breath in the face.

"Saving it all up for a book, eh George? Well fuck you." Seduction over, "You can't push a baby back up the womb."

The problem is, I have lost my objectivity: journalistic sin number two. Involvement is commendable for campaigners, but not for the seedy world of sports. From my privileged position on the bench, wedged in between Hutch and Johnny, I have allowed a natural empathy with the underdog, to become interwoven with the rise of Dockside, and the career of Freddy Feather.

All this exploded, as it had to, one cold January evening. Dockside vs. Leeds, already a promotion six pointer. A goal each from Arnold and Drew had moved the match beyond Leeds. When bananas started to fly onto the pitch. The ever present chanting turned to a torrent of vicious racial abuse, finishing up as a chorus of monkey noises. On the bench we shook our heads in hopeless despair.

At first nobody saw Freddy sitting alone in the centre circle, then the rest of the Dockside team drifted over and sat with him. The Leeds team milled about aimlessly as the Referee waved his notebook. Slowly some sort of realisation fell over the crowd. The three black players in the Leeds team joined with Dockside, sitting in the centre circle. The stadium had gone quiet, not silent, noises still came from the East stand.

"Monkey! Monkey! Monkey! Ooh! Ooh! Ooh!"

"Jewboy, nigger lover. We'll do you!"

Now the crowd knew. There was a movement of bodies that left the hooligans isolated, with nowhere to go but forward onto the pitch, towards the waiting police. Truncheons raised, the Law laced into the invaders with a ferocity normally reserved for striking miners or poll tax protesters. Five minutes that's all it took; until the thugs were gone like a bleached out stain. The Referee finished the match while the London hacks stood by, mouths open, notebooks closed, events falling outside their range of clichés.

After the game I sidled into the dressing room. Hutch, puffed up like a fighting cock, went straight for Freddy.

"That's it son. That's you and me finished. One mess too many."

The other players disappeared into the bath as Manager stood over Player, who sat on a bench, shirt off, sweat glistening on his body.

"Nobody's bigger than football, not you, not anybody."

Freddy looked up. "I've nothing to say to you Hutch. I don't care about your support and even less for your opinions." At this indifference, Hutch inflated even more, veins stood out on his face. One could almost see his blood pressure rise as he threatened to burst apart, smattering bits of his outraged self across the room.

"Can I say something?" Heads turned to me. "Now simply isn't the time for a personal slanging match. There's twenty pencils up there, all poised to kill. You need a united front, a statement, everything lovey dovey, keep the knives till later."

"No way am I apologising," Freddy said. Hutch grunted loudly.

"Alright, alright. Let me draft a statement." I was thinking this out as I went along.

"You Hutch can offer support for the principle of anti-racism; whilst stressing your non-involvement in this particular episode. Freddy, you will have to answer questions, do your best to get them on your side." Hutch gave another of his expressive grunts, but he was deflating slowly.

"And," I continued, "a signed statement of support from the players would be nice."

"No way, no fucking way." We turned to see Barney Anderson framed in the doorway. With his neat three piece suit and briefcase in hand, he looked like a respectable stockbroker whose Dow index had just collapsed. "You can hatch up all the conspiracies you want but leave me out. There's nothing in my contract about signing suicide letters. You do what you want, I'm damned if I'll be a part of this foolishness."

Hutch turned on him, grateful for somewhere to deposit his anger. "You'll be damned if you don't my son. Or you'll be on the transfer list, which at your age is pretty much the same thing."

Barney swopped his briefcase from hand to hand, contemplating this new twist to his future. "Okay, okay, show me where to sign," he muttered. We dug out a piece of club paper and Barney scrawled his autograph halfway down a blank sheet. "Can I go home now?"

"Yeah, piss off home son, and no talking to the press."

"I'll leave that to you, you're so good at it."

We huddled together, again. "Two more things," I said. "Hutch send up a bottle of whisky. Get them in the right mood."

"What?" he squawked, as if I had suggested sacrificing his eldest child.

"All for the cause of racial harmony Hutch." Freddy as ever, could not resist his little dig.

"And you," I turned on him, wanting to wipe the smirk from his face. "Here's a little advice from an old campaigner." I ticked the points off on my fingers. "Don't wear jeans and a tee shirt, don't try to be witty or rude, don't raise your voice, even if the questions seem provocative, just answer them quietly, stay cool."

"Don't turn up at all," came a voice from the shower room to general laughter.

The press was in convivial mood. Here was the story and here they were, what acumen, such nous. They sat dimly luminous under the cloud of cigarette smoke. I squeezed in between *The Independent* and *The Sun*. "We finally flushed the bugger out then," muttered The Sun. "Not too keen on him?" I said.

"Stuck up lefty piss artist."

"Good player though."

"Still a piss artist."

As a young reporter, I had longed for acceptance to this magic circle. Twenty-five years ago I would have thrilled to the chase. Now, I felt like an intruder, an outsider with secrets to keep.

"We'll get him, just you wait and see." The man from *The Sun* uttered these words with such chilling certainty that I shivered at the viciousness of his tone. Hutch bustled in, Freddy close behind. Seated at his desk Hutch surveyed his audience. "Well well, when was my office last so full?" he smiled, eyes shifting.

"No point buggering about. We'll say our piece, you ask your questions, then, maybe we can all go home." He read my words in a grey Northeast monotone. The hacks listened patiently, appreciating a decent bit of defensive play, waiting for the real show to begin.

My own position felt strange, almost detached. I had come to look upon Freddy as almost my own property. Had I not spotted him at sixteen almost eight years ago? Had I not pushed for his inclusion in the Dockside team? Been the first to urge England selection? Somewhere he had slipped away, his behaviour out of control. He was no longer the person I wished him to be, but an arrogant, wilful figure, romancing his own destruction. Now he stepped forward, placed a tape recorder on the table. "Just so there won't be any arguments later." There was a bristle of indignation amongst the hacks. Integrity impugned. How dare he?

"I don't regret anything I did tonight. It wasn't a premeditated action, not on my part. The only planned thing was the well orchestrated campaign of race hatred. But within that, I have to accept that innocent people could have been hurt. So firstly, I would like to thank the police for their prompt action. They got the right people. They got national front thugs; the same thugs who have had a campaign against black players all over London. I even recognised some of the faces. As I understand it, the police are charging them with carrying offensive weapons and inciting racial hatred. I tried to put their chants out of my head. I know the policy is ignore it, maybe it will all go away, and then I realised I can't play football while this is going on. It seemed like, by doing nothing I was actually a silent partner to it. But I didn't come on to the pitch thinking: 'Right let's have a showdown.' It just got to the point where I couldn't shut it out and I couldn't play. I'm not saying that what I did was right, there must be a better way of dealing with racism, but I don't feel I've anything to apologise for either. I guess that's all I can say. Anybody any questions?"

"As I understand it, you will probably be charged with bringing the game into disrepute. Do you have any comment on that?"

Freddy smiled. "That seems a question designed to get me into even more trouble, so it had better be no comment."

"Are you going to sit down every time the crowds chant something you personally disapprove of?" The Daily Mail spoke.

"There is a difference between chanting, even obscenities, and an organised demonstration of race hatred. To me that lies on the other side of unacceptable."

"So you would do it again?"

The hesitation was palpable, pencils were poised, breath held.

"I will be seeking advice from concerned bodies, Black organisations, the P.F.A. I would ask the opinion of Black journalists, except I don't see any. Maybe we'll all be able to work out a course of action together. I will try to be more in control of my impulses in future."

"Freddy, why don't you talk to us?"

"I am talking to you, here I am. What you mean is why don't I take your money. The papers here must have offered me at least fifty grand. If I'm honest...

With those words I should have gone home, made some cocoa and gone to bed. Instead I sat and listened as Freddy destroyed my scenario, wrecked whatever relationship he may have had with the press. Odd phrases floated in and out of my ear.

"Racist gutter press."

"Built on lies."

On and on, an epiphany of bad news! My swelling depression was confirmed by *The Sun*. "Got'cha my son, Got'cha good and proper."

Sod the cocoa, the real need is for a stiff drink, something, anything to prod these thoughts into perspective. So far Freddy... No I must stop that. The very act of thinking of him as Freddy reduces the distance between us, encourages a false intimacy. From now on I will refer to him as Feather. So far Feather's political activities have been small scale, locally based. Appearances at rallies, benefit concerts, interviews in underground magazines, nothing that could not be excused as youthful idealism, nothing he wouldn't grow out of. Tonight he came out of that particular closet, made enemies of people with long memories, set himself up as a legitimate target.

Earlier in the season, when all had seemed to be going so well. When the Dockside team, powered by Feather, brooded over by Hutch, was easing its way up the table I had gone to offer Hutch my congratulations. The team looked a good one. Hutch had dabbled in the market and brought Barney Anderson to supply experience and brains to the mid-field. Giant Scottish centre backs stood like blocks of concrete in the middle of the defence. On the surface all seemed well.

"So why aren't you smiling?" I asked him as we sat in his office sipping at his 'Manager of the Month' bottle of whisky.

"Don't ask George, you don't wanna know."

"I already know a fair bit Hutch. For example I went to see Sam Dolton, your beloved chairman, your boss."

"Oh aye, and what did he have to say?"

"Not a lot Hutch, a news item in itself. Sam Dolton spurns publicity; what do you think that does for rumours of a back stage power struggle. One only just avoids the phrase 'Coup D'état."

"Rumours, rumours, football's full of them."

"What about Dolton selling off his shares? Another rumour, I think not. Someone is buying in."

"I don't worry about upstairs. Not my business."

"Well, come down a floor shall we? Let's leave the question of who is actually running the club for the moment. I notice a few changes. A crèche, ramps for the handicapped, family enclosures, macho women about. Things are changing Hutch, this is a new policy in action."

"What do you want George, I thought this was going to be a friendly drink."

"It is Hutch, and I do think of you as a friend. You've let me sit on the bench, made me feel involved." The whisky was beginning to loosen my tongue. "I noticed you got a new coach in. Nobody I recognise from football, but the face is familiar, I think."

Watching Hutch swill his thoughts about, gave me a chance to study his face. Not that I think you learn much by a person's face, but he looked old, older than I remembered. Broken capillaries criss-crossed his drinker's nose. But then he had always been a boozer, even as a player in the not so swinging sixties.

"I'll tell you what it is," I said. "Every time I look round someone has shifted the furniture. I'm onto something, and if I am then the pack won't be far behind. And you Hutch," I went on, "why aren't you happy? This time next year you could be back in the first division. You've got a player most managers would kill for and all I see is a face full of misery."

He looked at me over the desk, the need to unburden himself was plain. Johnny, for all his virtues, his loyalty, his plain speaking, could never look outside his team of the moment. Strange really; as a player he had been the skilful one, blessed with a certain, if limited vision. Whereas Hutch, for all the brutality of his playing days, enjoyed and encouraged skill. If his teams went down, which they did, at least it was with skill and flair, playing football to the last bitter kick.

Slowly now, he started to talk. The words gathering momentum as they fell from his lips. "I've always bitched at chairmen and directors. Never liked 'em, never met one you could trust. Dolton was no different. But by Christ, at least he was there. I tell you it's a creepy feeling to have no one upstairs. I've known clubs get by without managers. I've managed teams that had no players, but I've never known a club without directors. If nothing else we've saved a fortune on drinks."

"Who handles the day to day running?"

He shrugged, reached into his desk draw and pulled out a folder, saying, "I've always been a Labour man, I read *The Mirror*, but I've never seen anything like this." He waved the folder in the air. "This is what runs the clubs." I reached across with eager fingers, but Hutch was quicker, snatching the folder away even as my fingers closed over it.

"I don't know George, this is high powered stuff."

"Come on Hutch, don't piss about."

"I'll read you a bit shall I? It's called *Charter for The Workforce* subtitled '*Guidelines for a smoother running work environment*'. You want more?"

"Read on Macduff."

He cleared his throat as if auditioning for Rada. "'*Any employer employing a workforce of more than twenty, will be asked to employ a certain percentage of minority and ethnic groups in the workforce.*' It goes on and on. Equal opportunities, consultation, shorter working week, not for the likes of you and me of course. So what d'you think?"

"Standard left wing policy," I replied.

"Is it? Is it by Christ? Perhaps I died for fifty years."

"Oh yes Hutch, the problem for any left wing council is making it stick. If there is a hostile employer, then it's all just so much paper."

"Ah..."

"What does 'Ah' mean?"

"Ah means that we, Dockside has been singled out as a test case for this... this... whatever. Ramps for wheelchairs, crèches for babies. I tell you before all this, I didn't know what a crèche was. It's a word that never crossed my path. Now I go to the gym and there's all these babies in there. Some woman I've never even seen looks at me like I'm the intruder."

"I see."

"Oh, and what exactly do you see George?" Hutch leaned forward aggressively.

"Well, in this situation, not uncommon, you would expect an unsympathetic employer to stomp on it, block it, tie it up with lawyers, pay off a few councillors. In the end, just ignore it. The question is why Dolton's low, almost invisible, profile?" I looked at Hutch but his face was set in stone. "I can make some guesses, a rumour here, a stray word there, leads us back to a certain shareholders meeting, at which a certain manager was present."

"And a certain player."

"And chairman of the board."

"Alright. You know so bloody much. I was there. I saw Sam Dolton destroyed, I saw it happen..."

"What, what happened? Don't stop now."

"George, I don't want to know, I do my job, the club ticks over, people get paid, we go on winning, everybody's happy." He poured himself another whisky, most of the bottle had gone by now. Still, another month another bottle.

"George, I tell you, I've had gamblers, womanisers, players who couldn't read or write. I've had poufs and psychos. Me and Johnny once had a player with an eighteen inch dick. We had to make shorts with a special pouch to put it in. But I've never had a player who..."

"Who what?" I prompted gently.

"Who took over a club. That's what I don't want to think about. I've been over that night, again and again, and it all comes back to one thing. Freddy was part of it all. Dolton was fitted up! Don't ask me how, but Freddy was right in the middle of it all. Just back from England, remember. What gives me nightmares is how can I bollock him in the dressing room? I'm looking over my shoulder all the time."

Hutch wasn't always so melancholy. Get him onto football and his spirit would show through. I grew to enjoy these chats. Hutch and I sifting through the thousands of players who had passed in and out of vision. Always returning.

"How good is he, Hutch? Can he perform on a world stage?" He leaned back, willing to share his wisdom. "I tell you George, I tell you. When I first saw him I thought 'Aye aye, we got a bit of talent here. Throw in a bit of the old Hutch know how, and we could have ourselves a nice little player."

"And now?"

"Well I tell you, I bought Barney Anderson, partly to give us a bit of know how in the middle, and partly because I thought Freddy could learn from him. Give it a season and a few things might rub off."

"And...?"

Two games and Freddy is doing things that took Barney twelve years to learn. Little things: making space, angles, giving people the type of passes that they want. Things an older player learns to save his legs."

"So," I said slightly puzzled, "he's a quick learner."

"NO! This is more than that. It's like he moves inside your skin, draws out your secrets and then moves on." He saw me look at him.

"Alright, alright, I know what you're thinking, but I know football. Listen, when I was thirty-four, playing for West Ham, I could see things happening on the pitch before they happened. I'd be up in their half looking back, and I could see the move playing itself out, and I couldn't do anything about it because I didn't have the legs.

"I used to think that if I had the knowledge of the thirty-four year old and the legs of a twenty-four year old I could have been a world beater.

"Well this boy's got it. He's the only player I've ever seen with the brains and the legs. Mind that doesn't mean I like him any better. He listens, takes it in, then goes his way." He sipped at his whisky, trapped in his own thoughts. "If only I knew then what I know now - the complaint of the old, eh?"

This was fertile territory, and the temptation was strong to let Hutch wander down his memories. But more than anything I wanted confirmation, or otherwise, of my own judgement. "How good is he Hutch? Can he live on a world stage? The World Cup?"

"The big one, eh?" He leaned back, smiled with all the wisdom of his thirty odd years inside the game, as opposed to my thirty odd years on the edges. "You want my honest opinion, off the record, just between us?"

"Yes, for Christ's sake."

"Well I tell you, I can't wait. Everybody knows he's good, the fans know, there's that buzz every time he gets the ball. Managers know, two men on him every game. But even they don't know how good. I tell you, I tell you..." Hutch was getting excited now waving his whisky in the air. "He's better. He makes people play and that's a gift given to very few. Look at old Barney, good player, good player, always has been. But now he's playing the best football of his life, he could even make it to the World Cup himself. Elton Drew, banging in the goals, Paddy Farrel down the left, Pete Stewert in defence; all looking good, better than they are. And England too. Martyn, Archer, Reid, good players, playing better than they have for years; playing their best. And he scores goals. He gets into that box, he's deadly as any striker." He stopped, put down his drink, looked straight at me. "Di Stefano, that's who he reminds me of, Di Stefano."

After the sit-in, an episode in which I considered myself rather badly mauled, I plied my trade in a semi-detached sort of fashion. Back in the press box, mistrusted by fellow hacks, I sat cocooned within a shield of intellectual cynicism. The observer, no longer a participant.

His standing as a footballer, pure and simple, increased as the season wore on. The win over Germany opened up a deeply buried seed of optimism. Friendlies against Italy, Argentina, Holland and Belgium caused hopes to rise to almost insane heights. We, England, could live with the best. This was the thought that filtered through the game, touching players and fans. If our international team, the standard bearer, was right up there then the players too were raised. Were they not playing alongside world class players? The supporters discovered new passion. After years of defeat and lethargy, there just might be something worth cheering about. At the centre of it all was the small, stocky figure of Freddy Feather. An unknown figure from the second division had taken his game and imposed it on the world stage, sending shock waves through the minute calculations of international managers everywhere.

In Moscow, Uncle Joe had played Feather and Westley together, an astonishing gamble in many ways, attacking the Soviets deep in their own territory. True, most of the match was played in the England half and the Soviets deserved their one goal lead, as rare England attacks fell into the Soviet offside trap. Then, with five minutes to go, Westley floated a pass over the top of the defence.

This time Archer and Martyn had come back with the defence, and it was Freddy running from deep within his own half, who collected the ball, swerved round a defender and moved in on goal. Voyanava, the Soviet Captain, came across for a last ditch tackle. He hit Freddy about thirty yards from goal, taking the ball and the man in a desperate lunge. It was a tackle that would have slowed a bull elephant yet somehow Freddy kept his feet as Voyanava, acknowledged as one of the best defenders in the world, clutched at his shirt and then his shorts. Now the goalkeeper was on the scene. Just before he fell, Freddy dug his foot under the ball, scooped it over the keeper, collapsed in a heap as the ball rolled with desperate slowness into the unguarded net. That goal confirmed Freddy's position as national hero, lifted him, almost, into untouchable status.

For a short time all was sweetness and light. The press boys were as delighted with their find as any proud bridegroom. Disillusion set in fairly quickly. The new bride was not behaving as she should, slipping out for the evening, consorting with undesirable company. Rumours filtering out of the Dockside area like dark shadows, insubstantial yet disturbing. Whispers of a left wing council; building a coalition of defiance. Vague stories of a meeting at which the chairman of the local club was effectively deposed. Shares bought and sold, the balance of power shifting.

Rumours given spine and shape by their very lack of substance. Secrecy means one thing: something to hide.

Whispers in the press box. Feather not behaving as a professional footballer should. No twenty things you never knew. No money changing hands. Around Dockside an invisible code of silence. Secrets: something to hide.

The episode of the sit-in left him remarkably unscathed. The deadlines were too close, the tabloids themselves too stunned by events to formulate policy. At that time of night just getting the story in was triumph enough. My own paper gave me all sorts of aggravation.

"I'm sorry dear, the pages are all made up now. Oh, sports, well I guess we can squeeze you onto the back pages, between the hockey and the sailing. Sorry, that's the best we can do."

Perched in my loft, away from the action, I became a Feather watcher, a breed of journalist I have always despised. On the field my eyes never left him, while my mind analysed his every move. Sad really, I took no pleasure from seeing Dockside rise up the table; obsessive behaviour, wasted time.

One evening, ploughing my way through the early evening London traffic, listening to P.M. on the radio, I half heard the announcer say: "We have reports of a demonstration outside a Government defence building in Mill Hill. Our reporter is there to bring you live coverage. Roger, what's going on down there?"

"Yes, Bob, I'm here in the middle of at least two hundred demonstrators. And so is international footballer, Freddy Feather. Freddy, what's this all about?" A pause and then that voice, no mistaking it.

"We're here to protest about a miscarriage of justice. Three months ago six comrades broke into this M.O.D. building. They came out with photographs of Government experiments on live animals. Experiments that are not only vicious and unnecessary, but also against European law as well as the laws of humanity. These six people admitted their offence, the crime of proving that the British Government is breaking the law. They were tried in secret, sub-justice, and sentenced to nine years. These people hurt no one, damaged nothing, stole nothing. These six comrades have just got nine years for exposing the M.O.D. as a bunch of law breaking sadists. Nothing new in that I suppose." His voice took on a mocking quality that I recognised.

"We're here to try and show people that this type of behaviour can't be hushed up. You can't use British justice to implement Government injustice. We're here to say that the wrong people are on trial. The Government broke the law. The M.O.D. are the ones who run electrodes through the heads of defenceless animals. Here are some photographs, take some, we've got plenty. If British justice is to have any meaning it will look at this case again. It will say, 'What are the Mill Hill six guilty of?' Exposing Government lies; exposing the evil secrets that go on, in our name, behind closed doors. We're here to say to the M.O.D. You won't get away with this in secret. We don't expect to change anything. If I wasn't an international footballer you wouldn't even be here, would you? We want to ask the M.O.D. 'what goes on behind your locked doors?' If there's nothing to be ashamed of then throw open your steel doors, let's all have a look. We're here to say that British justice has served its people badly. It has shown itself to be a tool and protector of sadists and torturers. The men and women in white coats who deal in death behind locked doors."

"Thank you, Freddy."

"Thank you, don't forget the photographs."

Yet again, he somehow slipped the backlash, letters to P.M. ran ten to one in his favour. At the very next match, away to Bristol City. The home fans displayed 'We Love You' banners, alongside the blown up photographs that appeared to be racing round the country.

He rewarded them with a virtuoso display, an array of flicks and mazey dribbles that left defenders caught in mid pose. The Bristol defence tried, they ran around with the single minded dedication of the English professional, expending their assets to the best of their ability. They blocked and fouled to no avail. He ran through them, round them, sent his passes over them. For Freddy Feather there was no hiding place.

I swear my phone knows when Gus Goodrich is on the other end. It seems to shake on its perch, shrill and imperious in its demand to be answered. "George?" Right enough it was my editor on the line. I could practically smell the alcohol. "Get over to Dockside, your mate Freddy Feather has just been arrested."

"No."

"Yes, busted for possession of drugs, right in the middle of some radio interview. What we've got now is some sort of riot situation. What are you waiting for George? Keep in touch."

'At least,' I thought as I guided the car through the London streets, 'I've been spared the indignity of hearing it over the radio.'

On foot now, weaving through the streets, grabbing at stray wisps of conversation, I began to piece the story together. Freddy had indeed been arrested at the headquarters of Radio Free Dockside, another of the seemingly unlimited stock of portacabins that circled the youth centre like protective wagon trains. Apparently, he had been holding an interview with the leaders of the local Rastafarian community, in the course of which the question of 'Ganga as a sacred herb' had arisen. Apparently, the 'sacred herb' had been produced, examined, discussed, and then smoked. The police, wailing their sirens and flashing their lights, had arrested everybody but finally settled for the two Rastafarian speakers, or smokers, Freddy, and the poor lad who worked the sound system. Two hours further on Dockside was verging on open rebellion. Hundreds of people stood outside the police station, singing and chanting. Police reinforcements had been called in. I was absorbing all this when my arm was grabbed from behind. I turned, guiltily relieved at seeing a white face, "You're George Barret?"

"Yes."

"We've been looking out for you, we want you to do an interview, background stuff. You know, Freddy, don't you?" As he tugged at my arm, I had a sudden insight, revelatory in its impact, then someone stuck a microphone in front of me and it was gone. Slipped away to the land of undiscovered inventions, missed goals, lost opportunities, wasted time.

"George Barret, you've written extensively about Dockside and Freddy Feather. Tell us your assessment of the situation here."

"I can see what you see. There are people here, probably in their thousands, there are police with riot shields, the police station is under a state of siege. The situation is that somebody is going to be seriously hurt unless an effort is made to defuse the situation." Damn, two situations in one sentence.

"Can you give an insight into Freddy Feather. What is it about him that provokes such extreme reactions in people?"

"Well, he is an anti-establishment figure, a rebel if you like; but more important, Freddy Feather is an integral part of the Dockside community. He is a local boy who, whilst becoming a superstar, has maintained his links with the community. He still lives here, has chosen to raise his family here. He is closely identified with the many real changes that have taken place in this tightly knit community. This is quite clearly seen by the nature of the crowd here, everybody knows him, he is one of them. More than that, Dockside has accepted Freddy as its spokesman, they are proud of him. In a peculiar way, the people here, feel protective toward him. When you arrest Freddy Feather then you strike a blow against the Dockside community."

"You make him sound almost a modern folk hero."

"Your words, but the trouble with folk heroes is they end up as martyrs."

"You're not suggesting he should be above the law?"

Had I said that? Surely not. "Absolutely not, but unless the law is seen to be responsive to people's needs, you will have just what we have here, a potential riot. It's going to take very little for this demonstration to turn ugly. On my way here I've seen skirmishes, flashes of violence. Authority and Citizenry in direct confrontation. At the moment it's singing, but that mood could change. As I understand it, Police reinforcements are flooding in, the whole atmosphere seems set for violence."

"What is the answer then?"

"If I knew that then I would be writing the editorials not the sports pages. But I do have a suggestion. I would get Freddy Feather and his fellow prisoners out here. Maybe he can calm the situation. I fear that unless someone makes a bold decision then we're going to see blood on the streets, and that would be the real crime."

"Thank you George Barret, sports writer for the er... erm..."

"Thank you."

The same arm pulled me away from the limelight, the voice whispered in my ear. "Good stuff George, if you fancy a change of pace give us a bell."

Far be it for me to suggest that the appropriate authorities (and well informed rumour has it that authority, in this case, was of the very highest, make of that what you will), were listening to my humble efforts, but haul Freddy out is exactly what they did. He stood, a small figure, sandwiched between the massed ranks of police shields behind him, and the crowd, threatening and unpredictable. I missed the next few minutes, there was a huddle of bodies, the television camera zoomed in to him. Then the bodies parted, Freddy was thrust forward. A moment of high drama, the crowd quietened. I distinctly heard one of the police horses whinny, the sound echoing down the street. Then Freddy started to speak, quiet and controlled.

"First of all, and I speak for the four of us, I must say how moved we are by this demonstration of support. The law tells us that we have a potential riot on our hands. The cameras are here as proof: *Riot Of The Day*, live." There was laughter, Freddy smiled then continued, his voice carrying as clearly through the streets as it did across the football pitch.

"If there is trouble tonight then it's our people who will be hurt. If there is blood on the streets, it will be our people's blood. And for what? Let's face it, four of us getting busted for smoking a joint. What I'm trying to say is that this isn't the time or place to confront authority. Hospitals closing, people dying of hunger, homelessness, poverty, racism. That should bring us into the streets, not a marijuana bust. I admit it, I had a puff or two." Wild cheering from the crowd.

"I broke the law. It's a fair cop. I'll survive, we'll survive.

"I want to ask a personal favour of everybody who has turned out tonight. It's late, it's the time of night when tempers fray, control slips. So, I want to ask everybody to behave with courtesy and consideration as you make your way home. Take care, be gentle, walk home safely, and who knows, if we get bail, we may even see you all on Saturday."

Within twenty minutes, the streets were quiet. A few technicians were putting away the last of their equipment, some stragglers still singing. For myself, dragged into a second-hand participation in this drama, there was only relief that no one had been hurt. I drove home through the quiet streets, putting paragraphs together in my mind.

The next morning, following an extremely late night hunched over the typewriter, my head felt heavy, the onset of depression. Gus knew no mercy, his antennae detected my presence as soon as I walked through the door. "George, in here." There was a muted ripple of applause as I entered the office. Gus was all business shirt sleeves rolled up, cigarillo firmly clenched between his yellowing teeth.

"I want you to watch this George, see how it jibes with your on the spot assessment. He switched on the office video machine, There once again was Freddy, in close-up talking directly to the camera. "This is a quick message for my children. I hear you are giving Grandma a hard time. Don't worry, I'm just helping these gentlemen with a few enquiries. I want you to be good girls, go to bed, remember to clean your teeth, and I'll be home soon." The mystery of the missing few minutes explained. Then the camera switched to the scene I had witnessed. It is here that my perception of events parts company with the televised version.

I am an experienced hack, well used to seeing my memory of a match contradicted by an action replay, or a written report so at variance with my own view that it could have been a different match altogether. The scenes I witnessed on the streets of Dockside were powerful enough, but what emerged through the television lens was magnified tenfold, or maybe real life is smaller than television. Gus Goodrich flipped a switch and Freddy was gone.

"What d'you make of this then, George? Is that how things went down?"

"Quite frankly I'm stunned," I said. "I almost can't believe what

I've seen. It's what happened, yet it isn't. It was all much lower key. Is that what people saw last night?"

"Even more powerful live," Gus said. "What comes over strongest is that single-handed this guy stopped a riot, purely through the force of his personality. Think about it George, take your time, about five minutes, then we're going to have an office discussion."

Five minutes later, true to his word, the whole team was gathered in his office.

"Okay," Gus started, cigarillo still clenched between his teeth. "We've all seen the pictures, let's sort out the facts. Was anyone unimpressed? No. So we're all agreed we have an extremely televisual personality on our hands. Why? What stood out?"

Althea Thompson, our token female writer was the first to offer a view. "I'm a parent, and that opening where he speaks to his kids was powerful and funny. I mean even in a crisis, here is a man who is thinking of his children. I was watching and I was moved, and I think every parent in the country would feel the same."

"So he appeals to parents, anything else?" There was a giggling from the back of the room. "Spit it out," Gus snapped, "No whispering in the ranks."

"Sex appeal, that's what he's got," said Janice, one of our typists, bolder than the others. Gus and I looked at each other, slightly embarrassed. In our generation sex appeal belonged to women. Gus waved his arms about. "Elaborate. Paul Newman, Boy George?" There were more giggles.

"See now, you and George aren't sexy."

"Thank you very much, remember to collect your cards on the way out," said Gus crossly. However, even I could see that with his belly smothering his belt and jowls covering his collar that Gus lacked the magic ingredient.

Janice was unabashed. "I'm sure that a certain woman might find you attractive, the mature, older type perhaps. But Freddy's got what I think of as 'Rip the shirt off your back appeal.'"

"This is the verdict of you all is it? Older women want to mother him, younger ones want to rape him. The question we have to ask ourselves is this: 'Is he genuine?' George, from one media superstar to another, is he for real?"

Gus' sarcasm slipped over me, something Janice had said, recalled my lost insight from the previous night.

"George, George, speak to us."

Instead I turned to Janice. "You think of him as Freddy. Why is that?" She shrugged, thought for a moment, "I guess because he's one of us. He speaks for us. When I see him like last night, or hear him on the radio, I think 'Yeah, that's right you tell 'em.' He could put his boots under my bed anytime."

"George, is this getting us anywhere?"

"Just thinking out loud. The public thinks of him as Freddy. Supporters do too. That's his persona. Now I can't think of a single similar example: not Stanley Mathews or Bobby Charlton, or any pop star although I may be wrong."

"Is this getting us anywhere?" Gus was becoming tetchy.

"It's surely an interesting thought," I said, and how often can one say that? "This is a sportsman, radical in his actions, who has so impinged on the 'National Consciousness', if you like, that the public thinks of him as Freddy. The image is clear, he's a rebel, he's sexy, he speaks for a generation, not ours, Gus. He's Red Fred, Freddy."

"He takes drugs, don't forget that." Gus added.

"He smoked a joint," Janice said firmly. "Everybody does, I do. But he's the first to come out and say so."

"So where's all this leading?" Gus sat back on his chair, put his feet on the desk. "I've seen him play. Christ, he's even got *me* out of this chair and I haven't seen a match for years. Then there's all this left wing crap. What's it all about?"

"Which brings us back to the question, 'Is he genuine?'" I smiled as I said it.

"George, I want more. You know him for Christ sakes, get in there. The tabloids have taken their line, but they went to bed before the final showdown. That makes it their view against the people's own perception."

"A close call," I said.

Gus nodded. "The thing is, the features boys want in and I want to keep it sports. He *is* sport, damn it, he's ours."

"He's tricky Gus, there's a whole trail of broken bodies behind him."

Gus slapped a hand to his forehead. "Broken bodies, that reminds me, Hutchinson, the manager. On his way to the scene, one over the top, drove his car into a wall. In hospital. Sorry."

In the car, driving back across London, not knowing quite where to go, my mood started to define itself. Moving through sorrow for Hutch, solidifying into anger against Freddy and the repercussions of his stupidities.

A phone call, told me that Hutch was out of danger, but not taking visitors. Then I drove to 'The Slum'. The not quite affectionate nickname for Dockside's stadium. It was locked up, closed for business. Still angry I then drove across Dockside to Freddy's home. Dowdy streets, pre-war houses, television aerials waving in the wind. Freddy's house was fairly typical. A three story building that, not so many years past, would have been crammed with families, firstly of Jewish, then of Asian and West Indian origin. Even as I raised the heavy black knocker I realised the futility of my gesture. Freddy would be out celebrating his victory with like minded cronies.

Then the door opened and he was standing there, smaller than I remembered, a half smile on his face. "George, nice to see you, I think. Come on in, cup of tea?" I followed him up the stairs, into the living room. Freddy disappeared into the kitchen, giving me the opportunity to prowl through the room, searching for clues, being plain nosy. One corner of the room was totally covered, some might say suffocated, with posters, leaflet's, photographs. There was a picture of a Mongol child, with the words: '*You say Mongol, We say Downs Syndrome. His mates call him David.*' Have to think about that one. There were posters of animals being mutilated 'Every six seconds an animal dies in a British Laboratory.' The room itself was a mess, as my eyes roved over the kids' toys, unwashed cups, books all over the floor. I had to restrain the impulse of the obsessively neat to start tidying the room.

When Freddy returned I had learnt nothing of any significance, except for the difference in our standards of cleanliness. "Social visit George?" he said, handing across a mug. "Or is this business?" Considering my answer I sipped from the mug. The inside of my mouth dried up as the liquid swilled around like chalk. Forcing a swallow I looked smiling, "Sorry about that George. Soya milk, you get used to it."

"Why? Why on earth should I want to get used to it? What's wrong with milk? Bob Geldof advertises milk."

"He should know better." Freddy shrugged, smiled again. "I don't really want to talk about it. I've never convinced anyone, I get too emotional. But, since you ask... The whole milk industry is built on exploitation and cruelty to an unacceptable level. Hang on, I'll dig you out a leaflet."

From the corner he pulled out an old suitcase the lid flew open and leaflets spilled everywhere. Finally he found what he was searching for, presumably a lecture on the iniquities of the dairy industry. Catching my look he said almost apologetically: "Hobby of mine, it started out not being able to refuse anyone committed enough to stand on street corners in the rain. Then I got so many I thought I may as well become a collector. You're lucky to find me in George, I'm having a day of self pity, sitting here drinking tea, feeling sorry for myself."

"I don't think anything I've got to say is going to make you feel any better," I said sternly, refusing to be charmed by his little boy lost act.

"Oh dear George, you'd better spit it out. I am aware that I owe you."

"And are you aware," I said heavily, "that Hutch is seriously ill in hospital. I don't think that's anything to smile about."

"No, no, George, you're right." He hung his head, a small boy caught doing wrong. "Except that Hutch isn't badly hurt. I went to see him this morning. He's simply not having visitors because the police want to have a few words. Having let me and the others go, they've got to arrest somebody. Hutch is 'lying low and sayin nuffin'.' However your basic point is correct. I've been a silly boy, Hutch could have been hurt. There could have been a blood bath, and it would have been my fault. I've been incredibly irresponsible, what more can I say?"

"Somehow an apology doesn't seem enough."

"Well, it's all your going to get." The flash of anger was over and the mocking smile back in place when he spoke again. "What is it you want George? An interview? I'll get out my tape, so it's all on record."

Did I want that? Censored, carefully constructed words. Possibly I could goad Freddy into rashness, but did I want that? Gus' last minute instructions whispered at me 'Two thousand words by yesterday.' But surely there is more than that. Perhaps a bit of honesty, in part to wipe the smirk from his face.

"Off the record then; it's true, I am angry. It seems to me that you're offering things you can't deliver. This whole Socialist enclave right here under the Government's nose. It's doomed to failure. A state within a state, it doesn't work, it never has. How long before the Government turns on you? What then, what about all the people who believed in you?"

"But I don't think we'll fail. And even if I did, is that a reason for not doing the things you believe in?"

"Okay, granting your sincerity, what I want to know is how far are you involved...?"

Freddy cut into my question "All the way George, up to my eyebrows and over. I presume what you're implying is: am I a front for sinister left wing forces who are using me, a naive, well intentioned footballer, caught up in forces beyond his understanding?

"Would that suit you George? Give you a handle on things, make my behaviour forgivable? Sorry to disillusion you. I was born here. My grandparents were refugees, my Zieder, a little Jewish tailor, who died before his time. My Buba, scrimping and saving to pay off the slumlord. The colour of the immigrants may have changed, but the slumlords stay the same. The Dolton family dynasty, gouging the poor for all they can get. Not any more, no fucking more, man!"

Dangerous territory, Freddy revealing more than he should. "You can leave," I said, in some strange way trying to protect him from himself. Too late. Once started, my words were no more than a spring for Freddy to launch himself into yet another black hole of invective.

"I can leave, I've got the money. I could buy a nice place in Chigwell, mortgage myself to Leatherhead. But I don't want to. Why should I be forced out? However, there is something in what you say. Moral dilemmas piling up like unpaid bills. If I use a National Health bed, isn't that taking one away from someone who can't afford to pay? I send my kids to the local school. Am I making them suffer for my principles? You're right I don't need to stay, but this is my home, I was brought up in this house. It was a bit different then: three families, one on each floor, one toilet between the lot of us. Now I own the house, thanks to Tory policy. I'm actually happy here."

Under attack from this formidable flurry of words, my anger was melting away, in need of fortification. I was approaching that twilight territory where no journalist should find himself, where objectivity is supplanted by personal feelings. "You remind me of a character from a children's book. Just William, I don't suppose you know him?"

"I know William," Freddy replied. "And I can't say I'm altogether pleased. The implication being that I'm into rebellion for its own sake, that I lack depth." I was about to answer this, to qualify it in some way, I should have known better. "You may be right. I'm more of an activist than a thinker, but I've been whisked away from the front lines and elevated to a position where my words carry more weight than they deserve. No one with aspirations or depth of character is going to get dope out over the air. If I had considered the repercussions then I wouldn't have done it."

"I think you exaggerate," I said. "The result has been to make you into even more of a hero than you were before."

Freddy gave me a sly smile. "Forgive me for saying this George, but that is almost tabloid in its simplicity, a certain lack of depth there."

"Oh?"

"The council, and behind the council there is a planning committee of which I'm a member, has been trying to reach some sort of common ground with the police. We say 'Don't keep busting the prostitutes on the streets? What about the pimps, and the child prostitution that goes on, that we all know goes on behind locked doors?' We're saying: 'What is the point of busting people for blow, giving kids criminal records, creating hostility? When was the last heroin bust?' The police say 'We'll do our job, it's got nowt t'do with you.' And we're saying 'We've got a mandate from the people...' I'm sure this is all relevant George, only I've lost track of my original point."

"You were discussing my lack of depth," I said dryly.

"Right, right, so all I'm saying is my arrest has landed in the middle of these negotiations like an unexploded bomb."

"Yes, that's quite interesting."

"I've hurt your feelings George, sensitive flower aren't you? Perhaps this vaunted depth is just an excuse for sitting on the sidelines, not getting involved. I can't do that George, I see life as a struggle in which you line up on one side or the other. At least I know which side I'm on. How about you?"

The situation had somehow switched round. Suddenly I was the accused: my respectable, liberal viewpoint under attack. I felt old. In the other armchair, Freddy smiled across at me, the face of youth, with all its energy, taunting me. Change the subject. Come back at him from a more oblique angle. "Let me ask you about football for a bit."

"Sure, that's why I let you in the door in the first place. You've written some nice things about me."

"I'm a fan," I said simply. "But I find writing about you unexpectedly difficult. There's no centre to your game. Most players build their game around a particular talent; tackling, passing, dribbling, power, whatever. But you quite clearly don't have that. Is that fair?" I asked, unsure of my own analysis.

"Yes it is. I think." Freddy looked solemn, turning over his thoughts. "What I am is... I'm a footballing Frankenstein. Everything in my game has been grafted on over a thirteen year period. I'm two-footed because I've learnt to be. I score goals because I spent three years as a striker, learning the trade. I take fifty penalties every day. I reckon to score at least ten goals a season from free kicks, that's learned - it's not a gift from God. The spinning passes I saw on T.V. and I worked and worked until I had them mastered. I lift weights for power. I still work with an athletic coach changing the way I run, developing my body for maximum pace. If I see something new in a game say on T.V., then I learn it, incorporate it into my game. So that it's part of my armoury, then when I need it..." He stopped, looked up at me, he seemed very young. "Does that conflict with your view of the game, that a player can learn the skills?"

I thought back to one of my many chats with Hutch. He had spoken of Freddy moving inside players, drawing out their talent. "No, it doesn't surprise me: I wonder how you manage to marry the two areas of your life, the political activism and the football."

"They're not married George, they live in sin. And they are only two areas of my life. Home, family, friends, relationships, all exist together. But I understand what you're saying. We live in the age of the celebrity. If I was still a nurse or a window cleaner no one would pay the slightest attention to anything I said. We actually tried to do a benefit for a Woman's Shelter; we wrote to every rock band in the country and we didn't get a single answer. Now all I have to do is pick up the phone, and it's 'Freddy Baby, how're you doing? A benefit concert, no problem.' We could be having a benefit for nuclear power. I've got lost again, what was I talking about?" I had lost track myself, caught up in the twists and turns of his conversation as sinuous as any dribble.

"What about the Labour Party?" I asked. Can you not achieve your aims inside the mainstream?"

He leaned back in his chair, smiled his trademark boyish smile. "Don't make me laugh. Labour gave up on Socialism in 1924, never regained it. I know their words: 'Broad Church, line up under one banner.' But step out of line and Central Office is on the doorstep saying: 'We don't want to upset things, not with an election coming.' You ask any housing association, 'Who built houses back in the 80's? and they'll all say 'Militant in Liverpool, the only council with a policy of housing its people.' Apart from a few individuals, Labour, The Labour Party, has betrayed the name of Socialism..."

I interrupted. The only way of ever getting a word in. "What worries me," I said, "is that all this is leading up to some sort of confrontation. I know you've just been arrested, but you're right. This will smooth over. What I'm talking about is a confrontation with the forces of Government and The Law."

"Only too easy to see George. If we had someone under Church Sanctuary like Viraj Mendis, then I like to think I'd be on the front lines. I've been on pickets, and I hope I would be again. Animal rights brings me out because animals can't defend themselves. Anyway it's a theory of mine, unproved as yet, that to be a Socialist, you must be Vegetarian.

"You might not believe this, but there is an awareness that my behaviour has been off the rails. There are even reasons for it, excuses maybe. I've been a bit carried away, seduced by celebrity. It's a tricky moment when your dreams become reality, when fantasy turns to fact. Just when all this change was happening, my partner left me. Not for good I hope, I'm proud of the work she's doing, but she's not here and without her guidance I have run a bit amok."

"A bit," I said dryly.

"A bit," he agreed. "I'm lonely George, no shortage of people, or causes, but still..."

This rare, reflective moment seemed a suitable moment to bring our little chat to a close.

"Freddy," I said. "You've been generous with your time, I appreciate it, I wish you were going anywhere but into the disaster that I see lying ahead." He laughed, his face lighting up, even though any humour had been purely unintentional.

"You've cheered me up George, I feel almost ready to face the day." He gave me a smile, slightly sad round the edges.

Back in the car it was time to edit together all the random thoughts, preparation for a protracted bout with the typewriter. Most annoying, in a literary sort of way, the word that insisted on forcing its way forward was Charisma. In my opinion an overworked, artificial concept. On one level, success breeds charisma; it comes with the territory. On another, self projection can be learnt. The 'Teach yourself charisma' school operates from a hundred seedy catalogues. But there it was, whatever it was, the effect filtering through the defences of a hardened cynic such as myself.

Fluency. 'Gift of the gab' my mother would call it. Freddy certainly had the gift, to a self-destructive degree. He overdosed on rhetoric like a greedy child left alone with a plateful of cakes. On the other hand, there was a mitigating degree of self mockery, and humour, and insight.

How we in the 'Quality Press' yearned for a politically aware sportsman, or woman for that matter. A break from the artificial outrage, the backhander, the exploitation of dubious reputation. Well now we had one; a footballer as far away from the normal furtive secrecy as it is possible to be: were we happy? Of course not, daft question, it isn't our job to be happy. Balances had been disturbed; roles stood in need of reassessment.

Passion, Freddy wallowed in it, like a hippo in the mud. His body language quivered with righteousness, with the inability of the fanatic to keep his convictions to himself. My passenger seat was covered with the leaflets that Freddy had pressed on me. A hurried glance showed 'The true causes of Aids' alongside 'The Cancer Research Scandal' partially covering a picture of a pig on an iron maiden. Hours of jolly reading to look forward to.

Predictions, every profile demands a prediction. Impossible to foresee anything but ruination. The only questions being from which direction and how long? The current situation: a club floating in limbo, a drugs charge, the promotion race in its final, most desperate stage, a community closing in on itself. All strands of a volatile whole. In the distance, the World Cup.

How far does one take idealism? I remember the footballs of my youth, heavy leather things, inflated by a pigs bladder, tied up with a lace that left its imprint on your forehead. Would Freddy have refused to play? Would the ball have been 'ideologically unsound?'

So we came to the last match of the season. The final play off. Sunderland, third from bottom in the first division, battle scarred, determined to retain their status. The words: 'work rate, effort, character, survival,' imprinted onto their footballing brain, elevated to the status of philosophy. Dockside, flash young dilettantes, still innocent, with their smooth passing, sweetly flowing moves, almost an old fashioned push and run. One match, winner takes all.

I chose to remain at Dockside, joining with twelve thousand of the faithful watching the match on giant screens. Sunderland laid out their scenario early in the match. Two mid-field destroyers attached themselves to Freddy with the accuracy of cruise missiles. In the third minute they caught him in a vicious sandwich, leaving him face down, semi-conscious in the heavy North East mud. The Referee called the three of them over, fingers were wagged, words exchanged. I asked Freddy afterwards what he had said. He grinned. "I said to them, 'Do what you have to do lads, just don't break me fucking legs.'"

At the end of the day, with romantic hindsight for inspiration, it seemed somehow right that Dockside should win. A fitting end to a season filled with trauma. Even more right, that Freddy should score the winning goal, taking his tally for the season to thirty, a phenomenal total for a mid-field player. Right that the country's top player should be plying his trade in the first division.

The season had left me exhausted, emotionally ragged. Dragged reluctantly towards the centre of events. I had become the possessor of unwanted secrets, the defender of the indefensible. A lone and lonely voice struggling against the mutant partnership of tabloid vendetta and outraged authority.

Thank God the season was over, but then again a sneaky little part of me was projecting forward. A new season. Dockside against Liverpool, Asenal, Man United. The World Cup... I need a holiday.

ELANE

Saturdays, I slip away from the village. Walk the half mile to the hut I share with three other workers. Then, closing the door and, holding the radio close to my ear, I do my best to tune in to the B.B.C. World Service Sports Special.

This particular Saturday, straining through the crackle and the fuzz and the dying batteries, to catch the second half of the match between Stranrear vs. Alloa, I was caught up in a sudden bout of homesickness, missing the girls, with a pain so piercing that for a moment I went dizzy and tears came to my eyes. I missed Freddy, wondered if the state of the house had passed the point of no return.

I couldn't understand the deep rooted Scottish power base at the B.B.C which allowed a Scottish second division match to broadcast to the whole of Africa. Maybe it was all code, a far reaching stage in Scotland's plan for world domination.

Maybe no more than a comfort to Scotland's lost tribes as they roam the earth, dreaming of Stranrear on an icy afternoon, calling the whole world Jimmy, searching for that perfect pint of heavy.

All I wanted was some news of Dockside, not much, just a snippet. Four forty-five Scottish time. The populations of Africa and Stranrear joined in mutual relief as the final whistle blew. Over to London and the latest football news.

"Well Mike, the attention of whole football fraternity, indeed the whole country, has been focused on one game today. I'm referring of course to the match at Dockside where Freddy Feather played what could conceivably be his final game." Oh yes, what's all this about then? "Later in the programme we'll be talking to George Barrett, sports writer for *The Protector*, but first of all give us your impressions of the match."

"Well John, Dockside won, as they had to do if their promotion hopes were to remain alive. Secondly, Freddy Feather scored, as was almost inevitable. Thirdly, the support of the crowd signalled quite clearly that the football authorities should think carefully before they attempt to levy any punishment of their own."

"Outside any action that the police and courts will take, you mean?"

"That's right, John. And it is looking more and more likely that Freddy Feather is going to evade any punishment from that quarter.

There is talk of deals being made behind closed doors, of a mutual saving of face. It seems that the police went in a touch prematurely, without the proper documentation. There's talk of the highest powers in the land becoming involved. No one, after all, wants an inner city riot. The scenes in the streets of Dockside just two days ago showed that..."

Twiddle, twiddle, squeak, squeak went the radio. Conspiracy theorists would immediately suspect B.B.C. censorship. London on the brink of civil war. And at the centre, the one person to blame? The father of my children, one of them anyway. Perhaps she could change her name and no one need ever know.

The radio still gave out the occasional high pitched squawk, but the message had come through something primitive, my family in trouble. Time to go home. True my work here was unfinished, but then Social Work, in any country, anywhere, is an ongoing process. Forever. The more you dig the more there is to discover! Professionally, I could go home. A network of community-based aid had been set up, a bit ramshackle, but forging ahead with an enthusiasm and belief far removed from the morally defeated cynicism of big city social work.

The journey to the airport took three days. Hard travelling by night, daylight spent hiding under camouflage. Plenty of time for revaluation, reassessment, a taking of stock. I had left home angry and confused, in danger of losing my sense of self. None of this had really changed. The anger and confusion were still paramount. My sense of self more fragile than ever. The difference being, hopefully, I no longer piled blame onto myself or those nearest to me.

The people of the village held a party. A going away/come back soon sort of affair. Nothing dressy, just slip into your best first world hand me down. The friendship shown, nothing asked freely given, had churned up some deep feelings. If I failed to maintain the bonds, then the fault would be mine.

As the trucks, trains and planes took me further from Africa, so my sorrow at leaving was replaced by excitement. Going home. Heathrow, cheap, plastic tack, and that's just the food. Down the corridor, through the red door, that's where they interrogate the illegals, or anyone with a black skin who doesn't take their fancy. Oh yes I know Heathrow, it's underside, it's dirty little secrets.

No one there to welcome me home. No one knew I was coming,

but still. From the taxi, a treat to myself, it could have been worked by bus and underground, London seemed much as I had left it: filthy, self important, caught up in an amphetamine rush of movement for its own sake.

The driver was in no mood to leave me with my thoughts.

"You from Dockside then?"

"Yeah."

"What about all this lark then? Whad'dayou reckon to it. I mean he's a bit of a pratt inne?"

Only one person I know answers that description. "To be honest," I said, "I've been out of the country for three months. I know less than you."

"Yeah?" He looked round, a half smile on his face. "Well it's all quiet now, simmering like. You know him then?"

"Who Freddy? Yes, I know him."

"Yeah, what's he like then?"

"He's okay, quite sweet really."

"Good player, I play a bit meself, mid-field destroyer like."

"Just what the team needs. I'll fix you a trial if you like, no problem."

As we sliced our way through the streets, the driver filled the gaps in my knowledge. The dope bust. "I mean you got to be a pratt to skin up on the air, right?" The scenes in the street that same evening. "The wife thought he was okay, like you said, a bit on the sweet side."

I got him to drop me off a mile or so from the house. I wanted to feel a bit of familiarity, put my thoughts into some sort of order. I wanted something from Freddy, but one doesn't come home after three months and make demands, it would have to be handled with tact.

The key fitted the door, no reason that should have been a surprise, it just was. Freddy's mother must have heard the turning of the lock, she popped out of her kitchen, saw me, came up and gave me a big hug.

"Lovely to see you back." She smiled up at me, maybe I had grown a few inches in Africa. "Shall I tell him you're home?"

"That's alright Beth, I'll surprise him."

She smiled again. "Shall I bring up some tea? I'd like to, if that isn't intruding."

"That would be nice, Beth."

I went on up the stairs feeling calm and in control. On the plane I had passed the hours with fantasies of finding Freddy in bed with some strange woman. Or the girls looking up at me and saying 'Who is this woman?' I opened the door oh so quietly. Reality was, and I imagine generally is, mundane. Freddy, Leroy, Animal Jim, and Pete Stewert sitting round the living room table playing bridge. 'A lads night in!' It took a while for my presence to filter through the dope smoke, the beer haze, and loud music; but then heads turned my way.

"Elane!" Four male voices chanting in unison, smart creatures.

I looked over at Freddy, his expression moved through surprise, rushed past guilt, finally settled on a sheepish smile.

"I want you to come back to Africa with me." Not the words I had intended.

"Now? This minute? Can I finish the hand first?"

On the edge of my vision I caught Leroy and the others exchange a quick, 'time we were somewhere else' sort of look.

"I'm sorry," I said. "I'm obviously not as calm as I thought I was. Sit down boys, don't let me drive you away." They sat obediently, frightened gazes never leaving my face. If they turned away I might strike. Switching back to Freddy I said, "I'm going up to see the kids." Even as I left the lads were gathering their things together for a lightning getaway.

Many cups of tea later, in the early hours of the morning, phone calls made, kids back in bed, Freddy and I were finally alone.

"I do want you to come back with me," I said. "I meant to approach the subject more subtly, but..."

"What about the girls?"

"We'll take them."

He nodded, looked thoughtful. "Sounds good," he said. "I've been to every Capital city in Europe, but I never see anything except hotels. Let's go."

"Just like that? I had a whole speech prepared." Freddy raised his hands.

"Elane, I trust your judgement, I've missed you so much, I've coped, just... But I've missed you. I love you."

Words. Of course they are just words, but still a girl likes to hear them every once in a while. "Do you know why I left?" I asked gently.

"Something about being smothered, lost inside Freddy Feather Incorporated feeling insignificant... dwindling away to nothing. Realising that..."

"Alright, alright, don't get carried away." I said feeling the snap come into my voice. "I remember when we first met, you were a callow young nurse, and I bossed you about. Suddenly I'm having babies and you're an England international. It all happened so fast."

"Not so fast, six, seven years."

"Be quiet just for a moment will you? I'm trying to say something nice." I took a deep breath. "I appreciate the fact that I was able to leave. Knowing that the kids would be alright. I shouldn't have to appreciate it, it should be taken for granted. If you buggered off for three months no one would bat an eyelid. But it isn't, so I do."

"That's it, is it? That's the something nice?" He smiled. "I do feel as if I've grown as a human being. I've fucked up almost everywhere else, but here, in the home, I've done alright, not brilliantly, not super dad or anything, but alright."

I laughed, how could anyone so innocent cause such chaos? "How's your sex life?"

"No worse than yours I hope. My stars did say that a time of famine was nearly over. I tell you something weird. Women of all shapes and sizes have been throwing themselves at me."

"Like lemmings."

Freddy laughed. "Maybe. Acres of female flesh wanting to smother me. Famous women: pop stars, actresses, Tory M.Ps. Women who wouldn't normally look at me."

"You stayed faithful to Big Mama, how touching."

The next few days were spent reacquainting myself with Dockside. A simple walk through the streets was enough to be intoxicated by the atmosphere. Half familiar faces calling "We're gonna do it." An unmistakable feeling of solidarity: Dockside was going to defy logic, the odds, the ranging of forces - its own poverty and history of failure. Dockside was going to show the world that the underdog can still triumph. God knows the town hadn't had much to smile about across the years.

Decades of economic depression, relieved only by the occasional war. The brief rise and long fall of the unions. The beginning of working class racism as Enoch lowered the drawbridge to black immigration. The problem was that Blacks didn't know their place, grew dissatisfied with sweeping the streets, driving the buses, cleaning up the hospital wards. And somehow Enoch overlooked the fact that Blacks just would keep breeding.

There is a thesis waiting to be written on the effect of a successful football team on a community. I understand how the wealth and success of the two Liverpool clubs can alleviate the general dreariness of life. I can understand the capitalist moving in, smelling profit like a shark at a shipwreck. I can even understand the Yuppie invasion. If I understand so much perhaps I should write the thesis. 'How to implement Socialism on the back of a winning team.' I think the answer is distract people's attention, then slip in the socialism when nobody is looking. I know men who make love like that.

This frivolous/cynical/realistic view was reinforced by a trip to Council H.Q. The ideas and idealism of the past year had ground through the system, finally emerging as policy. Decisions that would affect the lives of the Dockside community. H.Q. itself was in a high old state of excitement.

"This is it. This is the big one." Leroy pointed to a map on the wall. "No more fucking cars, no lorries. The whole area off limits. He smiled. "Finally gonna happen."

I looked at the map, at the squiggles and diversions, closed roads, no entries, bicycles only. The sheer cheek of it all brought a smile to my face. All this enthusiasm, it must be catching, like athlete's foot. I turned, mouth filled with questions, picked up on something - the way Leroy was looking at me.

"What?" I asked. He grinned at me. "We want you to take over this, push it through to the end. He rushed on before my objections could order themselves into a neat queue. "We've got four main arguments. Number one 'Damage to the road infrastructure.' We've got experts who'll say that the roads are on the point of collapse, that the damage reaches out for miles. Houses, underground pipes, you name it, it's in there. They'll bring in their experts to prove how safe everything is but it's good, we'll take it to court, delay things for months.

"Number two, 'Air pollution.' We got the bastards on this one. We're way over European safety limits. We got reports proving all kinds of linkage with cancer, leukaemia, plague.

"Number three, a bit sleazy this, but emotionally powerful, 'The number of kids killed in the immediate vicinity.' Handle this one with care, to be brought out at selected moments.

"Number four. At the optimum moment we'll hold a referendum on the issue. We're busy rigging the ballots now. Joke! So whadd'ya think?"

"I think I'd be insane if I went anywhere near being involved."

"Well Elane, I'm not putting pressure on you in any way, but, we've been waiting on you. It's been universally agreed, you're the very best person to see this through."

"You're getting good Leroy. What about our Africa trip?"

"No sweat, start the thing up, go away, come back just in time to catch the shit." He smiled. "Nice to see you back. We could do with your soothing hand, things are getting a bit... you know, down to the wire."

A few visits later, there was only one visit left to make. The one I had been putting off for the best part of two days. Curtains drawn, sunlight sternly kept at bay, the house of a sad man, a lonely man. "It's good to see you, Alf," I said when he opened the door. "Can we talk?"

He stood framed in the doorway, thinner than I remembered, a man at war with his own body, beaten down by illness, kept upright by moral rectitude. Would he even speak to me? He was perfectly capable of shutting the door, on me, on everything that betrayed his values.

"Best come in," he said finally, moving back into the gloom of his passageway. I sat at the kitchen table and watched while he put the kettle on. I had never been here alone before, sometimes with Freddy; sometimes with the girls, but never alone. The girls loved this house, with its cobwebs and sense of secrecy.

They could tear down Alf's defences by not acknowledging them; a gift of childhood. To them he was a grandfather figure, pockets filled with surprises. I should have brought them, at least there wouldn't have been this terrible silence. Of course silence was a key weapon in Alf's armoury. Let people talk on, betraying the shallowness of their views with every word.

"You got something to say, lass?"

An involuntary inward smile: the satisfaction of beating the master at his own game. "Where to start Alf, I feel like I'm standing on a riverbank, you're on the other side, and in the middle there is this raging torrent of hurt feelings, injured pride, righteous anger, self pity."

"I see. The whole thing is my fault." He nodded his head as if giving this theory its due consideration. At least he was talking, for Alf, that showed a certain willingness. "I didn't take drugs, betray myself as an athlete. Betray everything we've ever worked towards. I have no understanding of why he would behave in such a manner."

"No," I said gently. "I'm sure you don't." Taking a deep breath I moved into the lines, rehearsed on the way over. "I'm not going to sit here and tell you that what Freddy did was right. But it's done. So where do we go from here. How can you not be speaking after everything you've been through together?"

Alf sat on in stillness, grey eyes staring at me, unmoved. Time to move on to stage two. "You're right I am here to try and patch up what to me is a distressing situation. But for now I'll leave out personalities, leave out the fact that two of the people I feel closest to in the whole world are not speaking to each other.

"Let's talk about the feeling in the town. Let's talk business, the professional view." This is hard going, nothing to do but plough on. "We're on the edge of promotion, two games, one week, and this football team could be in the first division. The biggest thing to happen in this town since the Docker's strike. You're a politician Alf, you pride yourself on possessing a sense of strategy. You've got you're hands dirty while keeping your conscience clean. You've become an operator, a behind the scenes political fixer. Now you're in charge, everything we've all worked towards in your hands. You have an obligation, a responsibility to put aside your personal feelings. The manager of the team cannot be at loggerheads with his best player. As a professional it's your job to bolster him, have him at his peak. If you can't, or won't, do that, then drop him, suspend him. One or the other. The one thing you can't do is sulk in your tent."

"You're back, that should be enough."

"Maybe it should Alf," I snapped. "But it isn't. You think I don't feel that? You think it doesn't hurt? He's carrying a lot of pressure. He's young Alf, immature in many ways. Without your support, he won't have that something extra, that something special. You provide that."

A long silence, I poured more tea, stifling the temptation to speak with movement. And at last Alf did speak. "Manager, you said?"

"That's right Alf," I pounced, metaphorically. "Don't tell me you haven't thought about it. You're the man who thinks out all the angles, the one who peers into the gloom."

"The carrot, eh?"

"Business Alf, before I start in on feelings, respect, and love. We go up and I'll throw my weight behind you getting the job."

"You think a lot of yourself lass."

"No, not really, I'm desperate."

More silence, another ritual pouring of the tea.

"Every time," he said slowly, finally. "Every time I try to reach out. Drugs. I can't understand it. And I can't forget it. And I can't seem to forgive it." For a moment he seemed as helpless as a small boy crying out in bewilderment, 'Explain it to me, tell me, help me.'

I reached over and touched his hand. "There's no way I can explain it Alf. What can I say: everybody smokes, everyone round here, anyway. Escape, rebellion, the generation gap, nothing will excuse it in your eyes. I don't blame you, I can see that, for you, taking drugs must be almost the ultimate crime. I wish I could sit at your table and say 'We have sinned, we beg your forgiveness, it will never happen again.' I could promise all that, but it wouldn't be the truth."

In the end, all the fine words about 'Love and trust and mutual respect' would mean little. They might sneak through a barrier or two, but Alf had plenty more. He had built his life inside defensive shields. He listened politely to my fine plans, thanked me with equal politeness for coming, wished me well, saw me on my way.

The next day I gathered up the family for a day at the allotment. I wasn't pleased, to put it mildly. "What a state, how many times have you been down?" I snapped. "Look at my beautiful garden."

"A good few," Freddy muttered. Rachel sniggered behind him.

"You needn't laugh madam," I snapped. "You could have come on your own.

"Tell her Freddy, tell her what you told me. Don't be wimpy." My sweet little daughter.

"Yes, tell her Freddy," I said calmly.

"I did intend to come down. I did come down, to start with," he whined at me. "But then I realised I don't like gardening, never have. If I never see another slug, or stinging nettle again, it'll be too soon. When you were gone, one of my major pleasures was switching off

Gardeners Question Time. Sometimes I used to put the radio on, just so I could switch it off again."

"Well that's honest," I said. "While we're being so blunt with each other, there is something I want to talk to you about." I just love the expression on men's faces when they hear those words. The best time is when sport is on the T.V. Freddy made stabbing motions with the spade, as if only I and my little talk stood between himself and a good four hours digging.

"It's about this 'Operation Clean Air.'" Yes that rattled something alright. I smiled to myself as he rummaged through all his guilty secrets. "I've thought about it, studied it up and down, sideways and back again. It's not going to work."

Silence.

"All the time and money spent working it out," I said, "and we're going to be slaughtered. Nobody's thought about local shopkeepers, ordinary residents driving from home to work, handicapped cars. Shall I go on?"

"You've got the freedom to make any changes you want," he said. "You're in charge. The Boss lady."

"That's not the point," I snapped. "The point is: why aren't these problems in any of the files? Someone is trying to ram their own policy through. It's left wing gesture politics of the worst kind. Ban all cars and fuck the consequences." I was really working up a good head of steam now.

"So what is the right policy?" he said.

"Gradually, one street at a time, close them up for necessary repair and don't open them up again. Slowly, one street then another."

"Do it that way, you've got the authority."

"You're hiding something Freddy, you know I'll get it out of you sooner of later."

I expected a smile. Instead he said "You're not going to let it go, even though you'd be happier not knowing."

"Just tell me."

"This whole policy is Denice's. She took charge and nobody else could get a look in. Since you went, almost from the day you left, she's had some crack pot policy or other. She wanted to unseat old Joe Driver, she wants a city farm. Her latest is a carnival to celebrate 'Clean air day.'"

"And all you men have been helpless against her?"

Freddy spread his hands. "Absolutely, she's a force of nature. To stop her we were forced into a male conspiracy, meeting in dark corners, plotting careful plans that she would just kick to pieces."

"That's why you've given it all to me. I've got to deal with her."

"We couldn't do it," he said. "We just weren't ruthless enough, no one could wield the knife."

"And I can."

"Babe, you can stick it in, and they never even know they've been stabbed; it's your supreme political gift."

This was the moment when local politics, working for change, stopped being fun. With the distant support of the men, and at the expense of a friendship, I got my own way. It was exciting when they closed City street, but something vital had been sacrificed. There's always a price to pay.

Dockside won promotion. In retrospect it all seemed ordained. When I said this to Freddy, he lifted up his tracksuit and showed me his bruises.

"Tell that to my legs," he said. One week later we were all on the plane to Africa.

I had my plans, a vision of how things would be. Freddy and family would trail behind, full of admiration for my achievements. Not quite: on our second day, we went for a look at one of the field hospitals and Freddy simply stayed on.

Bringing his own brand of National Health expertise to the operation. Rumours must have trickled back to the capital. Suddenly the roads were crowded with trucks bringing long overdue supplies such as footballs and goal posts, and every teenage kid in the country who wanted to play football with Freddy Feather. We fed them, and put them all to work. In the evenings, when the heat melted away, it was time for the really important business: football, what else? You would think that after seven years I'd have grown used to it.

The best, the most fulfilling twenty days of my life.

In Africa, God, the conceit of saying something like that, as if I experienced anything but one tiny corner of one country, for one speck of time. In Africa it was nothing for someone to walk ten miles or so, purely to continue a discussion. In the West we have the telephone, working overtime. The perfect medium for bad news, no personal contact. The first call whisked Freddy away for pre-season training. A week in glorious, sunny Bognor Regis. The next dozen or so calls filled me in on all the petty personality clashes that had taken place. The problems that everybody seemed to think only I could solve.

"Think of yourself as 'The Manageress'," Leroy said. "In charge until you fuck up, Elane." His voice took on a more pleading tone. "You're the only person left whom nobody actually hates. We either keep control or lose everything."

"And you think I can do that?" I said doubtfully.

"You were right over the roads. That's one for judgement. You're black. That's two for ideological soundness. Stir in a bit of sex appeal and we got ourselves a package."

I tucked the phone under one ear while I opened a yoghurt, settled back. I always enjoy hearing Leroy on a roll.

"Leroy, what's your role in all this?"

"Think of me as a fixer, a mid-field destroyer. You want someone's leg broken, I arrange it. Incriminating photographs, I fix it. I crack heads and kick butt. It's dirty work but someone has to do it." I had no sooner put the phone down on Leroy's fantasies, than it sprang up at me again.

"Hello."

"Oh... ah... yes. I'm not sure if I have the right number."

"Well, you tell me the number you want and I'll tell you if you have the right one."

"This is 337462?"

"Yes, to whom do you wish to speak? You're not from some sleazy tabloid rag are you? If so then I've no comment, you can quote me on that."

"No, no, no, no," said the voice. "Actually, I'm Joe Taslin."

"Yes, so what?"

"The England Manager."

"England Manager. Manager of what? Oh." The penny finally dropped. "The England football manager. You want to speak to Freddy. I'm afraid he's not here. He's at training camp."

"Ah, yes, good. I was just wondering how he is, you know after..."

"You mean has he got leprosy or beri beri disease after venturing into the darkest jungles of heathen Africa? The answer is, no." There was a pause

"Young lady, are you this brutal with everyone?"

I laughed, suddenly liking the gentle voice on the other end. "Pretty much," I said.

The two calls, so close together, made me aware just how fragile it all was. A political crusade riding on the back of sporting success. Now Dockside faced its greatest challenge on both fronts. A slum team in the first division, like down and outs squatting in Millionaire Row. The council preparing to take on the Government in hand to hand combat.

As my thoughts wandered, it seemed somehow fitting that it should all come together. Hadn't we started together. A small caucus, still miraculously intact, a movement. Recognition that without Freddy, none of it would have been possible. I miss him, more than is good for me.

ON TELEVISION

Everybody was nervous as the lights went down in the studio. A delicate, directorial touch to sharpen up expectations.

High up in his revolving glass dome, the master of such moves was feeling his anxiety level rise. Yes of course, it was a scoop, and yes, one always welcomes a soupçon of controversy. That's the way reputations are made, short cuts carved. He lit up a cigarette. The problem was, nobody really knew this footballer, Feather chappie. One knew of him of course. Impossible to ignore the rumours; cupboards creaking with skeletons, trails littered with bodies, metaphorically speaking, of course.

Would he dry? Would he spit or swear? And drugs had to come up of course. As a youthful, thrusting, probing, live piece of television, the programme had a certain licence. 'Live television should have a Government Health warning,' he thought. 'Like fags.' He stubbed out his cigarette and lit up another.

Overstep the unspoken mark and Mary Whitehouse will be there, smiling amiably, teeth gripping like a pit bull terrier. That way lies a downward spiral. Past kids television, too old. Past morning television, too controversial. Down into the graveyard of afternoons, housewives and unemployed. His dreams extinguished like the little white dot that closed up the screen in the early days. Never to have his own chat show.

He'd wanted to do this interview himself, had been shouted down. "Too old, too fat, too bald, no street cred." Still one always welcomes good ratings. At the end of the day, Ratings Rule O.K.

Freddy Feather Inc. were nervous. Not that Freddy would cry or spit but his tongue might lead into areas best left hidden.

Stopping Freddy in full flight was like stepping into the path of a runaway truck. Still, nobody sells Socialism quite like Freddy.

Freddy Feather Inc. have tested the ground; this is as good as it gets.

The audience at that vulnerable, rather touching stage in their lives; just before reality moves in. To be blunt, the youth/rebel/anti-establishment vote is rock solid. This interview, carefully managed, is an attempt to reach out to parents, to the vaguely hostile, the uncommitted. They may not have known it, but their feelings were remarkably similar to those shared by thousands of football managers every Saturday afternoon. Dressing room instructions had been delivered, now all they could do was watch as Freddy strolled onto the field, out of their control.

This floating nervousness, combined and doubled, did not even register on S.T.'s private anxiety scale. As compère, chief interviewer, resident wit, he was feeling the strain. This was an interview that would be isolated and examined. His own role ruthlessly judged by peers and would-be peers. So far all had gone quite well. The rock bands had done their stuff, but the atmosphere had been lacking. Everybody was waiting for the interview: The Big One.

There was an upswing in the noise level. A cheering and stamping of feet as Freddy moved through the crowd. S.T. ushered him to the battered park bench, brought in for the informal touch. "Freddy," he said, "welcome to the show. I did have a big introduction worked out. 'Socialist footballer, or footballing Socialist?' but I see there's no need." This revealing of his thought processes was an integral part of his technique. "I've thought long and hard about my opening question. Should it be about football or politics? I want to ask this.

"You've been called everything from Marxist to Anarchist to dangerous subversive element in our midst. Using your sporting popularity to twist the minds of our children. Where do you see yourself on this sliding scale of human depravity?"

The figure at his side remembered his own last minute instructions. 'Smile, speak slowly, don't raise your voice, don't preach, relax. Be yourself.' He smiled. "Marxism is a label to wear with pride, if deserved. Unfortunately, my stay awake capacity is about three pages. Any Marxist theory that I have, is a hand me down, second hand Marxism."

"So Marxist is eliminated?"

"Reluctantly."

"Yet you are linked closely, intimately, one might say, with a left wing council at present locked in a titanic struggle with the Government."

Freddy nodded, smiled again. "It's comical in a way, Council Policies are no more than wishy washy Liberalism..."

"Surely not," S.T. interrupted, taken aback despite himself.

"Dockside Council is an elected coalition of Socialists, Environmentalists, and various Independents. To hold this base together, there is an agreed slate of five major policies.

"Number one: the Environment. A traditional wishy washy Liberal concern." He stopped, made sure the audience was still with him. "However, to turn environmental intentions into policy, that takes gut level Socialism."

S.T. was struggling to stay on track. "You're saying that there is a watering down of belief, a lurch to the right, whenever you achieve political office?"

"Yes. If you are a wishy washy liberal - and I'm not knocking it, it's a position with a lot of history - you worry about expenditure, inflation, not alienating big business. Officials flood you with papers saying 'Why this can't be done.' Maybe you get seduced by the trappings, the good life." He stopped, but went on before S.T. could come in.

"We did our research, we went to every Environmentalist group going. And all said the same 'You want to clean up the inner city. There's only one way. Eliminate the car and watch your air purify overnight. Eliminate the car and watch your children grow to adulthood.' We've had no traffic now for three months. Normally in that time four, five or six kids would have been killed. We have saved lives. But you tell that to the Ministry of Transport.

"Referendums - wishy washy Liberalism. Giving people a sense of pride in their community - wishy washy Liberalism. Caring for the disadvantaged within your boundaries - wishy washy liberalism. Turning these words into action against a Government who sits on the edge like a rabid dog, takes the commitment of people whose ambition has not yet become cynicism, who still believe in the possibility of change."

"Is that the most any Socialist can hope for? It sounds a bit depressing."

"To operate Socialism you need to have control of the factories and the economy. You need to tear down in order to build up. Otherwise all you are is a more humane operator of a capitalist philosophy. Which of course makes you a..." He spread his hands...

"Wishy washy Liberal." S.T. was getting to grips with this circular style of speech. It was clear that Freddy was media experienced. The flow of words, the expressive body language, the undoubted passion. All this kept the audience leaning forward, helped create a mood of intimacy.

"So how do other footballers see you, Freddy, when you come round the corner preaching Socialism and Animal rights? Do they run away? Do they take you seriously?"

Freddy smiled. To S.T. it seemed an artificial smile, contrived. "I don't have any expectation of support within football. Having said that, any support is more than welcome, I fall on it like a starving man on a crust of bread. Any factory, any workplace has its core of socialists, rebels, malcontents. And a football club is a workplace, so there is support, more than I would have expected. On the other hand," Freddy rode over S.T.'s hesitant interruption, "the more support there is within a club, the more I'm seen as a threat by club management. There was that whole thing with the benefit match, I was carved up like a sacrificial beast."

S.T.'s ear mike was squawking away. 'Times running out, move to audience'. S.T. obeyed with relief, somewhere the interview had slipped away from his grasp.

"Freddy we're going to turn you over to the audience now." And I hope they have more luck than I did, he thought.

"What about drugs, Freddy?" The audience moved straight to the centre of things. Hushed itself, settled down.

Freddy looked round, prolonging the moment, "Gimme a rope, I'll hang meself while I'm at it." Laughter. "I have smoked the occasional joint." Cheers and applause, on and on. Freddy raised his hands, "I can hardly deny it, I've been busted." More laughter. "I actually think of myself as rather clean living. I don't go to parties, I don't really go out much at all. My partner goes out - I look after the kids. So in my own house, in the company of friends, I'll have the occasional joint. I'm just an old hippie at heart."

Laughter, then a voice from the centre of the crowd.

"A couple of months back there was a picture in the tabloids of you coming out of a night-club with a woman. You've said this is a lie, but you haven't sued or anything, so we're left with the feeling that this is true and all your words are devalued." There was an angry rumbling from the audience. Freddy raised his hands for silence.

"I was hoping this would come up." More than hoping, this was one of the planted questions, carefully inserted by F.F. Inc.

"It just so happens that we've got the photo here. Can we put it up on the screen?" Of course. F.F. Inc. had seen to that.

"Larger; yeah that's okay. The first thing is, that's not me. It's my head alright, but not my body. Look closer, around the neck there and you can see the join, my head grafted on someone's shoulders. They've even got a word for it. Can everyone see it? Why didn't I sue? What would be the point? I don't have the necessary faith in the British justice system; I might be wrong, but that's how I feel.

"What if I say that the tabloid in question is a lying, scumbag, gutter rag? Now they can sue me.

"They say that the public have a right to know about my private life. And because I hold a position radically different from theirs, they think that gives them the right to print lies. As a last thought, can I just say that I'll really begin to worry when these rags say something nice about me. A last, last thought. I'm in good company. Tony Benn, Arthur Scargill, Bernie Grant, Gays, Militants, activists. The tabloids lie about them all. I'm proud to line up with them."

Hours later, sitting amidst the leftovers, the litter, the absence of life, S.T. and his producer were analysing reaction to the programme. "Positive, most positive," gushed the producer. "Compliments all round."

S.T. was more dubious. "I should have been firmer, imposed myself more."

"A difficult customer." The producer was all sympathy. He rewound the video. "He can rabbit can't he?"

S.T. didn't answer, he was studying the screen, his own worst impressions confirmed. He was tall, over six foot damn it, yet Freddy, smaller by six inches at least, seemed, in some way, to dwarf him. Watching himself on screen: he felt insubstantial, lightweight, a drifting, floating figure, a watcher. Beside him, stood a doer, someone who had placed himself on the line in a way he, S.T. had never done. Freddy positively bristled with commitment. It flowed from the screen, all that passion and belief. How S.T. envied Freddy; not the success, although that was there, but the ability to still believe in something, anything.

Yeah, okay, he'd been used, out-manoeuvred on his own territory, an away win. It wasn't so much that he'd come out badly, reputation in tatters, he simply hadn't come out at all. On the screen he seemed pale, background, unnecessary. It was all very depressing. He wanted to throw himself into some mighty cause. 'Oh, yes,' he would drop casually at some coincidental gatherings, 'I've just spent ten years working in a leper colony.' You bastard, you're not the only one who believes. Never had his practised air of bored cynicism seemed so inconsequential, so shallow.

FREDDY

Something in the way he fell; the way he rolled on the grass, sucking oxygen in great heaving gasps, hands reaching for, yet not daring to touch, the leg. The mind rejects the pain but the body knows the truth. Jim Craig had just broken his leg, his career shattered, dreams turned to nightmares. You could tell by the way we all, players, supporters, referee, refused to look as they stretchered him away, out of sight but still in mind.

There are moments when a side of one's character pops out and all one could wish is that it was somehow prettier.

There was a mixture of sympathy and relief. There was the replaying of buried memories; my own broken leg, the long months of uncertain healing, a time of doubt and fear and pain. Behind these natural feelings, sneaking up like a whisper in an unprotected night was the single thought. Now Craig was gone, through no fault of mine, I could be sweeper, do the job better. Truly I had hoped for more. I have seen people die, that should develop one's perspective. There should be an awareness of the differences between the truly important and the rest. Yet here I stood in the midst of a friend's disaster and the overriding emotion was 'This is my chance'.

I didn't tell Elane. Who needs one of her 'You've let yourself down yet again' looks. A good night's sleep failed to cleanse my soul. Whatever battle may have taken place in the overnight subconscious, the clear winners were selfishness, opportunism, ruthlessness. Not a pretty trinity.

Morning also brought a clear overview of the situation. "No one could say we didn't give it a go" would be the cry from the establishment. "Best go back to what we know", 4.4.2 or worse, 5.3.2.

Joe Doughty, Uncle Joe, would sway with the wind. He's been on the fence so long they are thinking of creosoting him. And Vic, I could hear his voice now. 'Sweeper? Don't make me laugh! Carpet sweeper, road sweeper, that's the only sweeping he'll ever do'.

Of course there was Alf, but these days he was a dubious asset. When I think of Alf I think guilty. I've let him down, taken drugs, succumbed to bad influences, betrayed his trust. Something delicate has been damaged, too many thoughts left unspoken.

Standing at his front door, almost ringing the bell, I realised how much time had slipped away. The good times, drinking tea and talking football, were somehow part of the past.

'What do you want from me? I'm only here because I want something, I've got two kids to look after. I'm sorry, I've said I'm sorry.' Oh ring the bell Freddy for fuck's sake, stitch a smile to your face and get it over with.

"Hello Freddy, best come inside." His voice turned me round. A lonely old man, wheeling his shopping trolley up the path. Inside, all was much as I remembered, abandoned cobwebs hanging in the corners, the necessary furniture with nothing to spare. We walked through the gloom to the kitchen and I put the kettle on while he unpacked the shopping; tea, bread, cheese, marge, no little luxuries for Alf. All this and not a word spoken. Worse to come, seated at his old wooden table, I couldn't look him in the eye. There was the feeling that the righteousness of his gaze would push my own guilt-ridden stare back down my throat. "What I've come about..." I started.

"If you're here about taking over Craig's position, don't bother." Flat, unemotional tones, discussion over. Rummaging around in my mind for some truth, memories of different times opened up with a sudden breathtaking clarity. Alf standing over me while I practised. Waiting with a stopwatch while I ran. Watching my every move as I brought new techniques onto the pitch. How could things have gone so wrong?

I remembered the fierce joy on his face when we discovered a game at which he could beat me: our version of tennis. Alf with a racket in either hand, hitting the ball to all corners of the court, me twisting and turning like a rat, returning the ball with my feet. Good memories, a closeness that nothing could ever break, or so I believed at the time. Elane says it had to happen, we had to grow apart before the bonding became unhealthy. Fortunately Alf was a socialist, but he could have been fascist and I would have been just as open to his truth.

Forcing myself into eye contact, not easy for someone with heavy weights on their conscience, I caught a shadow of something, Alf's bony old sense of humour, and I understood.

"Five games to make it work," he said. All the barriers, built up over the last few months, simply fell away.

"Are you doing this for me Alf? Or because it's the best thing for

Dockside?" Now it was his turn to hide inside silence. Those Mr. Quelch eyes that can still make me squirm were looking everywhere but at me.

"Elane came to see me," he said finally.

"Ah,"

"Ah, indeed."

"So what did she say then?" I demanded, uneasy at the thought of the two extreme areas of my life coming together.

"Not your business, enough to say that Elane and I actually spoke to each other as people. We did speak about you, just a little, about how devious you can be. We cleared certain matters up." He raised his hands, palms outwards. "Some things I will never understand. but..."

"So you are doing this for me."

He frowned. "In a way. You're becoming predictable, turning into a runner, as yet it's unnoticed, but I know."

"You think sweeper is the answer then?"

"We'll see."

That Saturday we lost at home to Aston Villa and the press moved in. They dug up Elton Drew from Spurs reserves.

"Freddy Feather made my life a misery."

Vic Smith stuck in his five hundred quids worth.

"Feathers' main value to England must be as a mid-field player. Of course it isn't up to me to tell his club where Freddy should play, but for the good of the international team with the World Cup less than nine months away we want Freddy playing in the position where he can be most effective for England. Where his strengths can best be exploited. It should be remembered that we gave Feather his chance when he was an untried second division player."

Another defeat at Everton and even the quality papers were busy writing of 'A brave experiment that failed'. On and on they went, drunk on their own words, never coming near to the truth.

When I was eleven years old, I had a mystical experience, nothing too fancy. I was standing naked in front of my mother's full length mirror. Not a pretty sight, breasts turning over like a budding female, rolls of fat almost smothering my timid little penis. As my reflection and I stared sadly at each other, the rolls of fat fell away, lines firmed up, my body changed before my eyes, becoming the body that is mine now. Sometimes, turning quickly, I catch glimpses of the fat person I should have been, he's hiding in a corner, waiting. Eighteen years later, in that match against Aston Villa I had my second mystical experience. The game was midway through the first half; no score. Villa pounding us with long high balls to their giant centre forwards; faceless beings, built to give and take pain. I took the ball from a rebound on the edge of our box, slipped a tackle and looked up. The game spread out before me, players moving in slow motion, three, four possibilities. As the Villa forwards closed in I retreated like an American Quarterback, mind and body fused into one I could see everything. The balance of the Villa team leaned towards me. I could see the expressions on their faces as I went back deep into my own area, waiting, waiting until their commitment was total. Then I floated the ball over their heads for Paddy Farrel to run onto. On video this moment flashes by, seems like panic but I knew, and Alf knew. At Norwich I shaped the game, pressurising to the left then to the right, probing at the weak spots until their defence crumbled. Moments like these and I knew I could do things inside the game that had been possible only in dreams.

Against Chelsea, in a local derby, I floated above and outside, existing in a timeless place where I could watch my own body in action.

Alf never denied the reality of these little moments. All our work was spent reshaping my game, studying film, living these moments again and again. Taking our plans onto the practice pitch, changing the team around until they learned to adapt. We brought Barney Anderson back, using his wisdom as a fixed point in mid-field. He didn't have to run, but he could hold the ball, draw the heat, play short passes until we could regroup. The other younger players, the Laurie Floods, John Pritchards, Ricky Miller, Paddy Farrell were forced to reach into themselves. Nothing came quickly but it came. The team learned to adapt to a new style. Hutch, for one, wasn't always happy, "Christ almighty, let's buy a centre forward. Hamilton from Manchester City, he does the business."

"The players we have are better," Alf replied with one of his fleeting smiles. Hutch could only shake his head, a reflection of changing times.

When Alf and I got together we pulled the shutters down on the outside world. Afterwards, I would emerge blinking and disorientated into the daylight, like someone who has sneaked off to the cinema in the middle of the day. Easy in these moments to tell ourselves that all was going well. In some respects it was. In others, there were small signs that 'They, the Establishment, those in power, whoever whatever' were biding their time waiting.

The other day a journalist from some glitzy music mag came knocking at the door. I was giving the kids their tea at the time. Failing to persuade them that vegetable casserole was not a 'mush' but a carefully balanced meal full of goodness and taste, and no they couldn't watch Neighbours but if they ate up there just might be ice-cream for afters.

Suddenly there was this exotic figure at the front door, tall and willowy like a house plant reaching for the light. Then I remembered an appointment made some weeks before. Part of Elane's Positive Media Rehabilitation (P.M.R.) interview with a yuppie magazine.

We started chatting over a cup of tea and out of nowhere the guy said, "You know they're going to get you. Sooner or later, one way or the other." I laughed nervously, half an eye on the kids still messing with their food.

"You remember," he continued, "the Miners strike, back in '84, '85?"

"I remembered."

"You remember the bomb that was planted at the Tory Conference? You know what I felt when I heard that?" 'Please God don't let it be the Miners.' That's how I feel about you."

"The miners didn't plant the bomb," I said somewhat stupidly giving him his cue.

"I know I know, but the perception is the same. I knew then that the miners were going to lose."

"And that's how you feel about me."

He stared at me with a sad, knowing expression on his face. "When I read about Dockside closing off the roads, there was that same feeling in the pit of my stomach. Now I know what you did was probably right. Ecologically sound and all that, but all I felt was, what a provocative action, like you push and push until they owe it to themselves to move against you."

"You're only partly right about the reasons," I replied. "Cleaning up the town was a part of it. Just as valid was two kids being killed in an accident, knocked down. Not by evil people, not even drunk drivers, just plain folk wanting to get home from work, cutting corners to cut time. We thought then that if we'd acted earlier, two kids would still be alive. So we did it. And because we're on the edge of the city we've got away with it. And it's nice: bikes and buses, prams and air you can breathe. I look at my own kid who has the road sense of a rabbit; why should she be in danger every time she leaves the house?"

"That's my point," he said. "You haven't got away with it, you've simply tightened the noose one more notch." Cheerful stuff but words that stayed with me long after the interview had faded.

The project closest to my heart; the one that hauled the two elements of my life together was Sport Aid. If second-hand celebrities, pop stars and Blue Peter appeals can raise millions, then athletes, as an equally privileged section of our society should be out there.

Our little group discussed it backwards and forwards and sideways. The extreme left say no charity at all. Every penny raised is a burden lifted from Government. But this argument seems, to me at any rate, a gigantic game of bluff with innocent people's lives as the kitty. As a group we already raised money in a small way. Rock concerts, auctions, sponsored this and sponsored that. Barney Anderson even had a country and western night for the local hospital. We helped fund a local charity (how I have grown to hate that word).

We had it all worked out: four matches, celebrities, former internationals, women's international, all star match. Throw in television rights, sale of the programme, auction of donated gear and we're talking a million pounds.

The easiest part had been the co-operation of the performers themselves. I think we had maybe three refusals.

Then one Tuesday, late in October, Alf handed me an official looking letter. It said, and I quote, 'The F.A. regrets that it is unable at this time to sanction the proposed match involving players from different associations.'

"Who asked them anyway?" I said to Alf, but he simply indicated the letter I was waving about, 'The F.A. regrets that as this proposed game falls outside its jurisdiction, it cannot allow Wembley Stadium to be used in such a fashion.' Signed by someone I had never heard of.

"What does it mean?" I asked stupidly.

"What it means my son is they've got you by the balls."

"Oh, have they? Well, we'll see about that."

His words floated behind me as I ran down the stairs, "Freddy, don't do anything stupid!"

Hauling out my bike, I raced along to the Community Centre where Radio Dockside, all legal and newly licensed, operated from one of the portacabins. Winston, the early morning D.J., was startled at my abrupt entrance, probably fearing another bust. Recovering his poise, he spoke into the mike. "Listeners one and all, guess who just stepped into our humble little studio? It's Dockside's main man, our very own Freddy Feather."

"Cut the crap Winston, when they come up with the silent D.J., you're for the chop."

"Oh, my man is in a mean mood today. Lay it out Freddy, what's on your mind?"

It's possible that a few words with Elane would have had a calming influence, but sweating from the ride and furious at the thought of those grey old men bending their brains to be as obstructive as possible, it seems I went over the top. I don't really agree, I've heard the tape and I think it was all quite reasonable. True, I did say, and I quote here from myself, "We were in the position of raising a possible million pounds. Halve that, call it half a million, and that is still a lot of powdered milk, medicines, nurses, tools, whatever. It seems to me that if faceless people, deep in their offices, put a block on this money being raised then they carry direct weight for the lives that could have been saved."

It may be that the reasoning is a little suspect, but in the heat of passion it seemed to hang together. However, as this tape made its way upward through layers of the media, it changed and grew, spawning like some monster child onto the front pages of the sleaziest tabloids.

"Red Fred accuses F.A. of murder!" Well possibly, not quite, I mean... I suppose... in a way. Talk about the shit hitting the fan, I think it missed and fell on my head. The F.A. laid their reflex charge of bringing the game into disrepute, making the hat trick. I'm going to have it inscribed on my tombstone 'He brought the game into disrepute'.

Worse, much worse was the mauling my own side gave me. Not that I had said anything wrong exactly, but at the wrong time, without consulting colleagues. Denice even seemed to take a sly pleasure in the situation. The problem with Denice is she will start every conversation with: 'The problem with you is' or 'You know what your problem is'.

"You know your problem, don't you? See, you've got some sort of Bob Geldof complex. Anything he can do, you can do bigger and better. It's not enough to raise money, you've got to be seen to be the man who saves lives. The great Red Fred. I'm not one to say I told you so." No? "But this is what happens when the movement is placed at the mercy of one individual's actions. We all suffer, the work we're all trying to do suffers. Everything we've achieved, placed at risk all because of one person's ego."

There were one or two murmurs in my defence, but these were swept aside by the force of Denice in righteous full flow.

"The problem is we used the success of a football club as a basis for social reform: but football is too shallow, too trivial to carry the weight. What happens? It crumbles and we all get buried. Now I don't know much about football." True, but why let that stop you? "But it seems to me that even here, this insistence on being sweep is an example of individual selfishness over communal effort." Pauvre Denice, her problem is she always goes that one step too far.

The consensus seemed to be that I had fucked up, consider me well and truly reprimanded. So place 'Damaged the movement' alongside 'Brought the game into disrepute'. Leave some room, there could well be more.

No one seemed to consider my feelings in all of this. They all acted as if I were some sort of behavioural experiment to be coaxed onto this path, or prodded onto that. Even in the intimacy of the bedroom, where one might hope for a little comfort, Elane was critical.

"If you hadn't gone mouthing off on that stupid radio programme then maybe we could have salvaged something. What you don't understand is that their letter was nothing but the opening shot in a long campaign. In going public you've used your final weapon. I worry about you. You've learnt nothing in the last five years."

"Alright," I said weakly. "So what now?"

"Nothing now, you've lost. All you've got is the moral high

ground. I hope you'll be happy there. And don't touch me that won't change anything."

Wednesday night, we trolled off to Highbury like working class yobbos visiting the Lords of the Manor. Something about Arsenal always brings out the best and the worst in me. That very first match three seasons ago when we beat them in the cup. That was a turning point, the first real sign.

Three seasons on the Arsenal faces may have changed, but the style remains the same. Mobility, strength, speed, and if these fail then turn up the button. More strength, more speed, more power, faster, harder. Behind this effort lies a dullness and lack of imagination that no amount of multi-million pound chocolate charlies can change. Their style of play fitted the sweeper system perfectly. Wave after wave of high speed, mindless attacks were absorbed by our defence, turned into swift counter attacks.

The sweeper role gave me a new freedom to move all over the pitch. An overall vision kept me one step ahead of clattering boots. Halfway through the second half, the balance of the game began to shift. Arsenal still came forward (what else do they know), like tired boxers throwing punches from habit. When I scored with a 25 yard power drive, it was my fourth goal in consecutive games, a blindside header gave me my twelfth of the season. A few minutes before the end, a defender chopped me down. Through the pain I could hear the Arsenal supporters jeering their own side, sweet music.

Lying in the bath after the game, playing it over and over in my head, running my mind back through the season. I understood I was reaching some sort of peak.

My career had taken off as a 23-goal-a-season striker. The need for more involvement had forced me back into mid-field, but Alf was right, the lack of space had taken thought away from my game, shifted the balance into bodily movement. Now as sweeper, there was a freedom that opened up a new vision, with a bonus, I still scored goals. Those years operating in the enemy area stayed with me, but fresh areas of attack had opened up. Free kicks and penalties, long distance power shooting, late timed runs into the box. Quick one twos with Paddy Farrel, Laurie Flood, John Pritchard. Every game in which I failed to score was a disappointment.

After wallowing in the Arsenal Jacuzzi for an hour or so, I trotted up to the Arsenal hospitality lounge. Typically Highbury, the best of everything in the worst of taste. Sleek leather, cutaway chairs, razor-thin women flashing expensive jewellery. The Arsenal players done up in their penguin suits. It's ten-thirty at night, Arsenal have just lost 2-0 at home, but for the lads the night is young. Night-clubs open, the good life still to be tasted.

I was looking for Ralph Machin, the Arsenal captain, one of the players I most admired. Ralph, (I like to think we were on first name terms) had been an Arsenal player for fifteen years, captain for the last ten. Managers had come and gone but Ralph had outlasted them all, survived to see the club taken over by the city wide boys. I found him in a corner, drinking something in lemonade; chewing gum. His face did not light up when he saw me.

"Hi Ralph, good game tonight." No reply. "What I want to talk to you about is..."

"I know what you want," he said, taking the tiniest sip of his drink. "You're here about this poxy charity match that I said I might play in."

"You don't seem quite so certain now Ralph, convictions slipping a little?"

Ralph look at me through narrowed grey eyes, chewed on his gum. "You are a pratt. A grade A wanker, with a mouth too big for your brain." Reaching into his inside pocket he drew out a letter.

"See this. This is from our beloved board of directors. What it says roughly is, on no account will any Arsenal player have fuck all to do with any event, football, blow football, that F. Feather esquire is in any way involved in."

"And you're going to sit still for that?"

He took another tiny sip of drink, turned those dead eyes on me. "You know what really pisses me off? You're the best player I've seen in years. You've got it all. How can you be so smart on the pitch and so stupid off it?"

"Right then, thanks for this little chat Ralph. I won't say I've enjoyed it."

Machin shook his head. "Fifteen years I've been in this game; fifteen years in the first division and not one cap to show for it. I've been in the squad a few times but not one fucking cap. And you with it all before you, you're going to throw it all away. In fifteen years what are you going to look back on. World cups, or a wasted career?"

"I take it this means you won't be playing in the match then?" Machin shook his head sadly.

"Every player in the first division has had one of these." He patted his pocket. "There ain't going to be no match. The sooner you accept that the sooner you can get back to doing what you do best, playing football."

"That's it then. Football! Nothing matters outside football."

"Look son, I'll tell you what, because I like you, I really do. A few years back I was after the Manager to buy you. What was his name?" He smiled for the first time, sharp, sharky little teeth. "Christ, I can't even remember his name. Owen, Norman Owen, good old Norm, got the sack soon after, never worked again. Anyway, even then the word was out. Any club buys you buys trouble. Look, I'll tell you what, because I like you, you get the match organised, square it with the F.A. and I'll play. Can't say fairer than that can I?"

That's it then, auctioned off like a dinner service.

Sooner or later there has to be an acceptance of failure. The match, the World Match was not to be.

Outflanked and outsmarted by the grey ghouls from Lancaster Gate, the political movement of Dockside retreated into itself. My own situation had changed. From being an asset, even a flag bearer, for a new/old small town socialism, I was now a liability.

When the tabloids printed a picture of me sneaking out of some night-club, nose halfway down the cleavage of some siliconed starlet, the publicity threatened to drag the whole of Dockside down into the gutter. All that remained was a certain sympathy vote. The older folk may not have been overly fond of me, but they recognised bullshit when they smelled it. We could have sued, but general wisdom said 'Lay low: trust the People.'

The fight back came back on three fronts. My own performances on the pitch, and here Joe Taslin's policy of one international a month gave supporters a chance to judge for themselves. Fact of life: one good game forgives an awful lot of sins.

Let it be on the record, as objectively as possible, that I was playing to the very edge of my capabilities. Sometimes, studying the videos, it was hard to believe it was me up there strutting around, calling the shots, scoring goals.

Secondly, the council held its nerve. The banning of cars from the town may have enraged long distance juggernaut drivers, but hit a popular spot locally. The twinning of local schools with third world schools. The building of a woman's shelter, licensing squatting groups. All the usual 'Loony Left' projects that could easily have been stillborn. Thirdly, it was decided that I make an appeal over the many heads of the press to a, hopefully, sympathetic audience. After much sifting, we accepted an invitation from Radio One. An hour and a half (subtle, these B.B.C. fellows) of my favourite records. Analysed down, this gave us twenty minutes between records to state our case in a loveable sort of way. Trying for objectivity once more: it worked. The audience figures were a Sunday afternoon record, and the L.P. of twenty protest songs even made the lower reaches of the charts. A pop star; who would have thought it? Not the fat boy in the corner.

Do I believe in God? Any God? Who wants to know? Who cares? Quite a few people, if one is to judge from the amount of mail that waits for me daily at The Slum. There is hate mail, not a lot, but vicious in its intensity and violent in its stated aims. There are sex letters, desperate, imaginative and, at a more base level, flattering. Fat boy lurking, cannot believe it - a sex symbol.

Then there is The God Question. Plaintive cries from the dark as if my belief will illuminate the writer's life. The answer is no, for the usual reasons. If there is a God, how can he/she allow such things as... supply your own list. I was actually reading one of these letters when the draw for the F.A. cup third round came through on the radio in best plummy tones. "173 Eastgate Athletic will play No. 46 Dockside Town." Maybe there is a God after all, some sort of ironic force with a crooked grin on its face. This was a tie to bring a smile to Dockside, to make the blood tingle.

Eastgate's run through the six qualifying rounds, their wins against Rochdale and Torquay had created more passion than our own struggle in the first division. Everybody loves a winning team. The media tried to climb aboard, but this was a private party with a subtle role reversal to add extra spice. After years as the brow-beaten underdogs Dockside F.C. were suddenly first division Flash Harry's, whilst Eastgate, (rapacious giant of their own East London League) was the gallant little fellow.

Only Dockside understood the closeness that had grown between the two clubs. For Alf and I, Eastgate was our first real team. That is something you don't forget. In his years as coach Alf had turned them from a bunch of semi-serious, overweight players into a sleek machine, a power within its own league. As Manager of Dockside F.C., he had polished these links until the two clubs were joined in a continental style club/nursery club situation. With an exchange of players, facilities and supporters that gave strength to both teams.

When Saturday comes, friendship means nothing. Eastgate stomped all over our neat passing game. On the half hour, roared on by four thousand fans they brutalised the ball into the net. Midway through the second half I curled a free kick around the wall for the equaliser. Ten minutes to go. I held a ball up on the edge of their box, swayed left, flicked it right for Laurie Flood to score. The next thing, I was lying on the grass, the linesman waving his flag, the Referee holding up a red card. Eddie Smith, the Eastgate assassin was walking, head bowed, to the tunnel. Scrambling to my feet I went over to the Ref, still posed there, one arm raised, the other pointing to the centre.

"Can I have word Ref? As captain and all that?"

The Referee, a six-foot-four-inch headmaster looked down as if I were a slug discovered on one of his prize cabbages. "Make it brief."

"I just want to say that up to now it's been a good game and you've handled it brilliantly."

"Thanks, is that it?"

"Not quite. All I want to say is I think you missed something. I held Smith back as he went to make his tackle, obstructed him. That's why he pushed me to the ground, nothing dirty, just inexperience showing." The man in black parted his lips in parody of a smile.

"Right then, I'll disallow the goal, give a free kick to Eastgate, plus here's a yellow card for the original foul." He held it proudly in the air. "Happy now?" he said.

"What about Eddy Smith?"

"Oh no. He's gone."

"So who's more to blame Ref? Me for fouling, Smith for retaliating, or you for missing the whole thing? Perhaps you should give yourself a yellow card, award a penalty against yourself."

It's a long walk to the dressing room, across the pitch, down the tunnel, studs tip tapping on the concrete. Through the open door of the opposition dressing room I saw Eddy Smith, head lowered.

"You alright, kidder?" I said softly. He looked up, face stained with tears. "Wassup? Match finished, who won?" He wiped a hand across his eyes; hard men don't cry.

"Nah, they're still playing. I got sent off, even up the sides a bit, besides I thought you might be lonely down here." I started to laugh. When the door burst open Hutch, Alf and John Walsh, the Eastgate manager, found us draped in each others arms. They stood for a moment framed in the doorway, fingers wagging, searching for the right words. Then they left, slamming the door behind them.

Having cheeked the teacher, Eddie Smith and I spent the replay in detention. I watched from the bench as Dockside wilted before the Eastgate aerial bombardment. Half time: 2-0 down. Hutch ranted and waved his arms, getting nowhere.

"I remember," I said softly into the silence. "Early in the season, you all said I was holding you back, that I was too critical, always moaning, that you were too scared to try things. It looks more like you can't play without me. The truth is I've been carrying you for three seasons now. Without me, you can't even beat a team of part timers. Without me you can't play."

Barney came off early in the second half, the only player I know who can limp on both legs at once. Neil Grey, the sub, brought long-legged enthusiasm to the mid-field. With Dave Ward, our other sub throwing his weight around in their penalty area, we finally started to play with some pride. Paddy Farrell scored from a Dave Ward knock down and with five minutes to go John Pritchard scrambled an equaliser. No score in extra time and the whole of Dockside held its breath for the third match.

We won 5-0 and I scored four. After the euphoria had worn off, other, more important side-effects crept through. The series of matches had generated a goodwill that repaid all debts.

The outside world caught a glimpse as the T.V. cameras picked up on a unity of spirit totally at odds with the usual tabloid trash. Dockside F.C. had reasserted its position as spearhead of the underdog.

Elane put it best when she said that in this time of struggle we were, at the very least, keeping the light of socialism shining. A small light to be sure, but as pure as we could make it. There was pride in being part of this movement. It may be that the responsibility lent an extra edge to my game. Every time I stepped onto the pitch I represented something worth fighting for.

At first, second, or even third glance, these performances were nothing to be proud of. It had taken three matches to dispose of non-league semi-pros. But deep down, amongst the jock straps and sweaty socks, there was the feeling of having been to the edge and survived.

"They've proved they can do it without you," was Alf's view. Barney Anderson, in particular, touched a golden patch, compensating, perhaps, for a serious lack of bottle in the first reply. Hutch laughed at my reasoning.

"Barney can read the signs. Possible World Cup call up. Old head guiding the youngsters and all that, his familiarity with the sweeper system. If he loses his club place there'll be no late flowering for Barney."

In many ways, in just about every way, this was the most fulfilling time of my life. Dockside F.C. had reached some form of maturity which paralleled the development of the Dockside political machine. We had grown, over the years, into experienced operators.

Decisions taken six years before were now Council Policy. Government turned its head our way. Battle was declared over the 'Clean Air, No Traffic, Free the Streets' policy. We were suddenly a threat. If we could get away with it then so could other councils threatened by the never ending flow that pollutes, kills: turns crossing the road into an art form.

To strengthen our legitimacy we held a referendum. Government and industry invaded us with facts and figures as to why the smoke and the speed was not only good for us but necessary to the smooth running of the economy.

After their defeat, the establishment went back to basics. The three R's of political life, they retreated, regrouped and retaliated by withholding our inner city development money. Fair enough in a grubby sort of way. If we had truly been inner, inner city then we never could have pulled the stroke in the first place. Our left wing lawyers headed by Leroy, took the Government Act apart clause by clause, and then we hauled the bastards up before the European courts, trouncing them as soundly there as we had in the local referendum. These were high political times.

As a council dependent on votes, we asked local people to decide on the style of community they wanted. Vote for us and you vote for hostels for the homeless, and the outsiders, and the handicapped. You vote for the Employee/Employer Charter. You vote for the right to breath clean air. You vote to keep the light of socialism flickering in a darkening world.

HUTCH

Ask me where I am: go on ask. I've been asking myself that very question ever since I woke up. Hospital, that's where. Now ask me how I got here. Another very good question. Finish me off with the cruncher, over the top, on the blind side. Can I leave? No! Here I am and here I stay until someone in a white coat says it is safe for me to re-enter the world. I wake, eat and sleep to the sounds of coughing, moaning and dying.

HE came to see me this morning. Did I mention that? Probably not. It isn't the sort of thing the mind cares to dwell upon. "Tell me how you do it son," I said to him.

"What's that, Hutch?" Not 'Boss' anymore, notice that.

"Oh y'know, you start a riot and I end up in hospital. You get arrested for smoking pot and I wind up with the police outside my door. How come I'm a villain and you're a bleeding hero?"

"I suppose it all depends on your perspective Hutch. Look on the bright side, we could soon be sharing a cell together."

'Only one of us would come out alive.' I thought.

"What I don't understand," I said, "is how come you're walking about free as a bird and I'm bloody well stuck in here? Can't get up, can't even use the toilet... show the slightest sign of life, and they're waiting to slap the cuffs on. I'm not one to moan, never have been, but it doesn't seem fair somehow."

"No one ever said life was fair Hutch. If you drive into walls at 60 m.p.h. and at least four over the limit, then don't expect the law to be pleased. Your best bet is to lie here injured, until they get fed up and go away." He smiled down at me. "If it makes you feel any better, we are pulling whatever strings we can."

Oh wonderful, just bleeding marvellous. Now he's doing things for me. The cause of all my troubles is pulling strings for me. I might even laugh if it wasn't so painful.

"So tell me," I asked, in what I hoped was a calmer tone of voice, "how come you're still parading the streets? Why haven't they locked you up and tossed the key down the nearest drain?"

"Bail, Hutch, a symbol of British justice."

"Isn't that against your principles? Wouldn't you prefer to go to jail for your principle?"

"I don't think so Hutch," he replied slowly. "I toyed with the idea, but it didn't seem quite the time or the place."

"You will be going to jail though, won't you? I mean you did break the law, they can't just let you go."

Another smile, sickly sweet, it haunts my dreams.

"Hutch my presence is obviously working you into a state. I'll come back when you're feeling better."

"No wait, don't go." Is it me saying those words to his disappearing back. He returned pushing a trolley.

"A little present here from the lads, a video, and some tapes. When you're better just leave it here for the ward." He stared down at me. "What should I do, stay or go?"

"Stay." The word squeezed out reluctantly.

"No tantrums, a state of calm, zenlike tranquillity."

"Yeah, yeah," I sighed. "How long have we known each other?"

"Two seasons and the back end of another," he smiled. "Not that long really it just feels like a lifetime."

"I've aged," I muttered. "Y'know that very first time. I knew you were the business."

"Get away. You didn't even know my name."

"Christ," I said, angry again. "You can't even leave an old man to his memories. You don't give an inch."

"Sorry."

I leant back on pillows made of iron. "Go on, piss off, leave me alone."

The days changed, at least I suppose they did, for me they drifted past like the clouds outside my window. Visitors came and went. Nurses attached things with wires to my head, wheeled me off for tests, rolled me back to bed again. Pills numbed the pain, but threw a mist across my brain. When HE came again, I was ready.

"So the fix is in." That wiped the smile off his face.

"What fix would that be Hutch?"

"Don't come the innocent with me lad. I know you. You've been plotting, manoeuvring."

"Spit it out Hutch, you got something to say, say it."

"Alright I will. Who's the new manager?"

"Acting manager Hutch."

"Oh I see, just keeping the seat warm. So who's the new acting manager then - Johnny?"

"No."

"You? I can see that. Freddy Feather, player-manager, it has a ring to it."

He smiled. "No, it's Alf."

I nodded. "Why not Johnny? He seems the obvious choice."

He drew a deep breath, even looked a bit shameface. "There are reasons Hutch, logical reasons. Statements have been issued about preserving continuity, keeping Johnny on the pitch working with the team, somebody they know and recognise, we don't want new faces in, not with the play offs coming."

"And the truth."

"The truth, the truth is we seized the opportunity when it came. We didn't ask for it. Nobody made you drink too much and roar off into the night. You should have stayed home, put your feet up and watched it on T.V."

"So Alf is your shield. Who picks the team - you?"

"Alf is nobody's shield."

"And you consider this acting with integrity do you? Integrity, now there's a word you're keen on. Do you still have any or has it been ditched like me, like the chairman. How is old Sam Dolton these days?"

"Hutch, you've just had a heart attack, mild, but real. What condition are you in to be managing a football team. Get your strength back. Sober up. Then we'll see."

"Ah, I understand, I'll step back into the job will I?"

"Not quite Hutch."

"Somehow I didn't think so - Go on piss off, you're making me tired." I watched him walk through the path of beds. As the door swung behind him all the strength seemed to leave my body. Propped up on my pillows, tears pricking the back of my eyes. I thought, 'This is where it all ends: useless and helpless in a hospital bed.'

But, of course, it - life - continues. Clouds still drift by, different shapes, same clouds. The end of season play offs absorbed some interest as Dockside squeezed into the final promotion place. I read in the back pages of transfer deals. Elton Drew off to Spurs for half a million pounds. Freddy never liked him. Chris Arnold to Newcastle for a quarter of a million pounds. And Jim Craig, the Man United and England centre back, on his way to Dockside. Alf and Freddy, two busy boys.

Finally, when it no longer mattered, they sent me home. An event that failed to make any pages, back or front. Home was even quieter than hospital. Nobody to break the monotony by dying. George dropped by, Johnny came, but the silence between us contained too many memories. I could feel his discomfort, him in work, me in nothing. Take away football and life was a huge hole with nothing to fill it: and if that isn't a sad comment on a wasted life then I don't know what is.

It must have been May/June sometime. I shuffled downstairs to pick up the mail. A letter with the Dockside crest on it, a ship coming in. I put it aside with the bills and all the other crap, left it unopened while I ate my cornflakes.

Well, well, who would have thought it? If I was expecting anything, it was the old heaveho. 'Thanks for your services: but...' Maybe even a nice little cheque: a last little earner, because I don't come cheap. Let me put it another way; I don't go cheap. Well, well. An invitation to tea, how quaint.

"Congratulations," I said, dredging up some sincerity from somewhere. "The Premier League, well done. Now, what do you want to see me about?" Alf sat in my chair, at my desk. He poured a mug of tea and pushed it across, nodding slightly, acknowledging my hostility.

"I'd like you to come back on board," he said slowly.

'I'm sure you would my son' I thought with a little inner smile.

"In what capacity?" I replied, betraying nothing. We stared at each other across the desk.

"Pick a title, it's yours, anything but manager."

"Nothing else worth having." Still we stared, like two ageing gunslingers, bluffing it out, too old to change.

"The Premier League." His words slid home with the smoothness of an assassin's knife. "You can wait for us to fail, knowing that the bulk of the work was yours. Maybe that will keep you warm on long winter evenings. Or," he held up a hand stopping my protest, "you can be part of a first division club. An important part: not the manager, but coach, adviser, general manager."

The first division, a foot in the door. Highbury, White Hart Lane, Anfield, good days long gone.

"I notice you've got some new faces in."

"Kids: bright, quick, mobile, fearless. We're going to the first division to play football, not kick and rush."

I sat silently, trying to develop a feel for the man opposite. He had nothing to thank me for. Taken on purely to keep Freddy quiet. His work, largely ignored, had been contained in a quiet corner of the ground. Still, there was no mistaking the steel behind those unyielding, tight features.

"What exactly do you want from me?" I asked. "Let's see it on the table."

"I want your experience, your contacts, your inside knowledge of the game."

"And what do I get?"

"Full consultation, a dressing room voice. You'll be in on team talks and tactics. Plus you'll still be working largely with the first team. My work will be done with small groups of players, two or three at a time. Final decisions will be mine. If I fail then I'll hand it all back to you."

I smiled. "That's inexperience speaking, Alf. Golden rule number one. Never accept blame: it's the chairman, the weather, the shape of the ball, never the manager; once hesitation seeps down to the players, you're dead."

Maybe a ghost of a smile moved on his lips, maybe not.

"What makes you think you can do it? Come from nowhere and run a successful club. It almost killed me and, let's be honest, you don't look in tip top shape, I mean we won't be seeing you in the London marathon this year. You married?"

He shook his head.

"That's something. I was married once, a nice Scottish lass. One day I looked round and she wasn't there. All that was left was football.

"Listen Alf," I found myself leaning forward, whispering. "I must say this, there are certain things, aspects about the club I don't like, or don't understand. I've got to say this, I resent the way you took the club away from me. I remember you from the shareholders meeting. I saw you standing in the background and ever since then I've felt the club slipping away from me. All that's in the past now." We sipped our tea in silence.

"I know I'm going to regret this," I said finally. "It's got bad decision stamped all over it, but the alternative, sitting at home growing bitter with thoughts of what might have been. That frightens me. So what's first on the old agenda?"

"Use your contacts to get top clubs here for the pre-season."

"I'll get on the blower. But first we should discuss the really important things, such as 'Do I get an office' and 'How much am I getting paid."

It's almost possible to believe that nothing has changed. Take away a drug bust, a riot, and a car crash. Turn one blind eye to the changes, the other to the frantic squealings of the press. Cling tight to what you have: a place inside the shelter of football.

To be honest there may even be relief in giving up control of a runaway club. A return to working with players. Take Laurie Flood, he can't read or write, but once on the pitch, no mathematician could teach him about angles and space and weight of pass. Poor kid, you have to smile, once training is over, he shrinks inside himself, it's time for school. Head bowed, wiping the snot away with his sleeve, he shuffles sadly away to his literacy class. Two hours of education that poor Laurie thought he had left far behind.

Alf and I did work closely together, up to a point. But I'd be lying if I said we were friends. He was a closed person. Maybe he smiled once or twice, but I never noticed. I said to him once, "What if things hadn't changed, what if I was still manager and I wanted to buy a player that you didn't rate. What then?" He just stared at me with his chilly grey eyes.

"Didn't happen."

"Yeah, but what if?"

In this murky world of football politics Alf's major weapon was his control of Freddy; because Freddy ran the dressing room. The older pros, Barney especially, kept their distance from all the shenanigans, the pop concerts, political meetings and the like. Barney motored in from Wandsworth, did his day and motored home, eyes firmly blinkered. But the younger players followed Freddy everywhere, on the pitch and off. Suddenly, it seems we've a team of vegetarian, bridge playing, Trotskyists. Don't ask me, I only work here.

True to his word, Alf did consult, sometimes he even listened. It was my idea to make Barney player/coach: someone on the management side had to be able to run. With reservations, we were agreed on the principle of the sweeper system. As Johnny said, "At least we'll have three at the back."

The season closed over us, like a coffin lid. Oh, there was Wimbledon. The test matches brought crushing defeat. British sport on its knees, a familiar position. Yet inside the game, and whisper this only, there was a feeling of optimism. Ringing around the clubs, calling in old debts, squeezing out thirty years worth of favours, the goodwill surprised me. I know the close season is a time of innocence, untouched as yet by groin strains, hamstrings, agents. I know all that but even so the whisper was that this time we could go beyond the semi-finals and maybe, maybe this time, we could even win the damned thing.

Uncle Joe Doughty was a regular caller.

"How's the boy then, how's he been behaving?"

"I'm well thanks Joe, nice of you to be concerned." There was a short embarrassed silence.

"Ah, that's good to hear Hutch, and how's Freddy, any injuries?" Hopefully.

"Wouldn't really know Joe, Freddy's not here."

"Oh." Anxious.

"Apparently, he's in Zimbabwe, some little village I can't pronounce."

"Getting away from it, eh? A bit of rest, a bit of sun, do the boy good." Wildly optimistic.

I smiled to myself, a smile of sheer evil, I could feel it in my teeth.

"Freddy's working as a nurse in some battle zone by the border."

Long silence, Uncle Joe digesting the news of his favourite nephew. "You're winding me up, tell me you're just winding my clock." Whinging.

"Afraid not Joe, we got a letter just this morning."

"Jesus, why didn't you stop him? You're his manager, you know what an important season this is."

"Not the manager anymore, surprised you haven't heard."

"Oh yes. Sorry to hear about your, ah, illness. When is he due back?"

"Yesterday."

His breath whistled shrilly at me down the phone, he didn't sound a well man. Time to twist the knife a little. "Barcelona have been on to us, and a little bird says Inter Milan are prepared to offer five million."

"Jesus."

"I don't think you have much to worry about Joe, the Manager's confident. He looks at it this way. If we don't know where he is, then he won't be going anywhere."

Joe's voice came through weakly, as if from far away. "I'm going to lie down for a bit, you ring me when he gets back, or if you hear anything."

Poor old Joe, but there was a certain satisfaction in spreading the medicine around. I've swallowed enough.

I had been cheery enough myself this morning, was it only this morning? A new season, my hopes already dashed.

"Where's Freddy?" I said to Alf. "I saw all the faces except one." For answer he tossed a letter across the desk.

"I'm not going to like this am I?" I said picking the letter up.

Dear Alf (written in haste),

Here we are in sunny Zimbabwe. Things haven't gone quite according to plan. Instead of roaming the country meeting people, I am working in an Emergency Hospital. Because of raids by the M.N.L.R. it's a case of all spare hands needed as bodies, alive and dead, come in daily. The second day here they opened up the side of a truck and there was this mound of bodies glued together with blood and flies; we carried them to the hospital sorting out the dead on the way. I hate the flies. I used to think that everything had a purpose on this earth, but not flies. To see them clustered round the eyes, and in the wounds of the children, is almost more than I can bear. I have two jobs really. Job number one - I'm taking charge of a feeding camp. Following Oxfam instructions I mix up the special milk and pass it out to the underweight children. Not as straightforward as it sounds, the possibilities for cock up are everywhere. But I can claim two tiny triumphs. Triumph number one - the kids do not like the special milk, the little sods went missing all over the place, but I instituted a system of bribes. Drink your milk and you get a sweet, works every time. (As I write this the realisation has dawned, I'm rotting their teeth, there's a meaning here somewhere.)

Anyway, triumph number two - two types of illness (Oxfam

again). Kwashiokor - electrolyte imbalance causing the body to swell up, and Marasmus - hanging flesh. Anyway, there was this little kid with a swollen out body. Everybody pouring extra milk down him until I spotted that this Bhudda child wasn't swollen from illness, but was in fact enormously fat from all the extra food. It gave me a certain spiteful pleasure to cancel his milk.

Watched the local people build a ward from sticks, straw and bamboo. The beds are shaped from stones carried by hand down from the hills, filled with earth, covered with straw and polythene. Which brings me neatly on to my second job, laying down a blanket of health over the dysentery wards. No one gets better until the flies go. If that means washing the wards three times a day if necessary, and carrying the bedpans a quarter mile to the ditch then so be it. Donkeys bring the water from one of the wells, appearing like a miracle just as we are running dry. Each day the hospital gets bigger.

I don't have any grand thoughts on all of this. The evil of the S.A. Government, the hypocrisy of our own. All one can do, is what nurses have been doing since the Crimea. Get on with the job.

P.S. Playing football every evening, the standard is amazing, I'll try to sign a couple of new players.

Yours,

FREDDY.

"What can I say, Alf? Some people take a holiday, Freddy saves the world." I held the letter, fanned myself with it while I said harshly, "I tell you this Alf, you got to punish him. It don't matter if he's been working with Mother Theresa. All that counts is he's late back." I gave him a hard look. "You can't be emotionally involved with a player. If you are then you come down twice as hard, otherwise you lose respect. Seeing his face I held out my hands in a gesture of defeat. "I won't say any more, whatever is between you and Freddy, and remember I was there at that shareholders meeting, I don't want to know."

"You seem certain that he'll be coming back."

I laughed long and loud, the best laugh I'd had in years. "He'll be back, I'm not dead yet."

"So you're back then, gracing us with your presence," I said to him, what, two days after the 'Day of the Letter.'

"No getting round you Hutch, the tiniest clue and you're on the case, like a rat up a drainpipe. He stood hands on hips in his usual cocky pose. If I had struck him, rumour has it that I wouldn't have been the first. Which reminded me, I hadn't phoned Joe yet: later, maybe tomorrow, or the day after.

"Tell me son because I really want to know," I said in a fatherly tone. "Tell me how you get away with it?"

"A pure spirit, a good sex life, and a clean conscience."

"No, no, seriously son, 'cause I've been counting the bodies, but I ran out of fingers."

"What's on your mind, Hutch? Don't be shy."

"Let me get this right. The F.A. had you up for bringing the game into disrepute, and up there you're the Antichrist, right?"

"You flatterer, you."

"Yet you get away with it, the mildest of slaps, a stroke, a caress even, no suspension, no fine."

"Do you want to know Hutch, really want to know?" He smiled showing sharp even little teeth. "We went in there armed to the eyebrows. Ready to take them on. We had writs for restraint of trade, we had precedents. We even had a little touch of blackmail. Not me you understand, I wasn't allowed to speak. But my team of left wing lawyers had this list of ninety-six managers, officials, directors, all convicted of drunken driving. It would have been ninety-seven but we left your name off."

"Thank you."

"You're welcome. Anyway you know what it's like up there, been a bit of a lad in your time. Grey offices, grey suits, grey men with grey minds. Wouldn't football be wonderful if it wasn't for the players. They sat there, Sir this, Wing Commander that. These people fought the war for the likes of me. And they simply caved in, no public flogging, no need for blackmail."

"Lucky boy," I said sincerely. "I've had the old finger wagging."

"That's what we thought; at first. Further analysis indicates that they'd been got at from above."

"No! Who?"

"We're talking Ministers, Cabinet, M.I.5. Who knows? What I

do know is, I'm lying in bed and this thought keeps flitting across my brain. 'Someone in high places is on my case.' This is not a comforting thought."

"So that's why you left the country so suddenly."

He smiled that butter-wouldn't-melt smile.

"Listen," I said, pulling him closer, "I got a job that calls for someone to be devious and tricky yet sincere. I think you're just the boy."

That 'Day of Letters', brought a telex from Barcelona.

'Four million for Feather,' signed Miguel Matthias. The next day another telex, this time from Italy.

'Five million for Feather.'

"He'll be on his way then," I said to Alf. "These boys mean business."

"No."

"What do you mean 'No' just like that. You can't stop it. They want someone, they simply up the price until they get him."

"He won't go."

"You know that do you? The same way you knew he was jetting off to Africa. The same way you knew he was on drugs. Still is for all I know. Would he let a little thing like being arrested stop him?"

"Point taken," Alf replied without changing his expression. "But he still won't go."

"Why? Because you say so? That sounds a bit like moral blackmail to me. Have you got the right to deny him his chance? This is Barcelona we're talking about; Inter Milan. Money, adulation, haciendas."

"Dockside is his home."

I shrugged. Alf would be saying that even as Freddy boarded the plane for Spain. Or Italy.

The plan was, bring these clubs to Dockside, play them off against each other, dangle Freddy as bait. You want him then come and get him. The flaw was the human element. No player in his right mind would, or should, deny himself the chance to play with the very best. I wish, I wish they'd come for me, in my prime.

Great nights for Dockside. A glimpse of The Big Time. Deep in the groin of the city, we played host to two of Football's giants.

Okay, we didn't win, but we competed, came out of the matches with pride. And it proved that I still had it, could still pull the odd stroke when it counted.

After the bribe, comes the payment. They led Freddy off, laid their dream on him. To be honest, I thought he'd go. Right up to the end. Even as we waved them goodbye at the airport, even as they mounted the stairs, shaking their heads, unable to understand their failure. I still think he should have gone. Lady Fortune is a cow, spurn her and she looks for revenge.

We started the season badly. The Milans and the Barcelonas of this world allow you time on the ball, have a certain respect for your ability. Chelsea savaged us like mad dogs. Birmingham stamped all over our neat, little passing game. The season felt three months old. The problem was, we needed time. On paper we looked promising, name me a team that doesn't.

HARRIS
CRAIG
STEWERT SHAHID
SAMSON KNIGHT
FEATHER
FARRELL FLOOD
PRITCHARD
WARD

Subs. Anderson, Grey.

The problem was simple: too many kids. One, maybe two, you can hide while they learn the ropes. We had five. Freddy of course knew different.

"If Craig doesn't bring the ball out of defence, then he's a third centreback. All we're doing is blocking up the defence with bulk." The management, plus Freddy, were gathered in the office on a Sunday afternoon, dissecting yesterday's 1-1 draw at home to Everton.

"I thought Craig was a rock," I said, unable to believe my ears. What was he doing here anyway? "Magnificent defending, held us together at the back."

"Agreed. No quarrel. He's a class defender, but he's not bringing the ball forward. It's like the halfway line is the eleventh commandment 'Thou shalt not cross'. If he doesn't run with the ball then we're simply not playing a sweeper system. All we are is five at the back."

"It could be you're a touch prejudiced. We all know who you think the best sweeper in the world would be. Who could possibly live up to your vision of yourself?" Johnny gave me a snigger in support, even Alf ghosted a smile. "The problem is we're not scoring. Nice football but lightweight stuff. It's you Freddy, you've got to get into that box."

"Then we're overrun in mid-field."

"You've got to be there too," I said.

"And picking up the ball from Craig. Perhaps I could be on the end of my own passes." Sometimes I felt that if I never saw Freddy again, it would be too soon.

Whatever went down between Alf and Freddy in private, we stuck with the system until the international against Italy. For that I blame Joe Doughty, Joe Doughty and his endless phone calls, 'How's the boy then?' Joe Doughty and his 'We're going to play one international every month against the best in the world'. If that wasn't enough he went on 'With the World Cup less than a year away I hope that supporters and management will be united in their commitment to giving England the best possible chance'.

Poor old Joe, still he was right in one respect, managers, directors, officials and supporters were united, just not up his direction. Behind the right noises managers were thinking, 'this is my job on the line.' Directors were counting out their lost money. Officials, well they resent free speech on principle. And the fans; long since grown stale on the promise of a better tomorrow.

I must say I was surprised when Joe won his battle. He must be a better in-fighter than is generally thought. Or else he sold his soul to the devil.

That's how come Craig and Feather were playing for England against Italy. And that's how Freddy got his wish. Sometimes Lady Fortune does smile twice.

It isn't that I dislike the lad, I wouldn't let my daughter marry him, but in many ways he's quite engaging. There are just these nagging thoughts, two of them, jostling together. The first one is 'What if he's right? What if, behind all that political posturing, there is actually substance to his words? Wouldn't that be awful? Almost too terrible to contemplate.'

The second thought was more a feeling. Where was all this leading? As the season wore on and attention focused more and more on England and The World Cup, everybody wanted a piece of Freddy.

"Look, We're willing to forgive," the media boys said. "Let bygones be bygones." Personally I agreed with them. The World Cup is simply too big. But Freddy was having none of it, and the population of Dockside rallied round to protect its favourite son.

To be fair, I believe that Freddy was unaware of the shield that surrounded him.

I saw this programme on Gandhi once, and God knows I'm not comparing the two of them; but Gandhi had this thing about walking around, being one of the people, without ever realising the colossal effort that went into preserving his freedom. People going before, people going behind, all trying to maintain an illusion. There was just a touch of that. Freddy walking the streets, whilst the population of Dockside worked in shifts to keep the media outside the city walls.

Nobody talked to the press. Individual journalists entered Dockside at their own risk. They tried. They came, armed with bribes and little rinky dink cameras, and got nowhere.

They even tried it on with me. But by this time I knew which side my bread was buttered. I was in for the duration, but I couldn't help wondering how long the ride would last, or where it would end.

With everything that was going on, it surprised me that Dockside was such a cheerful club. Even struggling near the foot of the table, we had hundreds in just to watch us train. Hundreds more cleaned up after every home match. This was nothing to do with Socialism, whatever Freddy might say, but there was a feeling that the club belonged to the community (I can't even believe I'm using that word) in a two way deal. We were a happy club, good dressing room feeling, and I've got to, I don't want to, put it down to Freddy.

Thirty years in the game and I still can't put a name to it: team spirit comes close, easy when you're winning. Everybody's happy when you're winning. But we're not, we're struggling, hanging in, but still playing football, still believing in the way we play. Much as I hate to admit it, this is down to Freddy. It isn't me or Alf, we do our bit, but neither of us is what you'd call in our prime. We're over the peak and well down the other side. Johnny kept an edge on things, but the driving force inside the club and on the pitch is Freddy. I may not like the situation but I have to deal with it.

This is my fourth season, which is as long as I've stayed anywhere. During that time I have watched his game grow until, and I'm calling on thirty years experience here, he is as good as any player I have ever come across. Now I have admitted that, I can go further. There are aspects of his game in which he is the best in the world. This isn't easy for me to say, even though there is a certain pride in the small part I have played in this development. Quite early on, we realised that Freddy was wasted inside the box, too small. The high ball leaves him exposed, taking up space. So we placed him on the edge of the box, hunting down the second phase ball. It's this position, attacking and defending, that Freddy has turned almost into a science. On the edge of the area he is quite simply the best in the world. Say we're defending a corner kick, we rely on our defenders to get the ball clear, we depend on Freddy to be first to the loose ball. He is the best in the world at reading edge of the box play, he is the best in the world at initiating counter attacks. If he doesn't get to the loose ball first then he is the best in the world at closing down the threat.

Now move the situation to the edge of their box. If they beat out our attack, then we look to Freddy to keep the momentum going. We discussed it many a time. The first thing he looks for is the shot, from anywhere up to thirty yards. See a gap, blast it, either foot. Second option, run right at the defence. Even as they come out looking for the offside, third option pass the ball keep possession, build it up again.

I would have to say he is the best in the world at riding a tackle. It's a gift a lot of little guys have, something to do with a lower centre of gravity. Once the defender has gambled on that final man and ball tackle, and lost, then space opens up. Other defenders are forced to come across. And he is the best in the world at identifying and exploiting the weaknesses of the opposition. Throw into all this twenty odd goals a season, eleven in seventeen internationals and you're talking the complete player. I know that this hasn't come easy. It's built on hard work, and practice, long hours on the training pitch, but that rubs off on the other players. If it works for Freddy then it can work for them. So we've got a club of ferocious grafters, that can't hurt.

This will be my last club. When the ride is over I'll walk away and not look back. My memories will tell me that I was involved in something just that little bit special, and as memory sorts out the bits and pieces, maybe I'll understand it all a little better.

JOE

The England Manager was a worried man. He sat at the bar of the plush hotel fiddling with his lemonade. Really the need was for something stronger, but the greater need was for a clear head. He swilled the lemonade round the bitter taste in his gums. "Ah, here they come" he muttered to himself "Ted and Stan, hatchet men from the F.A.' He watched as they moved through the crowd, casting suspicious glances right and left.

"Joe!" Ted greeted him heartily, too heartily, clapping him on the shoulder, almost hugging him. "Joe nice to see you looking so well. Shall we go straight in?"

Joe picked up his lemonade and trailed them into the dining room. 'No celebratory scotch,' he thought sadly. 'Not much to celebrate'. In his head, in the football part of his brain, he knew he should have jacked it in after the Europeans. He'd lost contact with the modern player. All those agents, filofaxes, deals, career structures; cold young men, earning more in a month than he did in a year. Where was the joy? The press bayed regularly for his resignation. Sometimes it seemed only his body dangling at the end of a rope would satisfy them. He even had his own Spitting Image puppet: senile Uncle Joe, the man who dithered, the guest who wouldn't leave.

In his heart, where dreams and ambition still lingered, he knew he couldn't/wouldn't quit. At best he hoped to face the chop with dignity, in the British tradition. Inside he might be screaming, but you wouldn't find him slagging off his successor in the press. Of course if the offer should come along, well, he had a few tales.

The men from the F.A. were deep into the prawn cocktails before Ted gave one of his little coughs. Joe sucked in his breath, straightened his back; he could almost feel the blade. But no; Ted merely murmured words of sympathy for England's evil grouping. "Germany, Russia, Sweden, Portugal, a bitch of a group." Joe understood their position, even sympathised, a little. Contracts had been signed, compensation was always a messy business. A start of the season sacking would be such an admission of failure that the buck could well slither upstairs. Best really to preserve the status quo, stand up to tabloid pressure. Hope things pick up. "However, if you feel the pressure is more than you can cope with, we'll understand."

'On your bike,' Joe thought, feeling the blade rise an inch or two.

They ate on, ploughing through the courses, avoiding, like many married couples, the one subject that could tear them asunder. Still, the message was plain, it hovered over the meal like an invisible bird of doom. 'The sands of time are running low, qualify or else.'

In his heart, Joe still believed they could do it. Even after the away defeat in Lisbon, the lucky home draw with the Ruskies. There was nothing wrong with the commitment, all that was lacking was that... something extra... something over and above.

Then it happened, like magic, like falling in love. A squad decimated by injuries. A call up to an unknown, untried second division player. A player there, purely to make up the numbers. A player Joe had never even seen. In a move of desperation, going with his gut, Joe flung the kid into the match, and watched, mouth open, along with eighty thousand spectators, twelve million viewers, not to mention thirty million Germans, as the kid turned the match upside down, sent a red hot flicker of hope through the ashes of English football.

There was a spring in Joe's step as the weight rolled away. To mix with the best, to pit his wits against the best, it would redeem every disappointment his career had suffered.

Ninety thousand people were at Wembley, to cheer on an England display of delicacy and daring; 4-2 against The Swedes. Then the smash and grab raid in the snows of Moscow and suddenly it was not one point from two games and everybody's whipping boys, but six points from five games, England back in the hunt, a force to be reckoned with. At Wembley against France, the cameras captured Joe dancing a little victory jig and for the first time in his memory he was popular with the fans. No longer dour and defensive he was a fan, taking pride in his teams performance. Now he was kindly Uncle Joe, wise Uncle Joe, the trust of English football safe in his hands.

Determined to preserve the magic, Joe threw out a protective net. The sit-in at Dockside: Joe was on the case, explaining in his uncley sort of way why it wasn't quite so bad, done with the best of intentions, a common struggle etc. etc. The drugs bust: Joe went to the wire with Ted and Stan, Eric and Simon and Winstone. Pleading, flattering, and in the end threatening. Now another dinner, same hotel, same table, behind the potted ferns away from stray cameras.

Pouring from the second bottle of expensive red plonk, Ted

coughed in preparation. "We need to think in a wider perspective." He waved the bottle around expansively. "When you pull on that England jersey, you represent your country to the world."

"I'm sure there was nothing personal," Joe said soothingly, still hoping to sidle round the edges of confrontation. "His intentions were good."

"Damn it. Man, he's called us murderers, right over the radio." He smacked his hand down on the table causing the plates to jump and red wine to run across the table like blood.

"Local radio," Joe muttered. "Be fair."

"Joe ask yourself. Is he the sort of person we want to act as an ambassador? Especially with the World Cup..." He left the sentence unfinished, 'The World Cup'. It said it all.

"If that's the way you feel, then suspend him," Joe said finally. "My job is football, not politics."

"In normal circumstances, that is exactly what we would do. But there's been pressure, interference from above."

Joe nodded, the reason for the dinner becoming clear. Shit shoveller wanted. "I'll not drop him," he said.

"Joe, Joe, we're not asking you to decide right now, but there are some things you should know. There are deals, we can't talk details now, but take it from me, there will be money coming in that can be used within the game." He tapped the side of his nose with two fingers." We don't want to jeopardise this, we need the money. Think about this too Joe. You'll be retiring soon, there are things we can do for you."

"I'll not drop him." Joe repeated the phrase like a mantra.

Ted looked at him, eyes hard. When he spoke, the persuasiveness had gone from his voice. "That's the second time Joe, make sure there's not a third."

Joe watched Dockside as often as he could. Anxious as a mother hen when Freddy made the switch to sweeper, excited by the free running young players as they stretched themselves in the first division.

He sat in the manager's office with Hutch and Alf. Hutch he knew of course, their careers had touched down the years. Many, many years; two or three eras ago, they had even played together, briefly, for Blackburn. As managers, they had wheeled and haggled. But who was this Alf? Where had he come from? Who had he played for?

'From the grave likely,' thought Joe. This was a man who did not look well. His face had a translucent quality, as if the skin had been stretched too tight, grey eyes stared at him. 'Whoever he is, he's giving nowt away." He cast a sideways look at Hutch, but Hutch had always been a joker, even in his Blackburn days.

"Good game," he said. "You got a good set of youngsters there. I liked young Flood, and the boy Stewert, very calm, very composed. And old Barney, who would have thought he could still turn it on?" Joe was aware that he was beginning to prattle, but there was something vaguely disturbing about this Alf character.

There were the eyes of course, grey and expressionless, and the thinness, no, it was more the stillness. Alf sat behind his desk revealing bugger all.

Joe tried again. "Look, this is just a chat, just between us and these four walls." He leaned forward. "We've both lost Craig. I'm sorry that it happened in an England shirt but..." He shrugged, that's football. "The question is: what do we do about it?" Alf said nothing and Joe rushed on to fill the gap. "You've pushed Freddy into the role. In a way that forces my hand." Joe was beginning to sweat, he was used to Managers not being pleased at his appearance. Nothing puts a player off his game more than the awareness that the England Manager is watching his every move. He felt that he and Alf were like two dogs squaring off over a particularly succulent bone. Joe may have been the larger, more powerful dog, but the bone was passed his way for only two or three precious days a month. The rest of the time, the smaller dog guarded it jealously, releasing it with reluctance.

As Alf started to speak, Joe thought he picked up the hint of a Welsh accent. He'd never liked the Welsh. In his opinion they ranked just a notch above the Scots, level with the Irish.

"The intention," Alf was saying in a tone so quiet that Joe had to lean forward, "is to give Freddy a free role. In effect we'll be playing with ten plus Freddy." Joe cast a quick eyes raised look at Hutch, but his face was purposefully blank, or maybe there was just a flicker of a smile.

"Be that as it may," Joe said, "that's not really why I'm here." He stopped, but as nobody asked why he was there, he had no option but to go on. "I understand your club needs, but I really want to ask something more personal." He hesitated, then plunged in. "Can you not just shut him up? At least until the World Cup. Because I don't know how much longer I can go on protecting him. I know he's entitled to his views and all that, and I know he's a lovely lad, underneath. But there's powerful people, very powerful, who want him out." This time he returned Alf's stare.

Alf laid his thin hands on the table, palms up. "Freddy's a grown man, with a family. Even if I wanted, I couldn't shut him up. I wouldn't ask him to, not to pacify the football establishment."

Joe felt as if he were swimming through mud. "What if he was a fascist or racist. Would he still have all this freedom?"

"I'd get rid of him."

Joe felt crushed, pressure from above, pressure from below. Vic was no help as they travelled together from match to match. "You're obsessed Joe. You've tied yourself so tight you can't even see it."

"I won't drop him Vic, I won't. It's how I've always dreamed an England team could play."

"This is what I mean Joe: we're over dependent. He could break a leg."

"I could cope with that. That would be fate, but I won't drop him."

Vic shrugged. "Don't say I didn't warn you."

The England Manager was a worried man. Sometimes the anxiety would vanish. Watching football his spirit could still soar, but then the worry would return, nagging away like toothache. In his bones, he had always known it would come down to this, the last match, A united Germany in Berlin, both teams needing a win. Only Alf had ever managed to put one across the Krauts, way back in '66, and even he had blown it in '70, thus beginning the long decline of English football.

Joe didn't want to, but he couldn't help remembering his boyhood during the War. Coming back from the shelter to find his home, gone, vanished, bombed into non-existence.

He had his team, a couple of problem positions. It was touch and go whether Craig would be back, and if Bobby Faulkner got any slower, he'd be going backwards.

No, what kept him awake was a tactical decision. Should he give Freddy a free role, in this the biggest match for years! In his bed, alone, the arguments ran across his mind, night after night as time ticked away. Freddy had given dignity back to The England team. Who cared if he was stealing tracksuits. Christ, beat the Krauts, and he'd buy Freddy a wardrobe full of tracksuits. But the Germans, they'd invented the sweeper system. Now Freddy was talking about going beyond that! A free role. Yes, if it worked. Freddy turning up in the box, causing mayhem and panic even in the highly disciplined German defence. On the other hand it would be only too easy to get lost on the edges of the game, to ball chase. Round and round went the arguments. Gamble, go for broke, but gamblers don't become England Managers. Keep Freddy back in defence, rely on the breakaway, safe, as safe as anything ever is in football. Attack them in their own back yard, keep their sweeper so busy he never comes forward.

A worried man; if he had any hair left it would be falling out.

FREDDY

Bear with me.

I'm going to ramble on a bit here. Touch on some subjects, linger over others.

Football first; there is this odd little coincidence which crops up more often than it has a right too. No, before that, it has to be said that these were thrilling times: Dockside in the semi-finals of the cup. The F.A. Cup. Much to my annoyance, I found myself rather gripped by the immensity of it all: the tradition, the history, the claptrap. I hope the Queen never drops in, I'd be bowing and scraping with the best of them. 'No, no Your Majesty, all that talk of non-taxpaying parasites, idle chatter. Abolition, wouldn't hear of it.'

Dockside was excited in a working class, pessimistic sort of a way, 'Enjoy it while it lasts' went the whisper. 'The bastards'll get us in the end.'

It had been a hard run. The three matches against Eastgate, two against Hull, a lucky win away to Newcastle. We have crept through to the sixth round almost unnoticed. Struggling in the premier league, the cup matches are a holiday, if we lose, we've still done well. So off we went to Goodison Park where, in front off forty thousand scousers, we dismantled their expensive, brittle Everton team. Took them apart, cut through them with easy flowing passing movements. Midway through the second half, Barney caught my eye. He smiled, nodded, this is football.

The semi-finals, Middlesborough, the unglamorous tie. Still mega media interest. Time to tuck the skeletons away, maybe make our own little film. Time to bring Fingers' Dolton back into the fold, for appearances sake. A busy time, lots of ideas running round my head.

That is why I missed it, too busy. So full of myself, I ignored the fluttery feeling in my stomach, pushed aside my early warning system. Three days before the semi, we meet Middlesborough in a near the foot of the table, six pointer, no holds barred, psychologically scarring, sort of a game. A dress rehearsal, nothing to get worked up about, happens all the time. Just one of football's little coincidences.

I was sitting in Alf's office at the time, he had to shake me out of some sort of trance.

"You've been staring out of the window," he said. "There's nothing there. What were you seeing?" All I could do was shake my head. It wasn't anything I saw, but heard, in the distance, faint but growing louder, the sound of chickens coming home, clear as anything.

If Dockside maintained its calm, refusing to yield to tabloid pressure, the same could not be said of the nation. England vs. Germany, one match, winner take all. Too much temptation for the tabloids, too many old battles to be refought, too much public feeling to be whipped up, papers to sell, money to be made.

Lots of money: "My agent's been trying to phone your agent, about a little deal being put together."

"I don't have an agent."

"Yeah, that's what my agent said."

Pete Martin and I were jogging round the Hendon track, a couple of days before we flew to Berlin. We ran on a bit, in silence, then he said, "So is it alright if Danny gives you a ring?"

"Who?"

"Danny, Danny Almond, my agent, Almond Enterprises."

"No, not really, I prefer to keep away from them."

"Well I've already told him he can, I didn't think you'd mind."

"Well I do fucking mind."

I would have dismissed the conversation, except that Pete hung around. We were having a quick hand of bridge when I noticed him hovering, studying the cards intently.

"Why didn't you win that?" he said suddenly. "You could've laid your trump there."

"I was trying to false card him, make him think I didn't have the trump."

"Oh right, sorry."

"It's okay, the boss is a gentlemen, he wouldn't dream of taking advantage. But do fuck off, there's a good fellow."

Later, at supper, Pete caught me again, just him and me, and two empty chairs. "Alright Pete, spit it out, what's on your mind?"

"It's about this agent business."

"I rather thought it might," I said.

"Well the lads thought..."

"Oh the lads, you're a spokesman then?"

"Yeah, if you wanna put it like that. Anyway, the lads have

agreed to put all England matters in the hands of one agency, a common pool, equal shares for everyone."

"Socialism in action," I said. "Don't you think all this is a bit premature? We haven't qualified yet."

"Keep your voice down." Pete made soothing movements with his hands, cast quick glances around. "This is all very hush hush, but if, if we qualify, there's no point hanging about. I mean the records' got to come out while the market's hot."

"What record?" Even as the words were spoken, I knew. The England World Cup Record. Please no.

"The record man, the record, we got demos waiting." He leaned towards me, licked his lips. "I tell you this man, in strictest confidence. We're talking Phil Collins."

"Oh well, that settles it. My doubts are gone. Make your record without me, good luck with it."

Pete looked at me, no longer the amiable, Chelsea wide boy, now his eyes were flat, hostile. He drummed a little tune on the table. "That isn't how it works man. Everybody puts in, everybody takes out."

"I won't put in, and I won't take out, then everybody gets the same, nobody's feelings are hurt."

"We're not talking pennies here, this is big money. My agent's talking forty, fifty grand apiece." He looked at me through shrewd little eyes. No one stands between Pete Martin and fifty big ones. "Can you afford to turn down that sort of money? What if you break a leg? What about your kids? What about team spirit? Fuck it, give the money to charity." He flashed me a tight little smile.

"The most I'll do," I said cautiously "is make a deal. We'll talk again, after the match. Till then don't mention it, not a word, bad luck."

Pete kept his part of the deal, many meaningful glances, just to let me know, but not a word.

Everybody knows we beat the Germans. The whole of Europe saw Pete Martin score two, lay on the winner for me, play a blinder. They didn't hear his words in my ear, as he picked me up.

"Fifty thousand quid man, that's what that goal is worth." He grinned at me. "There's a certain irony there, don't you think?"

That night, well bevvied, the lads paid me a visit, seven, eight of them, friendly, but meaning business.

"It's after the match," said Pete. "It's time, you in or you out?"

"Out."

There was a muttering in the ranks. 'Told you so'. Money changing hands.

"You've been betting on it," I said. "Who won? How much?"

"A monkey," said Norville. "I'm a big winner man, thanks."

"You were betting on my integrity, I'm deeply moved."

"No man, I was betting on your stupidity."

"Yeah, yeah, can we get back to the point," said Pete. "How can you turn your back on fifty thousand pounds? Use it to rebuild communism, feed the starving, but you can't say no. No one says no."

"Look lads, do your record, I hope it goes to number one, just leave me out. If we can't be married, we can still be friends."

"Why? Just tell me why?"

I looked at them; nice guys, friends. What could I tell them when I wasn't that sure myself? Pete's argument, using the money to do good, had touched a vulnerable spot. Give it all to Aid and it would be fifty thousand pounds that otherwise would never have been raised. If memory serves, I have played variations on the same theme.

"Alright," I took a deep breath, "None of this is aimed personally. Whatever you make, good luck to you, but for me, in my heart, I know it would be wrong. I'd look at myself and say 'You took the money, when it came to the wire, you took the fucking money. Maybe I could live with that, but there's this person I want to be, I never will, but... In moments of crisis I say 'What would this person do?' And he wouldn't take the money. He wouldn't, and he'd be right."

"He sounds a right pain up the arse, this fellow." Big Norve grinned down at me. "Listen, you don't want to be on *Top Of The Pops*, have groupies grabbing over your body, that's alright with me."

"Oh no, I want to be on *Top Of The Pops*, please, come on lads, be fair."

"No, no, no, no." Pete Martin's revenge, no *T.O.T.P.* no groupies. "We're getting a few beers in, Norville's room, be there," he ordered.

"You're gonna want to sneak out to some sleazy, Berlin Bar, full of whips, chains, women of easy virtue."

"Sounds good," Pete shook his head. "No, no, too much to lose, not good for the old image. I'm a married man now. Anyway, you coming?"

"Yeah, yeah, just give me a few moments alone with my integrity."

Pete was the last one out of the door, as he left, he turned, raised his fist. "Sunny Brazil man, here we fucking come."

And there it was again, louder, like a wind, blowing closer. No ignoring it this time. A fully blown premonition of doom, but from which direction? There are so many. Down in my gut, in my bowels, I knew. There would be no World Cup, no Sunny Brazil, not for me. No panic, quite calm, I just knew, that's all.

Sunday mornings, I go down the local park, watch the teams play, jeer the Ref, run the line. I've seen this written up as a working class affectation, preserving my constituency, man of the people and all that. What this misses is the fact that I've been doing it for twenty years.

The other night, well pissed, in Big Norves' room, Pete suddenly turned to me and said, "How do you have fun, man? I mean you don't go to parties, or discos, clubs, restaurants. What do you fucking do?"

Well this is fun, running the line in the rain. I must have been seven when it started. Slipping away from the Sunday morning row, dreaming that one day I would be out there. Then it was Alf and I, watching, planning, learning. Then, at last, stepping out, proudly, one fantasy come to life. Scoring goals, building up a little following, all of my own. Alf on the touchline, overcoat and hat, scribbling down hurried notes to be used as evidence. I've played for, or against, all of these teams.

Today, Alf is pushing Abigail, feeding her sweets when he thinks I'm not looking. Rachel used to come, but she said my shouting embarrassed her, so now it's the three of us. Alf is looking well, it's good to be close again. He's been very mellow lately.

When I got back Mum was waiting just inside the door, looking worried, "There's a woman here, asking for you."

"Journalist?" I said. "Who then? She's not said she's expecting my baby?"

Mother managed a weak smile "No, but she does mean business." "This is my card." A woman's voice from the gloom of the passageway,

"Valery Turner, Almond Agencies. Here to give it the old college try," I said, returning the card.

The woman, mid twenties, very sexy, sending out signals like a bat down an alley - spread her hands - smiled. "I'm here to ask for an opportunity to state our case. If, at the end of the day, we fail to persuade you, fair enough. Half an hour of your time."

She smiled again. I know that smile, it's a professional job. I've been to smile school.

My first mistake was looking up her dress as I followed her up the steep staircase. (She was wearing a short skirt, Your Honour. She was asking for it, Christ!) She had put sex on the agenda, my mini voyeurism merely confirmed it. I was putting the kettle on when I felt the drift of her perfume over my shoulder.

"Freddy," she said. "I'd do almost anything to get this account." Alarm bells ringing? I'd say so. She was standing so close I could have touched her breast, run my hands up her thighs. Let's be brutal, I could have spread her over the kitchen table and fucked her like a dog.

"Excuse me," I muttered, brushing past. I dashed downstairs to Mummy. "Phone Elane, tell her to get back here, fast. Tell her my vow of celibacy is under threat."

Upstairs again, it's firm line time. "Valerie."

"Val, please."

"Val, I'm going to put your innuendoes down to bad tactics, but you haven't made a good start. I don't want to preach, but it's selling yourself awfully short."

"Sorry, a mistake." She seemed unruffled.

"The other thing is, I won't discuss the subject any further until my partner arrives. You want to convince me, you have to convince her as well."

"Fair enough." She reached into her bag. "May I play the cassette of the shortlisted songs? Just to give a general feel of our thinking."

Elane came in halfway through, hurried introductions all round.

"What can I say, Val," I said when the music had finished. I looked over at Elane, reading her face. This whole deal smacks of sell out, one of the little bribes offered up by success, each one with its price to be paid at some later date. "You're continuing a fine tradition of completely naff world cup songs, congratulations." She looked so downcast that I actually felt sorry for getting in the way of her upward climb.

"Okay Val," I said gently. "You got your moment, on with the sales pitch."

She reached into her case, brought out a whole sheaf of paperwork.

"First off," she said, looking me in the eye, "there's an assumption that the end product won't be affected by your non-involvement. Research shows that this simply isn't the case. Normally we could expect a record to go top ten, maybe even top five. I agree that there are problems, but we're past the days when the squad got up and sang like an out of tune church choir.

Our research also shows that, for whatever reason, your lack of participation, in effect the withholding of your seal of approval, will result in drastically reduced sales. That's the reality."

"Your reality, not mine."

"No, it's the reality of the situation. And it goes further. It penetrates into every layer of our campaign. She looked up, saw we were still listening politely. "There are firms who have refused our overtures because they don't want their product/company whatever, to be associated with you in any way. They are not the problem. Our prospective partners..."

"Your financial backers," Elane put in.

Valery held up her hands. "Whatever. The point is, their input is dependent on your participation." She stopped, annoyed with herself. "I'm trying to choose my words carefully here. Our partners feel they've entered into an arrangement with the full England squad. We have F.A. agreement, we have the squad, we have everything except you. The Freddy Feather seal of approval."

"I think you exaggerate," I said. "I don't think people will care."

She shook her head. "When the video comes out, people will notice. That means newspaper headlines, stories of rows within the camp. Almond Enterprises don't want that."

"Get to it girl. How much you got in that briefcase of yours?"

Elane has been taking lessons in bluntness from Alf.

They exchanged meaningful looks, two sides of the sisterhood. Different choices made at different times, I just knew they'd hit it off. "Almond Enterprises has authorised me to offer one hundred thousand pounds to the charity of your choice," she said in a flat tone. "Obviously with provisos, but these can be discussed at a later date."

"Pots of money," I said. "What is that moral blackmail, bribery?"

"Bit of both," answered Elane.

"Perhaps it's a sincere effort to reach some area of agreement, some compromise." Give the girl some credit, she's fighting her corner.

"Valery. There is no compromise between our views. To you this is a deal, a money making exercise. Even if we were to consider it, by the time we've run your capitalist clients through our socialist computers..." I held out my hands.

Valery started stuffing papers away in her case. She looked up. "What's wrong with making the best deal for yourself?" she asked plaintively.

"Nothing Val. In this case it would mean me selling my self-respect, my credibility. It would be a bad deal for me."

"So why do I get the feeling you've been laughing at me, both of you?"

"Nothing personal, Val," I said. "Just the situation. The capitalist shark comes to call, bearing bribes."

"Is that how you think of us, sharks?"

"Almond Enterprises? No, more a little fish, aspiring to sharkhood though, having a go at the big time."

"We could go under," she said, standing up, straightening her skirt. "They're panicking at the office. Your team-mates won't be pleased if it all falls through."

"You'll stitch up a deal Val, I've every faith in you."

"Maybe you should think about lowering your profit margins," Elane added.

As we shook hands on the doorstep, she leaned forward, kissed me gently on the cheek. "Take care, Freddy," she whispered. "There are rumours, the sharks really are coming out to play".

Third and last warning.

Semi-final day: second up, we watched the first match on T.V.

Man United vs. Liverpool. The biggy: Brian and Ron are at this one.

We've got John and Gary, the second team.

"Both teams are playing with sweepers Ron. This is a real sign of the times."

Do me a favour Brian, both teams are playing with three centre backs, six in all. Over a quarter of the players out there are central defenders. I'd sooner quit than play like that; maybe not, but that's how I felt after ninety minutes of football built on fear. Prompted by Alf and Hutch the feeling was, 'We can do better. If that's the best: We can do better.'

Wherever you play, the local park, the school playground, you know when it's good. You want to applaud when the other side does a good move. You don't want the game to end. You understand, once again, why you love football so much. Especially when you win.

After the match, the excitement, the champagne, the interviews, comes the let down. The lads were sneaking away up West. I could see the guilt in Pete Stewert's eyes.

"Did Marx go to night-clubs?" I said to them. "Was Lenin ever seen in a disco?"

"Freddy, we're only going for a few drinks. We are in the cup final, after all. Correct me if I'm wrong but we did win."

"Lads, lads." I shook my head sadly as they strode off, heads high, into tomorrow morning's hangover. They never even asked me if I wanted to go.

Yet I didn't want to go home, so I went back to Alf's house. I wish I hadn't.

"Freddy, sit down and listen to me."

"Sorry Alf, sorry I can't be as calm as you. It's a new experience for me, someone telling me they're going to die. Look at you sitting there like you're about to read the six o'clock news 'Today Alf Evans, Manager of Dockside Town announced the date of his own death'."

"I thought about not telling you," he said. "I could have left a letter. 'To be opened in the event of.' In the end I realised that you've earned the right. I don't want there to be any guilt, or pity."

I looked away avoiding those eyes.

"Alf, you're not going to die. You're strong as a pit pony"

He smiled, shook his head. "Freddy, if I could avoid bringing you pain by not dying, I would. The choice isn't mine. I've had time to think Freddy. I've had a better, more fulfilling life than I had any right to expect; I owe that to you. You've made me part of your family; your children are like the grandchildren I never had. I thought you would outgrow me Freddy. All down the road, when you met Elane, when you started to be successful, when you had a family."

"That's all mutual Alf." I'm accepting the reality of his words. He really is going to die soon. Alf doesn't joke. He does have a sense of humour, it's a bit bony, sharp round the edges, but there nonetheless. This isn't humour, this is a man preparing himself for death, clearing his desk.

If Brian were here, he'd be pulling me to one side, thrusting a microphone in my face. How do you feel Freddy, knowing that your Father figure is going to die? Do you think that you bear responsibility for his death? Will it make any difference to your future plans? Tell us how you feel... feel... feel...

My mouth continued to make noises, words formed and fell out. We walked down memory lane a little. Gently, quietly, unwilling to kick up bad times, careful not to disturb the mood.

I had to tell Elane. For much the same reason that Alf had shared with me. Fuck it, why should I carry this alone? You've earned the right to share my pain. She cried when I told her how Alf had spoken of his strength slipping away. Of his calm, his inner peace.

I resented those tears. What right did she have to feel more than me?

That night, putting the kids to bed, Rachel said to me, "Freddy, are you going to be on television in the Cup Final?"

"Looks that way, babe."

"Well, promise me that you won't spit."

"Rachel I can't do that. I've been practising. I've got this really good one, where I gob all down my chin, then wipe it over my face. You've heard of goal of the season, well this is gob of the season."

"Freddy you're disgusting."

As I closed the door I realised how much I wanted to win for Alf. What else could I do? What else was left?

The Monday morning back pages had the football, but the big news, hold the front page, was '*Football Associations Great Coup*'. '*Thirty million for sponsorship of the F.A. Cup.*' '*The British*

Holdings F.A. Cup.' Then the phone calls started coming in. Animal Jim was first up.

"Do you know who British Holdings are?"

"Never heard of them," I replied. "But I'm sure I'm about to."

"Well you should read the fucking literature we put out. They're only one of Britain's biggest landowners. They run factory farms, animal breeding centres. They got this laboratory on Dartmoor that does nothing but animal experiments. Effects of radiation, and all that crap. They got a cosmetic testing factory in Cambridgeshire. That's where our people got busted."

"What am I supposed to do Jim?"

"That's up to you man."

It's too early in the morning for all this, I like to wake up slow and easy, lots of tea. Something else is happening today. Oh yeah, Alf is dying. Now the phone is ringing again. "This is an answering machine," I said. "If you've got good news, speak after the beep. If it's bad news. Don't bother."

"Freddy, don't fuck about."

"Leroy! Leroy is this a call that will raise my spirits?"

"No." There was a long silence before he spoke again. "I can catch you later. If this is a bad time?"

"No Leroy, things aren't going to get any better. This is the high point of my day."

"British Holdings, what does that name conjure up?"

"Animal Experiments."

"Ah," he said.

"What?"

"I rang before but you were engaged. I see now, Jim got there before me, right?"

"Right."

"Well Animal Experiments is only a small part of a greater whole, but none of it any cleaner." Another long silence, when Elane walked in, raising her eyes in question, all I could do was shake my head.

"Freddy, you still there?"

"I suppose so."

"The significance of all this is that this British Holdings deal starts with this season. That's most unusual. The F.A. must really be strapped for cash. I mean two weeks from the cup final. Sorry, The British Holdings Cup Final.

"You should see the stuff the computer is puking up. It's like a great big family tree; and guess who's Big Daddy, right at the top. I.P.C., International Petroleum Company. Number one on everyone's shitlist."

"Not everybody's, not the Football Association's," I put in.

"Get a pen and paper Freddy, you should get this down, at least the bare bones."

As Leroy dictated, something deep in my brain clicked into place. This is it. This is what I've been waiting for. All those warnings, all justified.

I.P.C.
(International Petroleum Co.)

T.P.C.S. Technological Plastics & Systems	B.S.P. British Swiss Petroleum BRITISH HOLDINGS	
A.M.S. Advanced Missiles System	Laboratories International	English Livestock & Poultry Lucky Chicken Fastfood

"So, what do you think?" I said to Elane, after she had studied the family tree. "Remember these companies are splitting like amoeba, more and more bastard little children, all chips off the old block, all up to no good, all born knee deep in corruption."

"I see that. But I don't understand what Jim and Leroy and everyone expect you to do about it?"

"They're throwing out the possibility that I make some sort of stand. That we gather the gang together: Animal rights, Socialist workers, the usual coalition. Then we'll all join hands and go down to the river to 'Yet another glorious defeat.'" I could hear the first whine of hysteria come into my voice.

"What do you want to do?" she asked softly.

"Want, I want to play. Otherwise what's it all been for? Half of my life. Elane, this is everything football has to offer. Everything Alf and I have worked towards. And now it's so close. Wembley, the Cup Final. The World Cup. There's a bit of me saying 'Get in my way and I'll fucking mow you down!' And there's another bit saying 'Just gimme the World Cup, gimme this and I'll do anything you want after.' All my being is centred round wriggling out of this, not letting it drag me under.

"The frightening thing is," I went on slowly as it all came together in my mind, "all the arguments, all this 'Should I, shouldn't I, do I, don't I' business. It's all been said, rehearsed. All that stuff with Pete Martin in Germany, and what's her name...?"

"Valery. Val to her friends, you remember, good legs, short skirt." Elane smiled and I smiled back, my first of the day. "I remember. And wasn't that all about 'Take the money or stick to your principles?' The difference being that was fun. Now, they're talking thirty million quid and somehow it doesn't seem so amusing."

"Just suppose," she said slowly "you fail to maintain a silence, bearing in mind that silence isn't one of your gifts. What sort of support could you hope for from the other players?"

I thought about it for a bit, Pete and Norve, and all the others. "Maybe if I'd pressed a bit more flesh, been a bit more 'One of the lads'. Realistically, I can see no great rush of support. Remember I'm the guy who cost them all money."

"Maybe a campaign on a sort of 'Save the Whale' basis, you being an endangered species."

"I'm glad you can take it so easily," I snapped. "Of course it's only football"

She reached across the table, took my hand, scratched gently with her nails. "I'm on your side, kid. Listen, I got to go, the revolution calls."

Normally I'm quite content to be alone in the house. This day the quiet seemed ominous, the rooms filled with a threatening stillness. Got to get out. To the gym, push some weights, have a sauna, clear my head.

I've been lifting weights since I was twelve. Alf put me onto it, after dieting reduced me to skin and bone.

Going at it in my usual way, I blew up like a mini Shwarzenegger, thighs so thick I could hardly run. I wanted to be a whippet, instead I'm a bulldog: short legs, deep chest, harder than the hardest hatchet man. Top dog in the alley.

The club was almost as empty as the house, silence echoing down the passageways. From the window I could see a few lonely souls going about their business. The pitch itself shrouded beneath a grey city mist. Empty, all empty. Everybody's celebrating, or recovering from celebrating.

I started to lift, gentle presses, nothing heavy, co-ordinating the breathing. Slowly building up the weight, letting my mind drift in and out, down alleyways, round corners, trying to make sense of it all.

And it came, almost like a religious revelation. If the F.A. had planned it all, down to the finest detail, then they couldn't have trussed me more securely. I had a picture of them sitting round a long table, chortling away at the sheer brilliance and scope of their strategy. Could hear their voices. 'We need a company that makes it impossible for him to play.' No warning. Secrecy and speed the watchwords.'

Dangerous thinking, we're talking conspiracy here, next door to paranoia. I've been there, stood on the edge, hand on the doorknob.

Still lifting, going for personal bests now, as if I could break their trap by sheer brute strength. So, what if I do nothing?

Keep my peace. How much of a principle is at stake here? A totally corrupt (in my eyes) group of corporations swoop down on football and pay unrealistic amounts of money to have their name on the F.A. Cup. Buying goodwill with blood money. British Holdings - Football's benefactor. A sugar daddy spreading sweetness with sticky money.

Slowly the lifting and deep breathing began to have its calming effect. Yes, I was scared, and angry. The consequences of putting myself on the line were potentially horrible.

Say I speak out, as Leroy and Jim want, what could they, the F.A., do? They could suspend me, ban me from any match under their jurisdiction - goodbye World Cup.

Could I force them to go back on their decision? No chance.

What would the people whom I admire do: Annie Besant, Paul

Robeson, Eugene Debbs. They'd speak out and damn the consequences. They gave up everything for their beliefs, died alone. But I think they would have wanted to play in the World Cup first; Robeson did his share of Uncle Tom movies. Maybe, like me, they would have tried to rationalise it out. How much more force my words would have after The World Cup; and that, friends, is the sound of the bottom of the barrel being scraped.

After sweating it out in a sauna, I went home, got busy with the scraper, gathered in the usual crowd. Leroy, Jim, Denice, a few other faces who had worked their way into the inner circle. I laid out my case.

"Yes, I agree with everything you've got to say. We're being done over by a bunch of scumfuckers but I'm not prepared to be the martyr, or sacrificed. If that is selfish, then so be it."

All things considered, they took it quite well. We all wanted to see Dockside at Wembley, the biggest day in the town's history, at least the biggest since the Dockers riot of '63.

And to be honest, by this time, after seven years in the murky world of political manipulation, we could all recognise a losing cause.

Next morning everything seemed deceptively back to normal. The kids getting ready for school, squabbling in the living room, telephone ringing. Elane got up to answer it.

"That," she said coming back into the room "was an anonymous friend, with a message. According to this voice, which I didn't recognise, Geraldine is an informer, a plant, an information gatherer. Apparently she's hawking a tape of yesterday's conversation around the tabloids."

"Gerry? But she was here just yesterday."

"Well, she ain't around now. I rang her place, no answer. Then I rang Leroy, if anyone can find her he can.

"You believe it?" I asked.

She stood in the doorway thinking it over. "Unfortunately, I think it's only too believable. I don't want to think about some of the things you said."

The next hours remain blank. Elane found me by Alf's bed, holding his white, bony hand in mine.

"I'm sorry, babe," she said gently. "Can I sit with you for a while?"

"Yeah, just don't cry, and no lectures."

Sometime later they came and took the body away. I stayed in the house, moving from room to room, holding it all close. Not my fault though, the house tells me that, the kettle still makes tea, the videos flicker in a dark and lonely room. Sometime, later still, Elane came, brought me home. I could hear voices but it didn't seem to matter. I was quite far away, out of my depth in memories, buried in pain, cutting off to survive.

Elanes' voice from a distance, pushing in, dragging me back. "Babe, we need you now. You don't have a monopoly on suffering."

"I can't Elane, you do it, you make the decisions."

"I've been doing that for two days. Now we need you. It's time Freddy." She came close. "Listen babe, everyone here is your friend, okay?"

I hauled myself into the living room, the buzz of voices faded, eyes flicking here, flicking there.

"I'm alright," I said, "I'm alright, I think." Even to me, my voice sounded rusty, frayed at the edges. "So bring me up to date. Who's going to be first with the bad news?" There was a quick exchange of glances around the room, then Leroy said, "It seems that Elane's anonymous tip was right on the button. Geraldine, if that's even her name, has been working for someone. Maybe the press, maybe some Government department of grubby tricks - whatever, it doesn't matter. It's too late. She has plastered that tape all over the tabloids. It's been doctored, a scissors and paste job, just like the photo."

I laughed, I couldn't help it. "I'm sorry," I said. "I'd forgotten all about her. In the middle of everything she simply slipped out of view."

"Well, she's back," Leroy said "And doing lots of fucking damage. They've got you on tape calling them scumfuckers. The whole issue is out in the open. The word is 'an indefinite ban' unless you retract every word, issue a public apology. They've gone beyond 'bringing the game into disrepute'. They're talking libel."

Some people even think you put the tape out yourself. At the risk of sounding like a doom merchant, my analysis of the situation is that this is a concerted campaign to get you, get all of us."

The faces waited expectantly, but for the life of me there wasn't a meaningful thought to be dredged up.

"May I say a word?" I hadn't seen Hutch sitting quietly in a corner. "I can't really add too much lad, except to say that this morning the players and workers at the club handed me a signed statement. If you are banned, then everyone connected to the club will go on strike."

He sat back while we all tried to take in this new twist.

"On the one hand," he went on, looking directly at me, "this is a touching show of loyalty. On the other, it means no Cup Final and as sure as night follows day, that means suspension, and the club itself, possibly being thrown out of the league." He spread his hands in a gesture of appeal. "I'm not here to make statements about the rights and wrongs of this, ah, situation, but you should know that there will be consequences."

Consequences; isn't that a kid's game? I've been playing it a lot recently.

"Can they do that?" demanded Leroy.

Hutch nodded. "You're talking about people who have been publicly humiliated, had their authority called into question. You hand these people a weapon and they show no mercy. A public apology might do the trick. Might."

He turned back to me. "I know we've had our differences and my advice probably isn't welcome. But, for what it's worth, here it is. Think about what's at stake here. You, the club, the town. That's all I want to say, ."

More people spoke at me, telling me this, telling me that, until the voices became a blur of noise, like a plane landing in my head. It all meant nothing, it should have meant something, but it was all faces and mouths moving. Finally they went away. Elane brought me a mug of tea. "I feel as bad about Alf as you do."

"No you don't."

She leaned over, ran her fingers through my hair. "You're right, I don't, but don't shut me out."

"What about all this with Geraldine? M.I.5. M.I.6. This is all fantasy stuff."

"She could be a reporter, she could be an agent provocateur, she could be a mixture of them all." She looked at me. "Do you want to hear my opinion?"

"Yeah."

"Alright. It's quite feasible that the agencies did plant someone. That to a paranoid right wing mind you are seen as a threat. A symbol. A figurehead for all the left wing activity that threatens their view of democracy. Take you down, and it's one more nail in the coffin of socialism.

"I don't kid myself, we've all worked hard in Dockside, played our part, helped it happen. But without you, none of it would have been possible. We know that. So do they.

"Think right wing for a moment. Communism collapsing all over the world. Now they're like rottweilers off the leash sniffing out the enemy within. You fit that description. Who else is left? The unions have been sorted out, the miners beaten, you're left, you're a threat. They're out to get you. Not only you, but everything associated with you. Look out the window Freddy, what d'you see?"

I looked, everything seemed normal enough, quiet.

"Yes," she said. "That's because the police have got the whole area cordoned off. But they're out there, the press and the media, waiting."

"Elane, I want to do the right thing, I think that's all I've ever wanted, but I don't know what 'The Right Thing' is. What do the papers say?"

"You don't want to know."

"That bad?"

"Worse." She looked at me, as if weighing my strength, then she shrugged. "They're blaming you for Alf's death, saying the strain was too much. They're after you in a big way."

"What do I do,Elane?"

"I don't know, babe."

Some things happen inside, where words don't reach. How can a sense of loss be described. I remember Abigail's birth and the making room for a new life. This is the opposite in every way. Then there was a personal growth. Now I'm shrinking inside. There are no tears, no way of expressing whatever it is I'm feeling. There's a gap, lashings of emotion with nowhere to go. What happens to love when it has nowhere to go? Does it curdle like milk?

Physically I feel like someone is reaching inside, twisting and pulling at something vital, pulling it out.

The minutes battled their way by, long days even longer nights. Then, out of nowhere: Tuesday, Alf's funeral.

"I'm not going. There's nothing to prove. It's a meaningless ceremony. He's dried bones and decay, I don't need to see it."

"You must go Freddy," Elane said. "It isn't open to negotiation."

"Why must I? Not for me, certainly not for Alf. He's gone to that great revolution in the sky."

She gave me a savage look. "You're going to make me say it aren't you? Alright. You dress up in your best suit, you pay your respects to the dead, because it's politically necessary. Because you can't survive any more bad headlines."

"They're shitty reasons," I said.

"Maybe." We stared at each other, across the kitchen table, hostile and angry.

So I let her strong-arm me into putting on my best, my only, suit for political reasons.

Lots of people, forty, fifty maybe. Dockside people whose lives had been touched by Alf. I saw them through a veil of non-feeling. Leroy got up and said a few words about political integrity. Then Hutch, then Elane, her eyes on mine, speaking for me, protecting me. She walked through the crowd, handed me a small urn, and I scattered the ashes into the sleet and wind of Dockside.

The show rolled on; smiling, shaking hands, putting on a political face.

Hours later, the crowd gone home, kids in bed.

"You alright, babe?" Elane's voice, gentle, concerned. I nodded.

"Been doing some thinking?" she asked. I nodded again. "So? So?"

I looked at her, seeing everything she had given me, so freely. "I want out," I said. She didn't reply, just kept looking at me, those big brown eyes. "I've been through it all," I said. "If I stay, then everybody gets dragged down. You heard Hutch, he's right and I'll be banned anyway. Elane I feel like a trapped rat, the only way out is to make a run for it."

I stopped, searching for some way to explain, to reach down.

"Possibly, before Alf, I might have battled it out, but I don't really care that much, not anymore, not now. It just isn't there."

"So what are you suggesting? You simply pack a bag and take off? Where do we, your family, come into this?"

"I haven't thought details Elane. All I know is I want to sleep for six months, wake up when it's all over. I don't want to see it on T.V., hear it on the radio, nothing."

"Freddy, I want you to answer this honestly, because I know that hitting the hippie trail is a romantic proposition. What would you say if I told you that we, me and the girls are ready at a moment's notice to pack up and go with you."

"Where would we go?"

"Night ferry to Holland, plane to Harare. By Saturday we'll be on a truck to where there's no press, no photographers. Be honest Freddy, be truthful with yourself."

"What about..."

"It's all taken care of Freddy."

"Yeah, but what about..."

She put her finger to my lips. "All taken care of. The only thing stopping us is you."

Something strange here. I was moved, almost to tears, by her loyalty. But at the same time a little part of me was thinking, 'It's okay for you to take off. You didn't hear me whining 'Oh let me come too!'.'

I could fancy six months on the road, just me and my rucksack. 'The old hippie trail.' I had to smile. Elane reading my mind before the thoughts are even written. I looked at her, seeing something new in her eyes. Always she had seemed so strong, so right, so sure of herself. Now there was vulnerability, even fear: Elane laying herself open, still with the courage to ask for the truth. You gotta respect that.

"Let's go, babe."

"You've got to mean it, Freddy."

"You want it written in blood? If I'm forced to flee the country, it's only right that family share the shame."

"No time for second thoughts."

"I can't answer for thoughts and feelings," I said. "They're private, not under my control. I just want out Elane, I almost don't care where, anywhere. I don't have any fight left, babe."

She took hold of my hand, lending me her strength.

"I don't see this as a happy ending," I go on. "We're not walking hand in hand into the sunset, this isn't a crap romantic novel. Love doesn't conquer all." I can taste the bitterness. "I've been set up, framed, and I'm too filled with anger - hate wouldn't be too strong a word - to even think clearly." I stop for breath. "I think what I'm trying to say is I can't promise to be happy. Football has been my addiction for most of my life. It's going to be hard to walk away."

She smiles at me, shaking her head in that way she's got.

"Freddy, how long do think it'll be before you've got your own team together? Then, who knows? Zimbabwe for the next World Cup? African flair with a touch of English discipline. I don't know about you, but I can't wait to see it."

I try hard not to laugh, fail. Accepting inside myself that it is time to go, nothing left to stay for. The final whistle just blew.